MURDER
AT THE
MANSION

MURDER AT THE MANSION

**A Logan & Cafferty
Mystery/Suspense Novel**

Jean Henry Mead

Medallion Books

Printed in the United States of America

ISBN: 978-1-9314515-99-6

First edition March 2015

Cover design by Bill Mead

Other books in the series:

A Village Shattered

Diary of Murder

Murder on the Interstate

Gray Wolf Mountain

Murder in RV Paradise

Medallion Books

Dedication

For my nephews and nieces: Bob, Patrick, Dennis, Charlene, Samantha and Monica; and their families

Chapter One

Bright mid-morning sun streamed through Dana's window, temporarily blinding her. Hands trembling as she prepared her tea, she nearly dropped the cup when the phone rang. Recognizing Sarah's voice, she attempted to calm her own.

"I don't like the way you sound, my friend. What's wrong?"

"The coroner just left, Sarah."

"Coroner? Who died?"

"I found a body near the garage this morning."

Sarah gasped. "Why didn't you call me?"

"I knew you'd drop everything to take the first plane."

"Did you know the victim, Dana?"

"My new gardener. A nice young man who did a great job—"

"How'd he die?"

"He had a chest wound. His shirt was soaked with blood."

"Shot or stabbed?"

"He appeared to have been stabbed, but I have no idea what the weapon was. I didn't dare get his blood on my clothes. I might have been considered a suspect."

"I'm on my way." Sarah clicked off without another word.

Dana sank into the nearest chair. Depressed since Walter's heart attack, she asked herself again why he had died so soon after their honeymoon. They'd had so little time together. Now this. Tears streamed as she rose from her chair to grab a tissue. The cup of tea waited on the kitchen counter, now cold and uninviting. Placing her cup in the microwave, she relived what had happened that morning as she watched the tray revolve.

Todd Warren had appeared at her front door asking which gardening chores she wanted him to perform. She mentioned the new rose bushes stashed in the garage. Yellow roses, Walter's favorites. Todd's grin briefly lifted her spirits and she watched as he descended the steps.

Why would anyone kill such a nice young man? And why hadn't she heard his cry for help? Dana placed her cup on the counter and rushed to the kitchen door, exiting into the garage. Punching the opener, she squinted as the door rose, flooding the area with intense light. Skirting the Jeep, she cautiously made her way to the driveway where she discovered traces of powder. The investigators must have dusted the garage door for prints.

Dana had been warned not to leave the county, which she knew was only routine. Surprised that she hadn't been taken in for further questioning, she realized that she was a person of interest. Closing her eyes, she envisioned the crime scene: Todd on his back, blue eyes wide as though in shock, blood staining his shirt. Who had reason to kill him? She berated herself for not investigating the type of wound, but she had immediately rushed to call the sheriff's office when she realized he was dead.

A CD had been playing 60's rock music to quell her depression, so she had only heard the Four Seasons singing their bestselling songs. When she glanced out the window, she noticed the garage door open, but Todd was nowhere in sight. Maybe he hadn't found the rose bushes. She noticed the body as soon as she started down the front steps.

Blood stains were visible inside the garage, the rose bushes still leaning against the interior wall. So Todd had been killed as soon as he opened the garage. But why had he been dragged onto the lawn, instead of the killer hiding his body inside? That made no sense unless the killer intended to flaunt his crime. Or she? Could it have been a jealous girlfriend? Dana couldn't remember a wedding ring on Todd's left hand.

The phone rang as Dana was inspecting the bloodstained concrete. Hurrying back inside, she lifted the receiver before it stopped ringing. It was Sarah with flight information. "I arrive in Casper at eleven-twenty-two tonight. I hope that's not too late."

"Of course not. I'll reserve a hotel room so we won't have to drive all the way back to the mansion. We'll have breakfast at our favorite restaurant in Casper, and do some shopping tomorrow, if you happen to be in the mood."

"Sounds good, Dana. I've missed you and the mountains. It's flat as a griddle cake here in West

3

Texas."

Dana was amused that her friend had acquired a Texas accent during her five month marriage. When she replaced the receiver, she recalled the deputy's order to remain in the county. Should she call the sheriff's office for permission to pick up Sarah? She wrote down the flight number, feeling even more apprehensive. What if the sheriff denied her request? It would leave Sarah stranded at the airport in Casper, if she couldn't rent a car at midnight. Dana's last encounter with the sheriff wasn't exactly a friendly one. She was sure an order had been issued to keep her under surveillance.

If she left after dark and stopped at the strip mall along the way, she may be able to elude anyone who might follow. Driving the Jeep, she could travel cross-country to the gravel road which paralleled the highway. She could then circle back at the next onramp. Her anger grew at the thought of the murder as well as her perceived suspect status. She decided to leave as soon as it was dark.

Dana busied herself preparing for company although Sarah was considered family. Other than her daughter Kerrie, who lived in Cheyenne, her friend was the only person left that she could trust. A single tear hesitated on her cheek when she thought of her late husband. Recently retired, Sheriff Walter Grayson had pursued her since she and Sarah lived in the California retirement village. She should have married him sooner.

Changing clothes three times as the afternoon dragged on, she prepared a light dinner and repeatedly checked her watch. It was still half an hour until dusk. Could she pull this off? Maybe it was paranoia and she wasn't actually on legal radar.

Then again, she must be the sheriff's prime suspect. If a deputy followed her to the airport, he would think she was attempting escape.

Biting her lip until it bled, she was paralyzed with indecision.

Chapter Two

Dana held a small, stubby flashlight between her fingers to mute its glow. Punching the garage door opener, she quickly turned off the overhead light. Creeping to the Jeep, she urged her wolf-dog Jenny into the backseat, then stood watching and listening for sounds of a foreign presence in her rural subdivision. Gasping for air, she realized she had been holding her breath.

Switching off the Jeep's headlights, she backed down the driveway at a crawl until she reached the street, glancing constantly in each side mirror. Dana saw nothing unusual but realized that a dark, unmarked car could follow unnoticed. She dared not use the brakes when she reached the corner, so she eased up on the accelerator and hoped she wouldn't drive over a neighbor's lawn. Heart pounding, she checked again to determine whether anyone had followed. The only lights she saw flickered from a TV set in the house on the corner. So far, so good.

The headlights weren't switched on until she reached the highway, and she was relieved that no other vehicles were on the road, unless someone had followed, without headlights. Constantly checking the mirrors, she set the cruise control at 65 until she reached the 80 mile an hour zone. No headlights appeared behind her, and by the time she reached the cutoff to the strip mall, she was damp with perspiration.

This is stupid. I feel like a criminal.

In the convenience store, Dana bought several packs of gum, Sarah's favorite candy bars, and a six pack of diet Pepsi, a departure from her own health food practices. A red GMC pickup was parked two spaces from the Jeep when she entered the store. A black Ford SUV was now wedged between them. Silently calling herself a moron for experiencing so much fear, she climbed back into the Jeep and drove to the last store in the mall. A moment later the SUV followed. Entering the magazine and smoke shop, she browsed for what seemed an hour before buying a magazine and leaving. The Ford was there and appeared unoccupied. It was probably a coincidence.

Backing onto the street, she made a sharp left turn into an empty lot. Peering ahead at the landscape, she shut off the headlights and bumped across an undeveloped field. She knew the general direction of the graveled road, which paralleled the highway, and steered in that direction. Headlights followed. Fear numbed her hands as she gripped the wheel, wondering who was following. The terrain was rough and she doubted the SUV could follow the Jeep much further. The two-wheel drive vehicle would high center or mire itself in the unleveled field. Crouching lower in her seat, she prayed the driver wouldn't shoot before that happened. If it were a deputy, a call for backup had already been placed, and she anticipated a roadblock when she reached the graveled road.

Dana wasn't sure she was driving in a straight line although her arms were rigid and she hadn't turned the wheel. The moon had risen above the mountains, illuminating the rough terrain ahead. Bouncing over clumps of weeds and rocks, the Jeep shuddered as Dana's teeth clattered. When she glanced again in the rearview mirror, she noticed the headlights following were pointed upward at an angle. Smiling, Dana realized the car was stuck, but was a patrol car waiting when she reached the rural road?

Jenny whined from the back seat. Dana knew the dog was as frightened as she was. Whispering to calm her, she switched on the Jeep's headlights and searched for another vehicle when the graveled road appeared ahead. It seemed no one else was around, so she stepped down hard on the accelerator, driving as though terrorists were after her. When she reached the highway, Dana scanned both sides of the road for a parked vehicle of any kind. An 18-wheeler roared past, its air horn blaring as though a warning not to pull into its path. Trembling, Dana halted the Jeep until her normal breathing returned. Leaning across her seat, she petted Jenny with a trembling hand. The dog woofed softly as though to console her.

"It must have been the killer," she told the dog. "But I can't call the sheriff's office to report being followed."

Once on the highway, Dana held her breath whenever the Jeep was passed by another vehicle.

Before she arrived at the airport, a car followed close behind without passing and she berated herself for neglecting to arm herself with her Glock. A recent concealed carry law allowed guns without a permit. But she hadn't used the gun for some time and had forgotten where she placed it. Her memory was growing stagnant with age.

Jenny was left to guard the Jeep when they reached the airport west of Casper. Sarah's plane was late, arriving at ten past midnight. A storm surrounding the Denver airport had delayed a number of flights, and Sarah was beside herself. Dressed in a loose fitting shift, she had obviously gained weight since her marriage. Cooking for her Texas cattleman husband must have made him happy, although it hadn't done Sarah any favors. Obviously exhausted, Sarah's usual smile and sparkling blue eyes were faded replicas of their former selves. So, after the two friends had hugged and retrieved Sarah's luggage, they sat in the airport café, drinking chai latte.

"It sounds like you need to hire a bodyguard," Sarah said when Dana filled her in on the previous day's events.

"You're probably right. Unless only one deputy works the county roads after dark."

"If it were a deputy following you, he could have called the highway patrol for backup."

Dana glanced about the café, noticing no one suspicious. "Even more reason to believe it was the same person who killed my gardener."

"But why would the killer go after you, Dana?"

"Good question."

Sarah leaned forward to whisper, "If I were the killer, I'd try to pin the murder on you, instead of making you another victim."

Dana nodded. "I think I'd better cancel the hotel room and drive back to the mansion before daylight."

"I agree. Shopping can wait."

Both women rose to carry suitcases to the Jeep. Jenny was sound asleep on the backseat and Sarah reached to stroke her head. "Good wolf dog," she said. "I'm glad we have you along for protection."

Jenny opened one eye and snorted as though aggrieved that she had been awakened. Dana wondered what the dog would do if they were attacked. Surely her ancestral instincts would urge her to spring into action. She hadn't applied for a dog license because she was uncertain whether a domesticated wolf would be allowed to remain in the county. Wolves had been delisted from the endangered species list for several years and could be shot on sight by anyone with a gun. Ronald Benson, a trigger happy neighbor, would use the dog for target practice. For that reason, Jenny was never allowed to roam free.

"Homeward bound," Dana said as she shifted into gear. It was nearly one o'clock and most lawmen were asleep in their beds. Unless there was an all-points bulletin out for her arrest, they should make it home without incident.

Almost an hour later they pulled into the mansion's circle drive. Punching the garage door opener, Dana noticed movement from the corner of her eye. Floorboarding the Jeep, she drove inside and braked, the door creaking closed behind them.

Gasping, Sarah said, "What was that all about?"

"Someone's out there and may have ducked inside the garage. Reach back and open the door to let Jenny out."

As soon as the door opened, the dog leaped out growling, apparently alerted to danger by the tone of the women's voices. They both ducked low in their seats to peer through the Jeep's windows, unable to see past the Escalade parked beside them. Dim overhead light from the door opener didn't reveal movement, but someone could be hiding on the far side of the three-car garage.

Jenny's sharp bark raised goose bumps on Dana's arms. She then heard the side door open and close. "He's gone, Sarah. Quick! Let's get in the house."

Sarah groaned. "I'm so tired I can barely move."

Leaving the Jeep, Dana helped Sarah into the kitchen. "We'll get your luggage later," she said. "I left Jenny in the garage, just in case."

Sarah plopped into a kitchen chair, requesting a cup of tea, which Dana was quick to prepare. Thank heavens her friend was there, albeit exhausted and grumpy. This was one night she didn't want to stay alone.

"Better call the sheriff's office," Sarah said, swirling the tea in her cup. "You don't have to tell him you drove out of the county."

"Good idea. I'll say someone followed me back from the mall."

"If a deputy shows up, I'll disappear into the guest room so you won't have to explain my presence."

Dana nodded and lifted the receiver. Hesitating, she wondered how much she should say. What if it had been a deputy following her from the mall? And what if he sneaked into the garage to frighten her into confessing to Todd's murder? She no longer trusted her instincts.

Sarah urged her again to call and she reluctantly punched in the number she had memorized months earlier. The dispatcher who answered yawned as though Dana had interrupted her nap. Not much happened in Stanton County, so she must get paid for sleeping on the job. When Dana identified herself, the dispatcher said, "Sheriff's been looking for you."

"Why?"

"He sent a deputy to your house to bring you in for questioning."

"I was shopping at the strip mall last night."

"The mall closes at nine."

Dana caught a distinct tone of disbelief in the woman's voice, and wondered when the deputy had arrived. She told the dispatcher her reason for the call and waited for a response. A radio transmission could be heard in the background before the dispatcher said, "A deputy will be there at eight this morning. Be prepared to accompany him back to the station."

Great. Just great. "Did he sneak into my garage to scare me?"

"I doubt it. That's not standard procedure."

And our deputies always go by the book.

Sarah stood behind her, sipping the last of her tea. When told of Dana's conversation, she said, "Looks like we're wading into this case up to our knee caps."

"What if I'm charged with the murder, Sarah?"

"You can afford a good lawyer."

"You're not taking this seriously, are you?"

Sarah attempted to suppress a yawn. "How many murder cases have we solved, my friend?"

"More than I care to admit."

"Then don't worry. You didn't have a motive to

kill the gardener, did you?"

"Of course not. And I'm no cougar. Todd was at least thirty years younger, if you're suggesting that we had some sort of relationship."

"You're still a beautiful woman, Dana, so much like Gina Davis."

"You're very kind, Sarah, but I'm not interested in another man." Dana placed her empty cup on the counter and left for the garage. Retrieving Sarah's luggage, she was nearly knocked down when Jenny raced through the kitchen door. She had forgotten to bring her in. Time for some memory pills.

"You might want to leave the dog in the garage tonight, Dana, in case the intruder decides to return. As I recall, that side door doesn't have a lock. You can remedy that tomorrow."

Dana nodded as she retrieved Jenny's bed and carried it out to the garage, along with her water dish. She then used a doggie treat to lure her back on guard duty. Saying goodnight, she climbed the stairs to her room. All she wanted was sleep, which didn't arrive for hours.

Sarah rapped at her bedroom door later that morning. "A patrol car pulled in the driveway, Dana. I'll make him coffee while you get dressed."

Dana groaned. She had forgotten to set the alarm. Jerking a pair of jeans and a blouse from her closet, she hurried into her clothes. She found Sarah sitting at the kitchen counter drinking coffee and mumbling to herself. Her friend had recently married but that wouldn't stop her from flirting with any man present. That could include the deputy, who had just rung the bell. She wondered what had taken him so long.

Chapter Three

Dana glanced down at Sarah's swollen ankles. It was a relief to have her there, but she hoped her presence wouldn't complicate matters. The doorbell rang again and Jenny's barks echoed from the garage. She couldn't bring her wolf dog inside. The deputy might turn her over to animal control. Wolves were fair game although Jenny had been domesticated as a pup.

She found a plump, blond, curly-haired young man standing on the landing. He could have been Sarah's son. Chubby cheeked and smiling, he tried unsuccessfully to arrange a stern face when the entry door opened into the foyer.

"Miz Logan or is it Missus Grayson?"

Dana nodded, ignoring the question. Was the deputy insinuating she had an alias? Yawning, she led him into the living room and offered him a chair, which he refused. Assuming a military stance, he whipped out a notepad and began asking questions about the murder. When she had satisfied his curiosity, she offered him a cup of coffee, which he also declined.

"We're not allowed to accept gratuities, ma'am."

He was obviously new on the job. But what was he waiting for? Hadn't he arrived to escort her to the sheriff's office? A tear slid down Dana's cheek when she envisioned her late husband wearing a similar uniform.

"I'm gonna check the crime scene before we leave," he said, turning toward the entry door.

Remembering Jenny, she asked the deputy to check the yard before he entered the garage. "My dog's not too friendly with strangers."

A slight smile crept across his face "I get along just fine with dogs. I have three of my own."

Not this dog, she thought, insisting that he follow her suggestion. As soon as he left the house, she rushed to call Jenny inside, wondering why she was reluctant to leave the garage. Sniffing one of the Jeep's back tires, the dog seemed more interested in investigating the Jeep than acquiring her favorite treat. When she finally acquiesced, Dana gave her the jerky and led her into the bedroom. Ordered to stay, Jenny whined. What was so interesting in the garage that she didn't want to leave? Dana retrieved a flashlight from a kitchen drawer and turned on the garage's dim overhead light. Shining her flashlight along the Jeep's tires, she could find nothing suspicious or out of the ordinary. Maybe she had driven over leftover food tossed on the highway the night before. She didn't think the dog was interested in road kill, but one never knew.

Opening the garage door, she waited impatiently for the deputy to reappear, wondering why he was conducting an investigation of his own. The previous deputy had been thorough in his interrogation. Maybe they thought she would change her story. When the deputy finally appeared, he briefly moved around the cars and shined his own flashlight on the side door where the intruder had escaped.

Obviously satisfied that everything was in order, he said, "Time to leave, ma'am."

"Allow me to grab my purse." Rushing back into the house, she discovered Sarah peering through the drapes. She hoped the deputy hadn't noticed. Pulling her away from the window, she said, "I don't know when I'll be back." Rummaging in her purse, she handed Sarah the keys to the Jeep. "Just in case they decide to offer me a jail cell."

Her friend frowned. "They have no reason to jail you, Dana." Hugging her, she said, "Jenny and I will stay here on standby."

Thank heavens the mansion was for sale. She would never live this down. The neighbors already avoided her because of her involvements in past murder cases. Hurrying down the front steps she opened the passenger door. Seated behind the wheel, the deputy started to protest, but she reminded him that she was a witness, not a suspect. A patrol car sitting in her driveway was bad enough. She refused to ride in the back seat behind the wire screen.

Swiveling his head, he must have noticed a neighbor standing in his front yard, staring at them. Nodding, he started the engine and jammed the patrol car in gear. Dana hoped they wouldn't take a tour of the rural subdivision before he headed to the highway. She knew she had a reputation at the sheriff's office for snooping into murder cases, and wondered if this trip was the sheriff's idea of intimidation. Scare the snoop into keeping her nose out of Stanton County's business.

Dana exhaled the breath she had been holding and relaxed against the seat. "Any suspects yet in the case?" she said, without looking at him.

"Not to my knowledge."

"It doesn't make sense that my gardener was stabbed in my garage, then dragged or carried into the yard in broad daylight."

He let up on the accelerator. "How'd you know that?"

"There were blood stains on the garage floor. I've investigated a number of homicides."

"So I've heard. Any others committed on your property?"

"No, thank heavens."

Continuing to gaze through the windshield, she felt him staring at her. "My friend Sarah and I are apparently murder magnets. We manage to stumble over bodies no matter where we go."

"Mighty suspicious," she heard him mumble. "I've never heard of anybody finding bodies wherever they happen to land. Unless, of course, they're serial killers."

Dana turned to face him. "You can rule us out. My friend and I are reluctant amateur sleuths." She then told him about their first murder case in the California retirement village, as well as the ones that followed.

"You don't expect to find a dead woman in a Mercedes along a northern Arizona highway when you're driving an RV. Or your own sister about to be cremated soon after her husband claims it was suicide."

"No, ma'am."

"You must have heard about the murders up on Gray Wolf Mountain last year."

"You were involved in that too?"

"That and a woman we pulled from a lake at a Texas RV resort a few months ago."

The deputy whistled. "The sheriff should make you and your friend honorary detectives."

"I'll pass on that one."

"By the way, where's this friend of your's now, ma'am?"

Dana hesitated. "On her way here from Texas."

"That's a long drive."

"She's flying in." Dana crossed her fingers to nullify the lie as they pulled into the small parking lot and made their way to the office.

"Sheriff here?" the deputy asked.

"Out having coffee with the mayor," a large woman with fizzy red hair replied. "Won't be back till noon."

"Until noon?" Dana checked her watch. It was only ten thirty. How much coffee could the sheriff drink in an hour and a half? She imagined him dunking a box of donuts while he conferred with the mayor. Were they plotting to deport her from Wyoming?

The deputy waved her into a metal chair against the wall. She then watched as he leaned over the secretary, if that's what she was, and whisper in her ear.

"Oh, sure, I can handle her," Dana heard her say.

The secretary appeared to be at least six inches shorter than Dana but a good hundred pounds heavier, so there would be no contest, if Dana tried to escape. Escape? What a silly notion. She had no reason to leave before she talked to the sheriff. At nearly six feet, Dana towered over the sheriff as well. Maybe that's why he had an attitude whenever she was around.

The secretary glared at her with narrowed eyes as though she were a suspect. But when Dana attempted to engage her in conversation, she was ignored. After forty minutes, her backside was numb but she dared not stand to relieve her discomfort. Was this the sheriff's idea of witness torture? Dana sighed as she gripped the sides of the metal chair and lifted herself a few inches off the seat.

The secretary rose from her own chair and stood over her. "What do you think you're doing, sweetie."

Dana gritted her teeth. She hated that name. A nurse had called her sweetie at the clinic when they read her chart and realized that she was sixty-one. She could pass for fifty, and that was another pet peeve. Age was just a number and people should be judged by their abilities, she thought, not the years they had lived. An Internet image of a hundred-year-old man running a marathon came to mind.

"I'm tired of waiting, *sweetie*," Dana said, standing. "I'll come back when the sheriff's here."

The secretary pulled a set of handcuffs from her desk. "I don't think so. Let's make sure you stay put."

Dana stretched to her full height to glare down at her. "Cuff me and you'll be talking to my lawyer before the sheriff gets back." Pulling her cell phone from her jean's pocket, she punched in his number.

The secretary grumbled as she sat down at her desk. Picking up her phone, she said, "There'll be a warrant out for your arrest the minute you leave this office."

Checkmate. The law always had the upper hand, even if it was just a secretary. Dana briefly rubbed her backside and sat back down. A woman's voice on her phone was repeating "Hello."

Dana placed the cell phone to her ear. "Maggie? It's Dana Logan-Grayson."

"Yes, Dana. What can I do for you?"

"I'd like to speak to Bill."

"He's in court today. May I tell him what your call is about?"

"I'm detained at the sheriff's office. My gardener was killed—"

"I heard about that. I'm sorry. I'll leave Bill a message to call during his next break."

Thanking her, Dana clicked off. The secretary was still glaring. Didn't she have enough to do without intimidating witnesses? Apparently not. There was a game of solitaire in progress on her desktop computer.

Dana had nearly dozed off from lack of sleep when her phone rang. Her attorney, Bill Randall, was on the line. When told what had happened, he said she should be patient. He would arrive at the sheriff's office as soon as the criminal court adjourned. Probably by three o'clock. Dana glanced at her watch. Five minutes until noon. Where was the sheriff? Still dunking donuts?

The office door opened moments later, admitting a stranger in a sheriff's uniform. She then remembered hearing that the former sheriff had retired several weeks earlier and another man had been appointed to take his place. Dana rose to greet him.

"Sheriff? I believe you wanted to see me."

He failed to return her smile but waved her into his private office. Once seated, he introduced himself as Steve Simmons, adding that he was sorry to hear about her husband's death. Dana bit her lip, holding back tears.

"Is that why you sent a deputy to escort me here, Sheriff?"

"No, I'm puzzled why you've been involved in so many murder cases. And this time in your own yard."

"It puzzles me too. I admit that solving the murders has become somewhat of a hobby, but now that Walter's passed on, I want nothing more to do with them."

"Any ideas about who might have killed Todd Warren?"

"Absolutely none. He was likeable and did a good job gardening. He had only taken over the gardening job last month, and I don't know any of his friends. Or whether he had an enemy."

"It's a small community. You must have heard—"

Dana's chin dropped to her chest. "I-I've been depressed since Walter's death and have only left home for supplies and doctor appointments. And I haven't been sleeping well."

"I understand that you've been out of the loop. If you hear anything about Todd Warren, I'd appreciate a call."

Dana managed a slight smile. A new sheriff with a little compassion. But why didn't he simply call or stop by?

Before she could ask, he punched an intercom button and told the secretary to arrange for Dana's ride home.

"Is that all, Sheriff?"

"For now, but don't be surprised if I call you in again."

"In that case I'd appreciate a softer chair to sit

on next time." She knew she sounded as grumpy as his secretary.

"Sorry for the wait," he said, rising from his desk. "The mayor called me in for a grilling. And it wasn't a barbequed steak."

Dana liked him. He reminded her of Walter. And he obviously appreciated her sleuthing skills. Maybe they could work together to solve Todd's murder.

Chapter Four

She found Sarah in the foyer when she unlocked the door. Excited, she said, "You'll never guess what's happened. I saw on TV that Wyoming wolves have been placed back on the endangered species list. That means that we won't have to worry about someone shooting Jenny."

Dana sighed. "I'm not so sure. Benson, the neighbor down the street, would probably claim he didn't hear the news. He won't pass up a chance to take a pot shot at Jenny, no matter how many laws have been passed."

"Then I can't take her for a walk?"

"Not past his house, Sarah."

"Ranchers are upset about the listing. I wonder if they'll continue shooting wolves."

Dana shook her head. "You can't really blame them when their livestock is killed, but open season has nearly decimated the wolf population, which unbalances nature. I think we'd better be even more careful with Jenny. There are always people who will defy the law."

"Like whoever killed the gardener?"

Leading her friend into the kitchen, Dana placed a cup of water in the microwave and retrieved teabags from the cupboard. Sitting on a kitchen stool, she said, "I have no idea who might have killed Todd, and I'm not so sure I want to know."

Sarah gasped. "You mean I flew all the way here to help in the investigation when you're not even going to pursue the case?"

"Is that the only reason you dropped everything to fly here, Sarah?"

Her friend paused. "I've missed you terribly and I'm tired of the hot, dry West Texas climate."

"What about your husband?"

Sarah appeared on the verge of tears. "It's not that I don't love him, Dana. But I love you more."

"*What?*"

"We're closer than sisters. I miss seeing you on a daily basis and solving crimes together."

"Oh, Sarah." She reached to hug her. "You're not considering divorce, are you?"

"We've talked about it. He knows I'm not happy living there in isolation."

"Maybe he wouldn't mind moving here."

"No, Dana. He's a Texan through and through. We never should have married."

"You know I'll welcome you back. It's been incredibly lonely since you left and Walter died."

Sarah smiled. "You don't mind?"

"Of course not. Go back to Texas and file for divorce. Your room's always waiting."

"Not until we solve the gardener's murder."

"That could take forever. I have no idea who

killed him."

Sarah suggested having lunch at the Blue Roost Café, where they could listen in on local gossip.

"Not a bad idea, but we'd better tune up our hearing aids so we won't miss a word."

"I'm glad you haven't lost your sense of humor, Dana."

"I'm not so sure I haven't." Sliding off the stool, she said they should dress for a meal on the town.

Dana felt elated for the first time since becoming a widow. It would be great having Sarah back. She might even take the mansion off the market. The only potential buyers had been lookie loos, and when word got out about Todd's death, no one would want to live there.

They changed clothes and gave Jenny a treat before leaving. It was a five mile drive to the small town of Concord, and few cars were parked at the café. The lunch crowd must have already departed to return to work. They should have gone earlier, but they could return for dinner if no one was inclined to talk about the murder.

Once seated, a petite, blond, older waitress sauntered over to their table to ask, "Ain't you the lady that owns that big house where Todd Warren was killed?"

Dana acknowledged that she was. She asked if the waitress knew the victim.

"Sure. Everybody knew Todd. He was an all right guy."

"Did anybody have it in for him?" Sarah asked in a surprisingly quiet voice.

"Nobody that I know of. Why?"

"We were just wondering who might have killed him."

The waitress looked about the small café before answering. "If I knew, I wouldn't be dumb enough to talk about it. I might be the next dead body." She walked away without taking their order.

Sarah's fingers drummed the table. "I'm afraid we're losing our touch."

"Maybe we should have dinner at the bar and grill down the street." There might be more people present, and liquor could loosen their tongues. Sarah suggested they return home where she would whip up Texas-size grilled cheese sandwiches. They could also plan that night's strategy.

Once they were seated in the Jeep, Dana asked if Sarah were certain about her divorce.

"As sure as I'm a natural blonde. I knew within a week that I'd made a mistake. And now that I'm here, I know it's the right thing to do."

Dana worried that Sarah would regret her decision. Glancing in her rearview mirror she noticed a black Ford SUV following half a block away. They would soon leave town for the open highway, and she didn't want to lead their pursuer home. Hitting the steering wheel open-palmed, she knew that everyone in the area was aware that she lived in her sister's former mansion. The killer must know as well.

"What's wrong, Dana?"

"Don't turn around to look. I think we're being followed."

Sarah dipped her head to stare into the side mirror. "Looks like a man with a baseball cap pulled down over his forehead. He has a dark caterpillar mustache."

Dana spotted a wide spot in the road and made a quick U turn. The other driver ducked his head when he drove past and negotiated the same turn.

"Did you get his license number, Sarah?"

Sarah lifted her shoulders. "I was too nervous. I didn't even think to look?"

Sighing, Dana accelerated and drove back into town. Turning into an alley, she told Sarah to leave the Jeep and run for the building's back door. Once inside, Dana locked the door and led her friend into a room where a secretary was seated at her desk.

"Bill's not back yet," the elderly woman said. She eyed them curiously before returning to her computer screen.

Dana told her they were being followed and asked if they could wait in the lawyer's office. "If a man wearing a baseball cap and dark mustache comes in looking for us, tell him we left."

The secretary nodded and must have thought better than to ask questions. Dana heard a phone ring as she and Sarah closed the door to her lawyer's office. Pushing a chair beneath the knob, they stood listening for sounds of another visitor. It wasn't long before the knob rattled. Dana held her breath as she pressed her weight against the door. She then heard a familiar voice.

"Dana? It's Bill. Open the door."

"What's going on?" he asked when she allowed him in. "Are you two playing detectives again?" His tone was exasperation. Folding his lanky frame into a seat behind his desk, he lowered his handsome, greying head.

"Not exactly," Dana said. "Todd Warren was murdered in my garage and the sheriff hauled me into his office for questioning."

"So you're a person of interest?"

"Apparently so."

"Do you want me to represent you, Dana?"

"Only if I'm charged with the crime. I don't think the sheriff actually suspects me, but he may think I have information I'm not willing to share."

"And what might that be?"

"I have no idea. I only saw the gardener three or four times. He answered the ad I placed in the newspaper." She then told him about the man in the black SUV who had followed her on two separate occasions.

The attorney told them to stay home until a suspect was taken into custody. When they protested, he said, "Send out for whatever you need and keep a weapon handy. I'll call tomorrow to check on you."

Thanking him, they left. Dana peered from the office's back door. Seeing no one in the alley, she stooped to look beneath the Jeep. When she saw that the backseat was unoccupied, she unlocked the Jeep's door. Hurrying Sarah inside, she cautioned her to watch for their pursuer. She then drove directly to the highway. Few vehicles were traveling the road during mid-afternoon and they arrived back at the mansion without incident.

"What about dinner at the bar and grill?" Sarah asked when they were safely inside.

"You heard what Bill said. No leaving the house unless it's an emergency."

Sarah smiled. "You can drive the Escalade and wear a disguise. It's dark inside the bar so no one would recognize us. And you can take your Glock."

Dana stared at her for a long moment before she said, "Are you serious? I thought when you married Harry that you were tired of investigating murders."

"You have no idea how bored I've become living in isolation thirty miles from the nearest shopping mall."

"You must have neighbors to visit with."

"I don't fit in, Dana. Everyone else has lived there all their lives."

"Are you sure you want to get involved in the murder case?"

"Absolutely. Especially because you think you're a suspect."

"Then we're going to have to watch each other's backs, even more than we've done in the past."

"I wish I'd brought my baseball bat with me for protection."

Dana laughed. "I'll buy you a brand new bat if you promise not to swing it indiscriminately."

"Only at people who deserve it."

Dana drove into her driveway feeling more confident than she had before. Together they might discover why Todd was killed and who hated him enough to end his life. Jenny was waiting for them when Dana unlocked the mansion's front door. Sniffing their legs, the dog led them into the living room. Wagging her tail expectantly, she waited for someone to pet her. Sarah squatted to run her hand gently over the dog's head.

"We won't let that nasty man down the street shoot you, Jenny. Too bad he doesn't have anything better to do. He has no idea what a good guard dog you are."

Dana plopped down in a chair next to her. "What kind of disguises do you have in mind for us to wear tonight?"

Sarah groaned as she pulled herself upright. "Let's search your closet to see what we can find."

Dana followed her into her bedroom where Sarah had invaded her walk-in closet. Pulling a pair of corduroy overalls and denim jacket from their hangers, she said, "Wear these and tuck that pretty auburn hair into a slouch hat. I brought a pair of overalls that I wore at the ranch."

"They'll think we're—"

"Who cares what they think. We'll sit in a back booth and listen."

"But—"

"And scrub off your makeup."

Dana made a face. "Why don't I just draw mustaches on our upper lips with eyebrow pencil?"

Sarah laughed. "Not a bad idea, but it's not Halloween."

"I'm glad you recognize the absurdity in what you're suggesting. If Todd's killer is watching the house, he'll know when the Escalade leaves the garage."

Sarah suggested calling a taxi. They could leave one building in town to enter another, under cover of darkness.

Dana surmised that her friend liked to live dangerously, which she had suspected all along. Hesitantly agreeing to Sarah's plan, they dressed in overalls with Dana's Glock tucked into her concealed hip holster. Sarah crept from the back door to pluck a hand-sized rock from the flower garden, which she placed in her drawstring bag.

The taxi arrived shortly after dark. Surveying the street, they climbed in. The cab driver seemed amused. They weren't sure whether it was their attire or their cautious surveillance of the neighborhood that made him chuckle.

"Where to, ladies?"

"To Concord," Dana said. "We'll tell you exactly where when we get there."

It seemed an eternity before they spotted the lights of the only gas station on the western edge of town. Dana had turned repeatedly to survey the highway behind them, relieved that no one seemed to have followed. She told the driver to stop half a block from the tavern, and tipped him generously before they left the cab. Then, stepping into the shadows, they hugged the storefronts single file until they reached Jake's Bar and Grill.

Few customers were present in the low-slung log building where two outside lighted signs said Coors Beer and Open for Business. The neon letters K and G were missing from the overhead Jake's Bar & Grill sign, which said volumes about the Wyoming wind and upkeep of the tavern. Two rough looking, greasy men were slumped over the bar, one of them eyeing Dana as she lowered her head and led the way to a dark, rear booth. The rotund bartender left his station behind the bar and walked over.

"Two beers," Sarah said in the deepest voice she could probably muster.

"You two in town for the rodeo?" he asked.

Dana nodded. "Menus please."

"Sure." The burly barkeep returned to his station to bellow, "Carla, you got two customers."

Sarah whispered, "Are you sure you want to eat here?"

"I heard the food's good but I've never seen the kitchen."

A dark-haired, middle aged waitress appeared, or was it the cook? Her apron had probably been white at one time but it was now grease-spattered and dingy. Hard to tell in the dim light.

"Chef salads," Dana said.

Large brown eyes peered at her, crinkling at the

corners of her lined face, reflecting light from neon signs behind the bar. "Salads aren't the specialty of the house. Burgers and fries are all we got."

They reluctantly agreed and watched the woman push through swinging doors at the end of the bar. No one seemed interested in talking, not even the bartender, so Dana considered leaving. Sarah, however, was determined to get something going. Squirming for a better look at the men sitting at the bar, she attracted the attention of the one nearest her. Winking at her, he rose from his stool and motioned to his companion to accompany him.

Dana groaned. The last thing she wanted was two greasy men joining them. "Now look what you've done," she said through clenched teeth. I can smell their aroma from here."

"Howdy," the first man said. "Mind if we sit with you ladies?"

"Well," Dana said, refusing to budge. "We're waiting for someone."

"How 'bout some company till he gets here?"

"Until *they* get here," she said.

"'Nuff for a party." He pushed in next to Dana while his friend slid in beside Sarah.

Dana waved her hand as though to fan the smell away.

Her unwelcomed guest laughed. "Sorry, ma'am. We just got in from the oilfield. Stopped in to wet our whistles."

"Why don't you go home and shower. We'll be waiting for you."

"Sure," he said, getting to his feet. Why don't you join us?"

"Our friends wouldn't know where we've gone."

"Okay, we'll be back in half an hour. Keep the

booth warm." Leaning, he planted a wet kiss on Dana's forehead. Shivering with repulsion and the whiskers that scraped her brow, Dana resisted the urge to slide under the table. As soon as the men disappeared, she slapped several bills on the table and grabbed Sarah's hand.

"This was a bad idea, my friend. Let's get out of here."

Chapter Five

Sarah was never one to pass up a meal, and protested leaving before their burgers arrived. She also thought it was worse than rude to stand up a date.

"A date? Are you serious? I think oilfield workers spend most of their time on location. They probably didn't even know Todd Warren."

"It's a small town, Dana. Everyone knows everyone else. Even me, if they see me in the daylight, without this newsboy cap." She pulled the hat lower over her brow.

Dana shivered. She dreaded being there when the men returned. But they might know something about the murder. News traveled fast in rural areas. Motioning Sarah to slide in next to her, she watched as the waitress rounded the bar and headed in their direction. The aroma of freshly grilled hamburgers was a distinct improvement over their previous companions.

As they were finishing their meals, Dana noticed a man wearing a wide brimmed hat and western boots enter the tavern. He stopped to drop coins into the ancient juke box before taking a stool at the bar. He looked familiar but neither she nor Sarah could place him.

Sixties rock music filled the dimly lit room as they sipped their light beers. When the newcomer looked in their direction, Sarah smiled, her head tipped at an inviting angle. Returning her smile, the tall, grey-haired man left his stool and slid into the booth facing them.

"Marc Bartlett," he said, extending his hand to Sarah. He then peered at Dana, who had scooted against the wall. "You ladies mind some company?"

Sarah shook her head as she leaned forward. "Are you a local?"

"Yes, ma'am. Born and raised on a ranch not far from here. How about you?"

Sarah grinned. "I'm visiting my friend from a ranch in Texas."

"That so? Is this your friend?" He nodded toward Dana.

Dana straightened her slump and attempted to appear friendly. She hadn't planned to mingle with the customers, but maybe this rancher knew Todd. "Still ranching?" she asked.

"Only thing I know. Cattle and alfalfa are my specialties."

Dana warmed to his melodic chuckle.

"I don't recall seeing you gals around town. You from Casper?"

"No, we live a few miles from town in a rural subdivision."

His expression darkened. "I hope it's not the

same place where that young fellah was killed yesterday."

Dana hesitated. Should she tell him the murder took place in her garage? She decided against it. "He died in my subdivision. Did you happen to know the victim, Todd Warren?"

"Matter of fact, I did. His family ranches a spread near mine. Good kid. Used to bale hay during the summers on some of the neighboring ranches."

"Did he have any enemies?"

"None that I know of. Why'd you ask?"

"Just curious why someone would kill him?" Dana glanced up to see the two oilfield roughnecks enter the bar. Cringing, she told the rancher they didn't want to be bothered by the men.

"No problem. I'll take care of them." He was out of the booth quicker than most men his age, which Dana guessed to be early sixties. A nice looking man, tall, neatly groomed and someone she felt they could trust—to a point. After a few moments of conversation, the roughnecks left the bar. They appeared to be grumbling.

Sarah remarked that they had cleaned up nicely, but a rancher in hand was worth two in the oilfield. Dana agreed.

"What did you say to get them to leave?" Sarah asked when the rancher resumed his seat.

"I hope you don't mind, but I said there were some young, good-looking gals down the street at the Ace Saloon." When he noticed Sarah's expression, he was quick to add, "Not that you ladies aren't attractive."

Sarah laughed. "You're not bad, yourself."

Dana nudged her, hoping she would stop her flirting. They needed to learn whatever he knew about her gardener. "So Todd Warren was a rancher," she said. "When did he decide to live in town?"

"To my knowledge, he never left. He worked at odd jobs in town when his ranch chores were done. His old man is sickly and can't work like he used to, so Todd had to take over. He was still in his late teens at the time, but he was a responsible kid who worked hard at whatever needed to be done."

"When did he find time to garden?" Dana asked.

The rancher said that he had no idea how he handled both jobs. "He was a worker, that one. I wish my own son was as ambitious as Todd." He hung his head as though he were ashamed of his offspring.

Sarah reached to pat his hand. "How does your wife feel about your son's reluctance to work?"

Dana gasped, embarrassed by her friend's aggression.

He sighed. "Marci died last year. And it's been awfully lonely at the ranch without her."

Dana's attitude softened. She could certainly sympathize.

Both women said they were sorry, and by the sly look on Sarah's face, Dana knew she was contemplating her matchmaking hobby. She was even more shocked when Sarah told him that Dana was a widow. Marc's face lit up and he wondered aloud why they hadn't told him their names. She could tell he was interested, but she wasn't ready for another relationship. She was still grieving Walter's death.

"Dana and Sarah," her friend said, pointing to her chest. "We'd really like to know more about Todd Warren because he was killed in our neighborhood. We could be next."

"Not much to tell. He was engaged to a nice

young gal who lives on a neighboring ranch. They attended school together. She went off to college and I know he wanted to go, but he had to take over chores at the ranch."

He frowned when Sarah asked the woman's name. Hesitating, he said, "Amy Porter."

"Did Todd have any known enemies? Anyone who might have wanted to kill him?"

"None that I'm aware of. He was the sort of young man that I would have been proud to call son."

Dana knew their questions were bothering him. She decided to invite him to lunch the following day at the Blue Roost Café, so that they could get better acquainted. She would have to tell him where the murder took place before someone identified her as the owner of the house where Todd Warren was killed. Now was not the time, and she hoped that no one would tell him first.

Marc readily agreed to lunch, offering them a ride home when Sarah reached for her phone to call the town's only taxi. Dana sensed that he could be trusted, but didn't want him to know where she lived. Not yet. Crossing fingers behind her back, she said they were going to visit a friend in town before going home. They might even spend the night.

When they parted on the street, Sarah whispered that they should have accepted the ride. They were visible targets if the killer were searching for them. She pulled Dana into the shadows of the building next door and punched in the taxi's number on her lighted screen. Dana watched the taillights of Marc's pickup truck disappear down the street to the east, then noticed a black SUV drive toward them a block away.

"It's the killer," she said, pulling Sarah into the darkness between the buildings, causing Sarah to drop her phone. Telling her to forget the phone until the car drove by, Dana placed her hand on her holstered gun. A shootout in town wasn't her idea of a good way to end their evening. She hoped it wasn't the same car.

Sarah's phone was face up on the sidewalk and she feared the killer had seen the light. She was right. They should have accepted Marc's offer to drive them home. The SUV turned the corner and Sarah dashed out to retrieve her cell. They then reentered the bar, taking the same booth in back.

"Couldn't stay away?" the bartender said. His sarcasm was evident.

They ignored him until he approached with two additional beers. The rule of the house must be 'Buy a drink or get out.' The face of Sarah's phone was cracked but she managed to call the taxi's number. She was told that it would be close to an hour before they were picked up, so they huddled together in the darkest section of the booth. No one else was present and they sat sipping beer and watching the door. Minutes later, the door opened and the two roughnecks appeared. Dana groaned as Sarah slid to the edge of the booth and beckoned to them.

"Just until the taxi arrives," she whispered.

The two young men stood next to the table until told to take a seat opposite them. "What happened to Hopalong Cassidy?" one of them asked.

"It was past his bedtime," Sarah said, smiling.

The chunky one said, "The old cowpoke lied. There wasn't any good lookin' chicks at the Ace Saloon."

"I guess Hopalong didn't want any competition

from younger men. And by the way, we're not cougars."

"We thought you was waitin' for customers."

Dana felt like throwing her beer in his face. "Sorry to disappoint you boys. We're waiting for Todd Warren."

They exchanged looks before the burly one said, "Haven't you heard? Somebody knocked him off yesterday at some rich broad's house down the road."

Putting on her best mournful expression, Dana asked if they knew who might have killed him.

"Hell, it coulda been anybody. There's a coupla meth labs on the edge of town."

"Are you saying that Todd was doing drugs?"

"No, but there are some rough characters hidin' out here. What better place to cook meth than in a small town?"

Sarah asked if they knew the druggies, and was told that oilfield workers could get plenty of methamphetamines at some of the remote drilling sites. They didn't need to mess with criminals. When asked if they knew Todd Warren well, they said they didn't hang out with ranchers.

"Cowpokes think drinkin' hootch is the only way to get high."

Dana cringed as she glanced at the lighted dial on her watch. The taxi wouldn't arrive for at least half an hour. They needed to keep the men talking in case the killer entered the bar. They might even have to leave with them and fight them off later. Pressing her arm against the holster, she reassured herself the Glock was still there. Whether she could shoot to kill bothered her. Shooting her murderous former brother-in-law in his groin was the worst she had ever done.

"Tell us about Todd," she said. "We heard he was getting married."

The thin one smirked. "Nice gal but not too smart. She coulda married a rich rancher on Casper Mountain, but she picked a poor cowpoke like Todd."

Both said they couldn't think of anyone who would want to kill Todd, but they would nose around and get back to her. Dana wouldn't tell them where she lived, but decided to give them her phone number. She could change the number later. The chunky one wrote the number on a napkin and stuffed it in his pocket. He then wanted to know, "What's in it for us?"

"A five thousand dollar reward when the killer's captured and convicted."

Their eyes lit up and they immediately agreed to Dana's terms. She said, "Don't tell anyone about our arrangement or what my friend and I look like, or you'll place our lives in danger."

"You'd have a hard time collecting your reward," Sarah said, "if we're six feet under."

"You think the killer might come after us?" the lanky one asked. "I mean if word gets out about us telling you who we think killed Warren?"

"Of course not. We'll keep this conversation between the four of us."

They both offered their hands to seal the deal.

While they were ruminating, the door opened and a man beckoned to Sarah. Was he the taxi driver? Dana waved him over to their table where he impatiently told them that he had another customer. If they weren't ready to go, he'd leave without them. They thanked the roughnecks and rushed to follow the driver. The clock on the wall behind the bar said

11:15, well past Dana's bedtime. The trip to town had been a fruitful one if the roughnecks came up with needed information. She was also looking forward to lunch with the rancher. He must know everyone in town.

Chapter Six

Dana knew she was paranoid. What if the killer had murdered the taxi driver and now sat behind the wheel? She glanced at Sarah, who seemed unconcerned. Touching her Glock, she tried to relax against the seat.

"You ladies have a good time in town?" the driver asked.

"Todd Warren stood us up," Dana said, hoping the driver didn't know he had been killed on her property.

"That right? One of my passengers said somebody killed him, but he didn't know where or how it happened."

Dana pretended shock before asking if the driver knew the victim. He said Todd had attended school with his son. "They were good buddies, but my boy joined the marines and they lost contact with each other. He'll be sad to hear that Todd's dead."

She asked if Todd had any enemies. The driver thought for a moment before he said a boy had bullied him in school. His name was Brad Langley and he was now part owner of the Ace Saloon. The sleuths glanced at one another in the dark. Tomorrow night they would frequent the saloon. Hopefully, the roughnecks wouldn't be present. Maybe Marc Bartlett could be persuaded to accompany them. Dana thought the rancher would make a good companion.

When the taxi left the highway, both women scanned the rural road for parked cars, primarily black Ford SUVs. A crescent moon loomed overhead and Dana was able to distinguish trees and other objects, but no parked vehicles of any kind. When they pulled into her circle drive, both women crept from the taxi after Dana paid the fare. Briefly scanning the yard, she led the way up the steps. When she unlocked the front door, they could hear Jenny barking.

"Good dog," Sarah whispered. "That deep bark would scare anyone away."

"Let's hope so." Dana retrieved a long-handled flashlight she kept inside the door. It was heavy enough to crack a coconut, a handy weapon to discourage an intruder. Jenny sniffed their legs before she would allow them to pass. Reassured that they hadn't been around other dogs, she led them into the living room. Dana sank into her recliner as Sarah hurried off to prepare them cups of tea.

A moment later the phone rang. Dana picked up and listened, but all she heard was silence. Had the caller hung up or was she losing her hearing?

"Hello?" She heard a click and the dial tone. Was the killer determining whether she was home?

Sarah returned with tea and small cakes. "I don't know about you, but I'm hungry— What's wrong,

Dana? You look like you've seen an apparition."
"Not a ghost, but someone called and hung up." Checking her watch, she said, "Who calls at a quarter past midnight?"
"Check the caller I.D."
Dana retrieved the phone and announced that it was a private number. "Are you thinking what I'm thinking?"
Sarah rose to close the drapes. "If we're being watched, he knows we're here. I hope you still have your gun handy."
"I do but the security system stopped working yesterday. The repairman will be here tomorrow."
"Then we'd better keep our eyes and ears open."
"Do you mind sleeping in one of the recliners?"
"I can sleep on the floor, if necessary."
Jenny growled and raced to the back of the house. They followed, arriving in time to hear a prying sound and splintering wood. Muzzling Jenny with one hand, Dana drew her gun. Whispering to Sarah to call 911, she feared that no Stanton County deputies were on duty at that hour. She knew the intruder could gain access to the house long before a deputy arrived.
"I have a gun aimed at the door and I know how to use it," Dana said in a loud voice. The sounds stopped and she thought she heard footsteps echoing on the patio. Jenny wrenched free of her grip and began a series of sharp barks. Had the man left? She ran to the living room where she turned off the lamp and peered through the bay window. Dana sighed with relief when she noticed taillights departing in the direction of the highway. But would he try again? As much as she hated the thought, she would have to hire a bodyguard. The last time she employed a

guard, other than Jeff Mailer, he was attacked in his car and later died in the hospital.

When Sarah returned, she was obviously shaken. "Is he still here?" When Dana shook her head, she said, "The dispatcher woke a deputy and told him to investigate."

"Call her back. Tell her the deputy can wait until morning. I'll leave all the downstairs lights on and Jenny will let us know if the killer returns."

"Are you sure?" Sarah plopped into an arm chair and picked up the phone. When she clicked off, she said, "None of this is making sense. Who would want to kill *you*? Have you made someone mad enough to do you in?"

Dana suppressed a yawn and reached for her cup. "The neighbors don't like me because of our murder investigations. They must think I'll bring criminals into the neighborhood to harm them."

"That's not enough reason to kill you."

"My trigger happy neighbor is incensed that I own a wolf dog and won't allow him to shoot her."

"What about the rest of the neighbors?"

"I'm sure they resent the fact that Georgie's mansion is nicer than their own homes."

"But the mansion belongs to you now, Dana. You weren't responsible for the fancy gables and gingerbread trim."

"They know that my former brother-in-law built the mansion and is in prison along with his drug lord brother, so the house must be tainted."

"But your sister was a famous mystery novelist."

"It doesn't matter, Sarah. As far as the neighbors are concerned, I'm as tainted as the house."

"That's not fair."

"I've gotten use to the fact that I'm an outcast in

my own neighborhood."

"So that's why you put the mansion up for sale."

"That and the fact that Walter died and you moved away. I've been rattling around in this huge house alone for five months."

"I'm here now and we'll face this mess together."

"I hope you're not making a mistake by leaving Harry."

"It didn't work out, Dana. My place is here with you."

"Okay, Watson, what's your take on the murder."

"I'll tell you, Sherlock, I've been wondering about the killers we helped to send to prison, including your brother-in-law. Maybe one of them escaped or was paroled."

"Escape is possible but I doubt any of them were paroled."

"Another convict escaped just before I left to get married. Remember?"

Dana set her cup down so hard that she spilled her tea. "There must be a way to check on their whereabouts."

"We can do that later this morning. I'm exhausted." Sarah rose from the chair and climbed the stairs to her room.

Was Sarah right? If one of them did escape, why kill Todd Warren? Was it a warning that he was also going to kill both her and Sarah? She needed to convince Sarah to return to Texas and her husband.

Jenny lay at her feet, prompting Dana to pet her. The dog had probably saved their lives. The mansion was so large that they would have never heard the break-in. Rising from her chair, she checked that the windows and doors were securely locked, and followed Sarah's lead.

<><><>

Tossing for what seemed hours, Dana realized that she had become an insomniac. Checking her alarm clock, she saw that it was almost four o'clock. How was she going to function that day? Propping the pillows behind her back, she sat up in bed and began to meditate. Before long her head lurched forward and she slid onto her side, sound asleep. Sarah woke her later that morning, announcing through the door that the deputy had arrived. She hurriedly dressed and joined Sarah and the deputy on the patio.

"Looks like somebody tried to pry the doorframe loose," he said. It was the same chubby-cheeked deputy who had escorted Dana to the sheriff's office.

Sarah suggested that he dust for prints. His expression said that he knew how to do his job. Backing away, she offered to bring him a cup of freshly brewed coffee. He refused. Again. Dana thought, Give him a few more years and he'll gratefully accept a hot drink after his job has worn him down.

The deputy retrieved a camera from his patrol car and spent several minutes clicking off photographs. When he finished, he said, "We only have seven deputies to patrol over eighteen hundred miles of county roads. I suggest you hire a private guard to patrol your property."

Dana agreed. She wondered whether Jeff Mailer was available. He had protected them through two other murder cases, but Sarah had a crush on him. She would have to persuade her to refrain from flirting with Jeff. He was probably the best personal guard she could hire. Dana found his number on her speed dial and listened to three rings on the other end. When he picked up, he sounded pleased to hear her voice and immediately agreed to take the job.

Sarah seemed happy that Jeff would provide security, which prompted Dana to remind her that she was still a married woman. She sensed déjà vu when Sarah rushed upstairs to her room to change clothes and apply her makeup.

The phone rang. Hesitantly picking up, Dana recognized the number and sighed with relief. She briefly feared that Jeff had changed his mind, or that the killer was calling again.

"Hi, Dana. It's Bill calling to make sure you and Sarah made it through the night."

"Someone tried to break in last night, Bill. But we managed to scare him off."

There was silence on the other end. The lawyer then said, "Perhaps you two should take a vacation—somewhere under a palm tree—until the killer is apprehended."

"Tahiti would be great but Sarah is determined to solve the case on her own. I can't leave her to her own devices."

"Have you thought about hiring a bodyguard or two?"

"Jeff Mailer's on his way."

Her attorney sighed. "Good man, Jeff. You couldn't hire a better bodyguard."

"I know. We'll breathe a lot easier when he arrives."

"Then I can stop worrying about you."

Dana smiled when she hung up. She was lucky to have such a caring attorney and bodyguard. And she hoped to add Marc Bartlett to her circle of male friends. Sitting at her desk to take notes while she waited for Jeff to arrive, Dana remembered her lunch date with Marc. She hoped the rancher would agree to a platonic relationship. She worried he would be angry when he learned that she hadn't told him the truth about her interest in Todd Warren.

The doorbell rang moments later and Sarah rushed to the door before Dana could leave her desk. Smiling, Jeff Mailer strode across the room to grip her hand and give her a brief hug. He had expressed an interest in her instead of Sarah. But when she married Walter, Jeff had backed away.

When they explained the situation, Jeff took notes and asked about the security cameras.

"For some reason they stopped working yesterday," Dana said. "The repairman will be here tomorrow."

"I'll have a look at them to see if they've been tampered with."

"Thanks, Jeff. It's good to have you back."

He smiled and placed a warm hand on her shoulder. When he squeezed, she moved away to retrieve her notes. She then asked if he had known Todd Warren, and received the same answer that everyone else had offered about his character. Todd was a great guy who worked hard and had no enemies that he was aware of.

Jeff frowned when Dana mentioned Brad Langley. "He's not someone you can trust. An alcoholic who hangs out at the Ace Saloon where he owns a piece of the action. It's not a place for the two of you to frequent. Drug pushers and users are the main customers."

Sarah plopped down next to him on the leather couch. "Then how can we discover who murdered Todd?"

The retired police detective sighed. "Leave it to the sheriff. You're lucky that you haven't gotten yourselves killed during previous investigations."

"That's why you're here, Jeff. Whoever tried to break in last night will probably try again."

Rising from the couch, he said he would retrieve his clothing from the car and settle in Dana's former brother-in-law's room, where he had stayed before. They would then plan their strategy. As he was leaving, Jenny jumped to lick his face, surprising Dana that the dog remembered him. It was good to have Jeff and Sarah back in the mansion. Partial sunshine had replaced the dark cloud hanging over her head since Walter's death.

Chapter Seven

When they had dressed for lunch, Dana asked Jeff about the rancher. Marc Bartlett was given a thumb's up, although Jeff's expression was strange when told Dana was meeting him for lunch. Jeff suggested they make it a foursome and Sarah agreed. But how were they going to explain Jeff's presence?

Before they left for the café, the phone rang again. When Dana answered, the voice on the line sounded vaguely familiar but she wasn't sure of the caller's identity until he said, "I'm ready to collect the reward money."

"Who is this?"

"Jack Norton. We met you at Jake's Bar and Grill. Chad and I think we know who killed Todd Warren."

"Who?"

"Bart Bailey and Todd Warren had a fight at the gas station last week."

"What were they fighting about?"

"The station owner said that Todd dropped his credit card while he was pumping gas and Bart picked it up and used it for his own truck."

"Did anyone tell the sheriff?"

"Not that we know of. When can we collect the reward?"

"When Bart Bailey is convicted of murder."

"But that could take forever."

"Sorry, that's the deal. I suggest you call Sheriff Simmons with the information." Dana hung up before the caller could protest further.

Their bodyguard drove them to the café early to acquire a table with a view of the parking lot. Within minutes Marc Bartlett's dusty Dodge pickup pulled into the lot. He soon appeared at the café door, western hat in hand. Dana left the table to welcome him and explain that Sarah and Jeff were joining them. Jeff stood to extend his hand when they reached the table, and Dana compared the two men, who looked remarkably alike in both height, age, and body mass. Both were tall, handsome, and well-built with greying hair. They knew each other and shook hands as though old friends.

"Don't tell me you're guarding these ladies," Marc said.

When Jeff nodded in the affirmative, Marc glanced at them both. He didn't ask why, but Dana filled him in on the sketchiest details of the murder and the reason for Jeff's presence.

Marc frowned. "So that's the reason you were questioning me last night. I thought—"

"That's not the only reason," Sarah said before

Dana nudged her.

"You're someone we'd like to know," Dana said.

A smile crept across Marc's face. He asked what he could do to help with the murder investigation. He had already told them everything he knew about Todd Warren.

"We'd like to talk to his fiancée."

"I know she's broken up about Todd's death and might not want to see anyone."

"I'm sure she is, but maybe she can tell us who might have killed my gardener."

Marc agreed with Jeff that they should leave the investigation to the sheriff. He understood that they were personally involved in the case, but thought it too dangerous for them to tempt the killer's wrath by investigating.

When Dana told him that Jeff had accompanied them on other murder investigations, Marc shook his head, wondering why he hadn't heard about them.

"We don't broadcast our investigations," Dana said. "The fact that we seem to attract murderers and drug lords doesn't make us popular with people who know. I'm my neighborhood's Typhoid Annie, so to speak."

"And we've even been suspects in some the murders we've investigated," Sarah added.

"But I don't understand why two such nice, attractive women would become amateur sleuths. Is it because you crave excitement?"

"We're unwilling sleuths, Marc. And this time the killing took place in my own yard."

Sarah's eyes gleamed. "Sometimes it's exciting. Once we were caught in a flash flood. Another time Dana had to crash the motorhome to escape a killer.

We were also on a serial killer's list in California, where he murdered a number of our friends. But that's not all."

Marc turned to Dana. "You must have feline blood to escape death so many times."

"Pure luck," she said. "I thought I had given up amateur sleuthing until I found poor Todd in my yard. My neighbors will probably set fire to a cross on my lawn or ride me out of town on a proverbial rail because the murder took place in their subdivision."

"I don't understand why you would continue sleuthing, unless it's an obsession."

"It may be with Sarah, but it certainly isn't with me."

"Nor me," Sarah said. "We don't go looking for murder cases. They just seem to find us, no matter where we are. And solving the crimes has always been a challenge. But it's a hobby we'd both like to avoid from now on."

"I see. Well, under the circumstances. I'll volunteer to help Jeff guard the mansion. My alfalfa crop was recently harvested and my brother and the cowhands will look after the cattle."

Dana thanked him and offered a guest room in the mansion. Glancing at Jeff, she realized that he wasn't pleased. She hoped Marc's presence wouldn't lead to conflict. She wanted to keep her relationships strictly platonic, if that were possible. Why did life have to be so complicated?

The men did most of the talking at lunch, the women unusually quiet. Because they were in a public place, the murder wasn't mentioned again, but Dana strained to listen to other patrons who might discuss Todd Warren. It wasn't until a big, disheveled man, with a few days' dark beard, sat at the lunch counter that someone talked about the case.

"Brad Langley," Jeff said in a low voice when the man bellowed his order. The tiny, white-haired waitress behind the counter scurried about as though waiting on the governor. When she returned with his order, he engaged her in conversation.

"Anybody arrested yet for killin' Warren?" he asked.

"How would I know, Brad? I'm just a waitress."

"I know you hear plenty of scuttlebutt here in the café. Sheriff been in lately?"

The waitress frowned. "Yeah, but he doesn't discuss his cases with me."

The big man laughed. "Warren was a wimp. I whipped his ass when we was kids."

"He was a nice guy," she said, scooting into the kitchen.

Langley turned on his stool to direct his attention to Dana's luncheon group. She disliked him on sight and lowered her head to finish her meal. He was still a bully and she doubted he had many friends.

Marc said hello and asked how he was doing. Big mistake. Langley pulled up a chair and made himself at home. Dana could smell the alcohol on his breath and knew the others did as well.

"So, Brad," Jeff said. "You used to abuse Todd Warren when you both were young?"

"Hell, yes. He wouldn't stand up for himself, so I taught him a lesson."

"Have you seen him lately?"

"Nah, he never comes to the saloon where I spend most of my time." The big man squirmed on his chair. "I ain't seen him in months. Maybe even a year."

"But you must have heard talk in the saloon about his death," Jeff said.

"Sure, I heard somebody killed him at that rich broad's mansion. Maybe she put the make on him and he rejected her."

Jeff's face filled with anger. "Don't go around spreading vicious lies, or you will wind up the defendant in a defamation of character lawsuit."

Langely gulped down his hamburger and claimed pressing business. No one said a word as they watched him drive away in his rusty pickup.

"Poor man," Sarah said at last. "He doesn't have much of a life."

Jeff said, "Alcohol does that to a man."

"He's been an alcoholic since he was a teenager," Marc added. "I've never known him not to drink."

Dana asked if they thought he might have killed Todd. And why hadn't the sheriff arrested him to prevent him from killing someone with his pickup?

Marc sighed. "He's been arrested so many times that he has his own cell."

"Does he ever get violent?"

"Sure, that's when he winds up in the pokey."

Had Brad Langley killed her gardener? Or was she grasping at straws? There didn't seem to be another suspect unless it was a random murder. But it didn't make sense that someone would drive in from the highway and hide in her garage to kill the first person he saw. What if Dana were the intended victim and Todd the innocent bystander? Cold chills made her shiver.

"What's wrong, Dana?" Jeff reached across the table to place a hand on hers.

"I was just thinking that maybe Todd was killed by mistake since, by all accounts, he had no enemies."

"That's something to consider."

Dana suggested that Jeff pay the sheriff a visit to learn anything he could about the murder investigation. Jeff would normally agree, but was Marc's presence making him hesitant? Turning to Marc, she asked that he return to his ranch to pack his things while Jeff visited the sheriff.

Jeff protested. "And leave you two alone?"

"Sarah and I will sit here and visit until you both return. No one's going to bother us in the café."

Sarah whispered. "Dana has her Glock."

Both men argued that it wasn't a good idea, but Dana reminded Jeff that she was an excellent marksman. They hesitated before leaving together.

Dana watched as both men drove from the parking lot. Sarah then said, "They're both interested in you, Dana."

"Don't be ridiculous. I'm not interested in anything other than solving this case. I've still got eight months of mourning Walter before I can consider a new relationship."

"That's old fashioned nonsense. But if that's how you feel, you'd better tell them."

"I intend to." Dana pulled a notepad from her purse. "Let's reconstruct the murder and figure out who could have killed Todd Warren."

Sarah said they didn't have much to go on. They needed to talk to Todd's fiancée as well as his parents. Dana remembered Marc saying that Todd's father was in ill health, but he might still live at the family ranch. Maybe Marc would arrange a meeting with Todd's parents as well as his fiancée. Surely ranch people visited their neighbors to pay their respects, if Marc hadn't already done so.

The waitress returned to their table to refill their coffee cups. She asked if they wanted dessert. Sarah wasn't one to pass up sweets and ordered chocolate cake. Dana declined. The image of Todd lying on her lawn had ruined her appetite. She only wanted to find his killer. Presumably at a dead end, they talked about Sarah's brief life in Texas. They then recalled their last murder investigation at a north Texas RV resort, where they found a woman's body in one of the lakes.

"You never know who's capable of murder," Dana said. "Most killers look like everyone else, although they have a hidden agenda."

"Some kill on the spur of the moment. A sudden rage."

"Do you think that's what happened to Todd?"

"I doubt it, Dana. Whoever killed him was hiding in your garage. That seems premeditated."

"That's what worries me. What if the killer was waiting for me and Todd just happened to appear at the wrong time."

"Don't even think that way, my friend."

"Whoever killed him must have followed us and tried to break in last night. Why would he have done that if Todd was his intended victim?"

"Maybe he thinks you witnessed the murder from your kitchen window."

"So you think he's trying to get rid of potential witnesses?"

"Maybe Todd was cheating on his girlfriend."

"Everyone I've talked to says he was an honest man, Sarah. I doubt he would cheat on anyone."

Half an hour later, the café door opened and Jeff walked in. His expression was one of worry. When seated, he said, "The sheriff's holding his cards close to his chest, but he seemed relieved that I'm guarding you. He agrees that you might have been the intended victim, Dana."

"You've validated my fears, Jeff. Todd was an innocent victim."

"We need to discover who wants you dead."

Two cups of coffee later, Marc rushed in. He also appeared worried. "Storm's coming in, might even be a tornado headed our way. I didn't have your phone number to let you know I've got to help drive the cattle to safer pasture."

Dana wrote her cell number on the note pad and handed it to him. "Call when you've finished," she said. "We'll be just fine." She watched him leave, then turned to Jeff. "We need to fortify the mansion. Let's pick up whatever we need on the way home. I anticipate cabin fever before this murder's solved."

Jeff presented his own list and escorted them to his car. They had all been through this security procedure before. Hopefully, her wolf dog had prevented a break-in while they were gone.

Dana couldn't take her mind off suspects while they were shopping. Who had she and Sarah helped to place in jail that wanted revenge? The serial killer in California? Her former brother-in-law who was responsible for her sister's death? His brother, the sheriff, who headed a vicious drug ring? Members of the home grown terrorist group in Arizona? The Texas killer who drowned his female victims? Or the deranged man who killed wolves to cover up his murders? It could also be their family members bent on revenge. Dana felt as though a large target had burned into her back. She should have known retribution would happen, and wished that Sarah had remained in Texas. Her life was also in danger.

Chapter Eight

They could hear the dog barking when they exited Jeff's car. Their guard left the driveway at a run, surprisingly fast for a man in his early sixties. He disappeared around the house in the direction of the rear patio, yelling for them to lock themselves in his car. Moments later Jeff returned, holding a shorter man's arms behind his back. Dana nearly fell from the car in her haste to reach them.

"Let him go, Jeff. That's my neighbor."

"He was looking in a back window."

Ronald Benson had been a royal pain since she moved into the neighborhood. He complained constantly, especially about the presence of her wolf dog. Dana demanded to know why he was in her yard.

Rubbing his wrists, he glared at Jeff. "I saw some guy sneak in your yard, and I thought he was gonna break-in."

"Why didn't you call the sheriff, Ronald? And

when did you start worrying about my welfare?"

Pushing thinning white hair back from his brow, he turned his glare on her. Gray eyes narrowed, he said, "If there's a burglar in the neighborhood, my place might be next."

Jeff asked for a description of the burglar and was told that he was tall with an athletic build. "He was wearing a baseball cap and sunglasses so I couldn't tell his age."

"How long ago?" Jeff's police experience was apparent.

Benson checked his watch. "Not long. Maybe fifteen minutes. I grabbed a baseball bat from my garage and came around back. I didn't take time to call the sheriff."

Jeff said he had seen the bat leaning against the back wall and assumed it belonged to the killer.

"Killer?" Benson said. "You mean the one that murdered Todd Warren?"

"Possibly."

Dana insisted that Jeff let her neighbor go. She didn't think Benson disliked her enough to kill her. But the retiree seemed half a bubble off. She suspected that he suffered from some form of dementia. If he did, he wouldn't make a good witness when the killer came to trial.

"I'm gonna call animal control to come after your wolf," Benson said. "I'm tired of hearing him howl."

"*She* saved our lives last night, and she doesn't howl. Jenny has never harmed anyone, but I'm sure she'd attack a burglar if he broke in my house."

"If I see that wolf on the street, I'll shoot him."

"I advise you to curb your trigger finger, Mister Benson. Wolves are back on the endangered list.

I'm surprised you didn't rush over here with your shotgun."

"I didn't have time to unlock my gun safe," he said, his face crimson.

Attempting to resolve the matter, Dana thanked her neighbor for investigating and reminded him to call the sheriff, if he saw the man again. He left grumbling as Dana unlocked her front door. Jenny greeted them in the foyer and barked when she noticed Jeff. Extending the back of his hand, he allowed the dog to sniff and lick him before Jenny trotted off. He then carried their supplies into the kitchen, followed by Sarah. Exhausted, Dana collapsed into her leather recliner. She had decided to sell the mansion whether Sarah moved in or not. The neighbors would probably throw a party to celebrate her departure.

Jeff appeared with a cup of tea that Sarah had prepared. Sitting in a nearby chair, he said, "Todd's family might rest easier knowing that he was killed by mistake."

"But are we sure of that, Jeff?"

"I'm not a hundred percent certain, but I think the killer was blinded by the sun when the garage door opened, and he struck at the person in front of him. You and Todd were about the same size."

"So you think he didn't know who he killed until Todd collapsed?" When Jeff nodded, she said, "Then why drag the body onto the lawn?"

Jeff leaned to place a hand on her arm. "Maybe as a warning that he's coming after you. To scare you into making mistakes that would make it easy for him—"

"We need to find out who he is, Jeff."

"We will by systematically going through your

suspects' list. My friend at the P.D. can find out who's still in prison. That will narrow the list down considerably."

Dana closed her eyes, leaning her head against the high leather back. Beginning with their first murder investigation at the California retirement village, she named each suspect and he wrote them down. When she finished, he said, "That's quite a list. I'll email this to my friend to see what he can find."

When she opened her eyes he was gone. She had probably dozed off. *Now what?* She rose from the recliner to find Sarah. She found her in the kitchen talking on her phone. Raising an index finger, she signaled Dana to wait. When she clicked off tears were visible in her eyes.

"He doesn't want a divorce, Dana. He wants me to come home."

"Then maybe you should. Talk things out before you make a decision."

"I can't leave you here alone."

Dana sighed. "I'll have two men to protect me. The neighbors will probably think I'm taking in borders or running a bordello."

"Stop worrying about the neighbors."

Dana hugged her friend and offered to help her pack. She would ask Marc to drive Sarah to the airport and pick her up, if she decided to return. Meanwhile, she could help Jeff investigate the suspects, which she knew would take some time.

The phone rang while they were packing. Marc called to say the cattle roundup hadn't gone well, forcing him to stay at the ranch another day. Dana told him not to worry, but to concentrate on his herd. Jeff was there to protect her. She hung up worrying that Sarah had no ride to the airport. When told, Sarah decided to wait until Marc was available. She said her husband would understand. But would he? Dana didn't want to contribute to a marriage breakup. She resolved not to influence Sarah either way.

Later that afternoon, Jeff said it might be days before his friend could learn the whereabouts of the inmates. Sarah seemed relieved and said she would unpack her things. As Dana was helping her unpack, an earsplitting siren startled them.

"Tornado warning," Jeff said, rushing into Sarah's room. "Hurry. Let's go down to the basement."

The dog was barking hysterically and running in circles, making her difficult to catch and leash. Jeff grabbed their arms and pulled them toward the basement stairs as they heard a roar akin to a freight train, and the sound of projectiles hitting the outer walls.

When they reached the basement floor, Jeff told them to crouch in the east corner, away from anything metal. Spotting a box of winter bedding, he tossed them quilts to roll up in and pillows to cover their heads. He had barely covered himself when the lights flickered off and they heard the mansion disintegrating above them. Dana screamed for Jenny and the dog came running. Wrapping the dog in her quilt, she prayed aloud that they wouldn't be buried alive.

"Cover your heads," Jeff yelled again, his voice barely discernible above the noise.

Something crashed into the basement and Dana prayed it wasn't her grandmother's heirloom piano. Although it was late afternoon, the basement was as dark as a moonless night. It was growing increasingly difficult to breathe, and Dana knew the mansion had been destroyed. Would anyone find them before they suffocated?

Jenny squirmed in her arms, making it difficult to pull her cell phone from her pocket. A hand then lifted the pillow from her head and a bright light blinded her. Jeff asked, "You all right, Dana?"

"I'm fine. See about Sarah," she said, coughing.

A moment later, Dana heard him say, "Oh, no."

Pushing the dog away, she managed to get to her feet. Jeff was crouched over Sarah's quilted form, the pillow held in one hand, a small flashlight in the other. "She's been injured and appears unconscious. Call nine-one-one. Tell them we're trapped and need an ambulance."

A lump formed in Dana's throat, so large that she couldn't speak. Handing her cell phone to Jeff, she motioned for him to call. Wiping grit from her eyes, she took the flashlight and knelt to examine her friend. A timber had fallen, hitting the pillow, which must have softened the blow. But was Sarah badly hurt? Cradling her friend's head in her lap, she felt hot tears cursing down her checks. She could hear Jeff requesting an ambulance and sheriff's assistance, but would they reach them in time to save Sarah? Dust hung in the basement air like dense fog in the flashlight's glare, boards creaking above their heads. Would the main floor collapse, burying the four of them?

When Jeff clicked off, he said, "Help's on the way but no one knows how extensive the damage is. The tornado might have destroyed the entire subdivision. That means we'll have to wait our turn to be rescued." His resultant cough sounded like a severe case of bronchitis.

If I didn't know better, I'd think the killer was responsible for this. Dana glanced down at Sarah's face when she groaned and moved her head. Thank heavens she's still alive. Gently patting her face, she asked if she could hear her voice. Sarah coughed but didn't answer. She must have a serious head injury.

Jeff asked if Dana had a first aid kit in the basement. When she said no, he decided to search for a way to escape on their own. It could take hours for rescuers to reach them. Jenny followed him, sneezing as though she had been sniffing pepper. Dim light filtered in from the floor above where something had fallen through the main floor. Maybe they could escape that way.

What remained of the mansion creaked and moaned as Dana shielded her nose and mouth from the dust. Should she call her daughter Kerrie to tell her goodbye? She decided to wait. No sense worrying Kerrie if there was a chance they would be rescued. Squinting, she watched the small flashlight Jeff wore on his belt, searching the basement for a way out. Long moments later her bodyguard returned.

"No escape route that I can find. The basement walls seem intact but the staircase is completely blocked. I tried moving the grand piano but it's splintered into jagged pieces."

Dana groaned. The piano had been a family treasure. But all that was important now was getting Sarah to the hospital. She then realized that the dust had begun to settle, making breathing easier. The sound of sirens could be heard from the highway. What if the killer was among the rescuers? She mentioned that to Jeff.

"Look at each person carefully," he said. I'll keep

my gun handy in case you recognize anyone."

Dana nodded, fighting tears. She had coughed so hard that her throat burned.

"I'm afraid it'll take a while before they can get to us. So stay calm and keep Sarah quiet when she regains consciousness."

Sarah's eyes remained closed but the sounds she made were like cats mewing. The irony was that Sarah disliked cats. In fact, she was afraid of them. She must be having a bad dream. Whatever she was dreaming couldn't be worse than what had actually happened.

What's taking the rescuers so long? Dana remembered that they were situated at the end of the block, each residence located on five acres. It could be midnight before they were found. Her cell phone rang and she dropped it on the concrete floor when she tried to answer. Fumbling in the dark, she realized it had stopped ringing when it landed. It was probably broken. When she found it, she lifted it to her ear. No one was on the line. Who had tried to call? The rescuers or the killer? Maybe it had been Marc or her daughter Kerrie.

"I'm afraid there's not much left of the mansion, Dana." Jeff crouched beside her, the flashlight muted between his fingers. He reached to place an arm around her shoulders. She knew he wanted to comfort her, but the enormity of what had happened made that impossible.

"I'll never forgive myself if something happens to Sarah," she said. "Losing her and Walter is more than I can bear."

He squeezed her shoulder, saying, "Sarah will recover. She's strong and fit for her age. Let's say a prayer. I haven't been to church since my wife died, but I remember a passage in the Bible that says when two or more people gather to pray, the Lord listens. I thought it was strange at the time that it didn't mention one person praying."

"I'm sure He listens to everyone," she said, gripping his hand. Bowing her head, she said, "Dear Lord, please help my friend Sarah recover—" Dana opened her eyes when she heard muffled voices.

A loud banging noise from the floor above startled them both. Jeff got to his feet and yelled, "We're down here."

Dana could hear footsteps through the basement ceiling. "We'll get you out," a deep voice yelled. "Stay away from the middle of the room." A moment later she heard a chopping sound and wood splintering. Jeff shined the flashlight erratically at the ceiling until they could see a hole forming. When it was large enough for someone to crawl through, a padded sling was lowered to the basement floor.

"Anyone injured down there?"

Jeff told them about Sarah and was instructed to lift her into the sling. An ambulance was standing by. When Sarah was safely lifted through the hole, the voice asked how many others were in the basement.

"Two adults and a large dog," Jeff said.

Jennie had begun to bark when she heard the man's voice. Dana tried to calm her, worried that whoever comprised the rescue team would turn her over to animal control. There was nothing she could do, except to lie about Jenny's breed.

Dana was rescued next. She was shocked by the floodlighting and the mansion's destruction, and stammered about her wolf dog. "She-she's Australian Shepherd and Husky mix, but she looks like a wolf. She's very gentile so don't be afraid when you lift her out of the basement."

The volunteer firemen nodded but they looked skeptical. Dana heard one of the men say, "I wonder if that's the wolf that old man Benson complained about."

"Where's my friend, Sarah?" she said to distract them.

"On her way to the hospital. Someone will drive you there as soon as we get Mailer out."

The dog's head appeared at floor level and Dana reached to pet her. "Good girl, Jenny." *Please don't bark or snap at these men.* The dog must have been traumatized for she nuzzled Dana's leg and whimpered. Dana knelt to hug her as Jeff was lifted though the hole. When he was able to stand on the damaged floor, she insisted they leave for the hospital.

"A deputy will drive," a fireman said. "I'm afraid all your vehicles were destroyed."

Dana looked about her former home. The chimney still stood, the only recognizable object. Bits and pieces of furniture and artwork were strewn about what was left of the main floor. The rest of the subdivision appeared equally damaged. She asked if everyone had survived.

"So far as I know, only the Benson woman is in critical condition. But we may uncover bodies when we search the rubble." The firemen collected their rescue equipment and moved on to the next property.

Dana's knees buckled and she would have fallen if Jeff hadn't caught her. They needed to reach the hospital. The road was strewn with all manner of debris, making it nearly impossible to reach the highway. A patrol car was parked in her circle drive and Jeff helped her into the backseat, along with Jenny. He then briefly talked to the deputy before joining her.

"It's going to be all right, Dana. We survived and the insurance will help to rebuild the mansion."

"Where will Sarah and I stay where the killer can't find us?"

"You could come with me but I live in a one bedroom apartment."

Dana said they could stay in Cheyenne with her daughter. But she didn't want to place Kerrie and her grandson in danger, if the killer found them there. And what if Sarah had a long hospital stay?

A dusty red pickup truck maneuvered down the street toward them. It had to be Marc. Jeff told the deputy to wait as he left the patrol car to talk to him. When he returned, he said that Marc had insisted they stay at the ranch with him. Jeff didn't appear happy about the arrangement, but agreed that it was probably the safest place in the county.

Dana sighed as she surveyed what was left of the mansion she had inherited from her sister. She wouldn't have to place it for sale now and she certainly wasn't interested in rebuilding.

Chapter Nine

Marc drove them to the hospital and sat next to Dana as they waited to visit Sarah. They had been told that Sarah had a concussion and an overnight stay in the hospital would speed her recovery.

Dana questioned Marc about his invitation to stay at the ranch. She was afraid it was an imposition. Shaking his head, he said his housekeeper was preparing for them. "I hope you like Mexican food. Rosita makes a mean breakfast burrito."

She smiled. "Does she also make tamales and chimichangas?"

"She's a great cook as well as a housekeeper. I'm sure you'll enjoy your stay."

Dana bit her lip. She still worried the killer was among the rescue workers, and might have seen them drive away. It would be easy to learn where the rancher lived, if the killer didn't already know. She hoped that Marc's ranch was fenced with barbed wire and that ranch hands would patrol the area.

Jeff sat hunched across from her in the waiting room, not saying a word. Dana knew he wasn't happy about the arrangements for her to stay at the ranch, but wouldn't object because he was on the payroll. She hated to see him so somber, and hadn't realized until then how he cared about her. She would have to remind both men that she was still in mourning.

Sarah was conscious and groaning when Dana was allowed to visit her room. She had no memory of what had happened and asked if the mansion had been destroyed.

"It doesn't matter. I planned to sell the place, anyway. I was tired of rattling around in that museum."

"Museum? You mean all that beautiful furniture aand artwork your sister left you?" Sarah appeared on the verge of tears. But when told they would stay with Marc, she managed a slight smile. "I'm a ranch girl," she said. "I'll be right at home."

Dana groaned. *You've only lived on a Texas ranch for five months, Sarah.*

Jeff arranged for an off duty deputy to guard Sarah's room until she was able to leave the following morning. Dana hated to leave her friend, but was exhausted and anxious to get settled at the ranch. But first she needed to replace her toothbrush and other necessities lost in the tornado.

It was nearing twilight by the time they reached the ranch, which was located in a tree-lined area in the foothills. Aspen leaves shimmered red and gold in the setting sun, a creek bubbling over rocks in the rear yard. Dana's temporary trance was shattered by the barking of a large dog, which bounded toward her the moment she left the pickup. The chocolate Lab greeted her by nearly knocking her down as Jenny leaped from the truck growling. Another problem to solve. Marc managed to grab the dog's collar and apologize for his greeting.

Jeff took her arm and escorted her to the house, which appeared quite large in deepening shadows. The rough-hewn logs formed an A-frame frontage with massive windows, which faced the mountains. Dana imagined Marc sitting in his recliner chair staring at the peaks.

Their host led them on a tour of his domain, including the upstairs bedrooms where she and Sarah would sleep. Jeff was to occupy the room across the hall, with a view of the surrounding area. Feeling as though she hadn't slept in weeks, Dana climbed the stairs to her room after dinner. Marc had assured her that his ranch hands would patrol the ranch twenty-four-seven. So she should be able to sleep. But sleep didn't arrive for hours. Suspects' faces continued to run through her mind as she considered each one and the possibility they would want to kill both her and Sarah. She wouldn't sleep well until Jeff's friend at the police department called with his inmate research.

<> <> <>

She awoke next morning to the scents of coffee and frying bacon. Hungry, she hurriedly dressed and combed her hair before descending the stairs. Following the scents, she made her way to the kitchen where she found a small, dark-haired woman with olive skin standing at the range. Dana asked about the men and was told they had recently left to check the area.

"No worries," Rosita said. "Senor Bartlett is a good man. He will take care of you."

Dana flushed. Did the housekeeper think she was moving in with Marc to share his bed?

Jenny had followed Dana into the kitchen and sat begging at Rosita's feet. She seemed satisfied when the cook handed her a strip of bacon. While she waited for breakfast, Dana called the hospital. A receptionist informed her that Sarah was to stay an extra day for tests. She hadn't slept well and was experiencing headaches. Dana asked to speak to her friend but Sarah was in the X-ray lab preparing for a cat scan.

Glancing down at the large plate of hash browns, bacon and scrambled eggs, Dana realized that she had lost her hunger. Rosita's large brown eyes were watching her. She would have to eat something.

"If you do not like American food," Rosita said, "we will have my country's food from now on."

Halfway through her meal, Dana heard the living room door open and stamping feet. It wasn't long before both men were standing in the kitchen eyeing her. They appeared perplexed.

Marc said, "One of my men found something interesting under the dining room window that wasn't there yesterday."

Before she could ask what it was, he said, "Looks like electronic wires."

She gasped. "For a bomb?"

"Not necessarily. Whoever dropped these must have been scared off by one of the men patrolling the yard. I've asked everyone here if it belongs to them but—"

"I don't want to place anyone else at risk, Marc. When Sarah's out of the hospital we'll find somewhere else to stay."

"Nonsense. We have plenty of well-armed men here to protect you."

"But you don't need to be involved."

"I want to make sure that you and Sarah are safe."

Jeff checked his watch. "Isn't it about time to pick up Sarah at the hospital?"

Dana told them about the phone call to the hospital, and suggested they shop for transportation. Telling them she could disguise herself so the killer wouldn't recognize her, she left for her room before they could argue. She had acquired a baseball cap, several shirts and pairs of jeans as well as a large pair of sunglasses following the tornado. Her purse and financial statements had been lost in the tornado, but she was able to withdraw money from the bank to finance her new wardrobe. Dana hoped she wouldn't be recognized, although her height might give her away. The nearest car dealership was in Casper, which required permission from the sheriff. Surely, under the circumstances, he would allow her to leave the county.

When she returned downstairs sans makeup and her shoulder length auburn hair tucked beneath her cap, Marc tried to talk her out of leaving. The ranch was safe, he said, and a stranger in the area would soon be noticed and interrogated. His argument made sense but she wasn't convinced that others wouldn't be caught in the crossfire.

She finally agreed to stay. At least temporarily. The most pressing problem was transporting Sarah safely to the ranch. She wished her friend would return home to work things out with her husband, but that didn't appear to be on Sarah's bucket list. Dana needed to contact her insurance agent and stop by her former home to determine whether anything left was worth saving. But would the killer expect her to do just that?

Jeff called the sheriff and managed to get permission for her to buy a car in Casper. Her bank officer would transfer the money. Sighing, Dana settled into the backseat of Marc's truck behind the two men, where she scribbled notes of needed actions. Patting the Glock in her holster, she was relieved that it hadn't been lost in the basement.

Peering from the darkened side truck window as they left the ranch, she looked for parked vehicles. Along the way, she called the hospital to check on Sarah, who was reportedly resting comfortably after her tests. But no one seemed to know when she could leave.

They arrived in Casper at noon but Dana was too anxious to acquire a new car to stop for lunch. Marc drove to East Second Street where the majority of car dealerships were located. After browsing the lots, she decided on a burgundy Jeep Cherokee. After the papers had been signed, they drove to the General Motors lot where Jeff bought a Sierra pickup truck. They then had lunch at a local café before Dana followed Jeff's pickup to the Stanton County Hospital.

Sarah was cheerful and smiling when they entered her room, but the guard at her door pulled Jeff aside to whisper to him. That worried Dana and she wasted no time asking about the conference when the guard left for coffee.

"Some guy was here last night wanting to see

Sarah, but the guard wouldn't let him in her room."
Dana asked if he had a caterpillar mustache.
"The guard didn't mention one. Why?"
She told him about the driver who had followed them before the tornado. Dana also wondered whether Sarah overheard the conversation or glimpsed the man at her door. When she asked, Sarah said she hadn't seen anything but her favorite TV show. She seemed ready to leave the hospital but would have to wait until morning after the doctor made his rounds.

The guard's smiling face appeared at the door, and Dana left the room to question him. He was already sipping his steaming coffee and ready to plant himself in his chair in the hall. He reminded Dana of a tall Pillsbury doughboy.

"Ma'am?" he said, setting his cup on the chair.

"Please describe the man who came to see my friend Sarah."

"Tall and trim with a wide, dark mustache and beady blue eyes."

"And a baseball cap?"

"Yeah. As I recall it was a Denver Broncos cap. You see a lot of those in this part of the country."

Dana nodded. She had one of her own in the new Jeep. "Could you tell his hair color?"

"Salt and pepper, kinda like Jeff Mailer's."

Dana caught her breath. "Do you remember the time?"

"It was just after visiting hours. I remember looking at my watch."

The description didn't seem to fit any of her suspects although, with a disguise, it could have been her former brother-in-law, who was convicted of murdering a teenage girl he had impregnated. He was also implicated in Dana's sister's death. But he couldn't have been paroled already. Perhaps he had escaped. Or maybe it was one of the home grown terrorists who kidnapped her and Sarah. Dana wrung her hands. It was probably a hit man hired by one of the convicts from his prison cell. If that were the case, they weren't safe anywhere.

She heard Sarah call her name and thanked the guard for his service. "Don't allow anyone in her room unless they're hospital staff. Especially if they look anything like the man you described."

He nodded and patted his belly. "No problem, ma'am. Nobody's gonna get past me."

Chapter Ten

Dana left her Jeep in the hospital parking lot and rode with Marc to the tornado-devastated area. Several trucks were parked on the road, including two from the county. Men were clearing debris from the rural subdivision that appeared to have been struck by cluster bombs.

She followed both men to the remains of her former mansion, which had already been stripped clean of valuables that escaped the tornado's wrath. Shrugging, she walked back to Marc's pickup where she scanned the area for any houses that may have survived. One, on the edge of the subdivision, had a portion of the roof intact and three partial walls still standing. She then noticed one of the workers staring at her. Tall and well-built, he ducked his hard hat when he realized she was staring.

Rushing to her bodyguard's side, she said, "That's the man. I'm sure of it." But when she turned back to point him out, he was gone. Craning her neck, she thought he may have hidden in one of the county trucks. When Jeff and Marc accompanied her to where she had seen him, the county workers claimed not to have seen the man she described. Had he shaved his mustache, or had he been wearing a false one?

Dana knew she hadn't imagined him? She then noticed a black SUV parked at the end of the road. When she indicated the car, Jeff led her to his new pickup. He then yelled to Marc that he would investigate the SUV. The street was still littered with debris, but Jeff managed to maneuver his truck over lawns as well as the road until he approached the black vehicle. The driver's door was unlocked, the SUV unoccupied.

"It's a rental," Jeff said when he had conducted a thorough search. "That tells me he's from out of town, maybe just out of prison. We should be able to trace the driver."

"But where did he disappear to?"

Jeff drew his revolver. Telling her to lock herself in his truck, he trotted back toward the workmen. Dana watched him in the side mirror, then swiveled in her seat to survey the area. Everything had been flattened, with the exception of the one house and two damaged chimneys. Could the killer be hiding in one of them?

Shivering, Dana pulled her cell phone from her jean's pocket and punched in Jeff's number. When he didn't answer and she could no longer see him, she decided to disregard his request to remain in the truck. Dana crept from the pickup with her Glock in hand. The nearest chimney was less than a hundred feet away. When she reached it, she called out in her deepest voice, "Throw your weapon down and crawl out of there before I shoot." Her suspects all knew she could handle a gun, so the killer would know she wasn't bluffing.

When nothing happened, Dana considered shooting into the ground near the chimney. But before she could pull the trigger, she heard Jeff call her name. Behind him one of the county trucks was bumping over debris in the direction of the highway. She watched as Jeff spun his pickup around in pursuit as Marc ran toward her. She felt foolish standing there with her gun pointed at the chimney, but Marc pretended not to notice. When he reached her, he informed her that Jeff wanted him to drive her to the ranch. He would notify the sheriff on the way.

When they reached his pickup, one of the county workers asked, "What's this all about?"

When Dana briefly filled him in, the stout, middle aged man frowned. "I thought it was strange that the office sent a new employee out to help with cleanup. He didn't even have a regulation hard hat."

Dana asked if the man wore a mustache.

"No, he was clean shaven and seemed a little nervous."

Turning to Marc, she said, "It was him all right."

"Let's go to the ranch before he shows up again." Marc told the man to call the sheriff.

"Already done. He stole a county truck."

It was well past noon when they arrived at the ranch. Rosita scolded them for not stopping for lunch and set about making burritos. Dana smiled and sank into a kitchen chair. She curbed the urge to call Jeff, knowing a phone call at the wrong moment could place his life in danger. She called the hospital instead. Told Sarah was sleeping, she asked to speak to the guard. When he came on the line, she questioned whether anyone had tried to visit Sarah. No one had but she warned him about someone masquerading as a medic. Sarah wasn't safe. They needed to rescue her from the hospital. When she asked Marc to accompany her, his wrinkled brow told her that he wasn't keen on the idea, but if she insisted he'd comply. They left the ranch shortly after their meal.

During the trip to town, Marc asked about her relationship with Jeff. She replied that she and her late husband had been Jeff's friends.

"That's it, nothing more?"

"He's my bodyguard, Marc, and an old friend."

He nodded. "I hope we can be good friends, Dana."

Before she could answer, a county truck passed them on the road that led to the ranch. Dana gasped as Marc slowed to negotiate a turn to follow the driver. If it were the killer, why wasn't Jeff following?

"It's probably not him," Marc said. "But I'm not taking any chances."

Dana flipped open her new cell phone that she had acquired at a discount store. The sheriff's not-so pleasant receptionist said her boss wasn't available. When told what had transpired, the woman promised to notify the sheriff via the radio. Thanking her, Dana clicked off, hoping the county truck was a false alarm.

Marc pulled out his own cell to call the ranch. His men needed to know the circumstances. Rosita took the message, And a few minutes later, Marc's foreman returned his call. All available men would be on the lookout for the county truck. Sighing, Marc turned his pickup around and headed back to the hospital. During the drive he questioned Dana about her suspects.

"I can't believe that anyone would want to kill you," he said.

"I guess when you help to place people in jail, eventually someone is going to retaliate and want to take revenge."

Marc shook his head. "Interesting. I hope you're ready for a new hobby."

"I am but Sarah isn't, and I'm afraid to allow her investigate on her own. I thought when she remarried a few months ago that she would settle into Texas ranch life, but—"

"She found it boring," he finished for her.

"I think Sarah felt left out when I married Walter. And she misses our companionship. Living in West Texas was like moving to another planet and she simply couldn't adjust."

"Would you feel the same way?"

"Please don't go there, Marc. I have to stay focused on Todd Warren's death. And I'm simply not ready for another relationship."

"Fair enough," he said, turning up the radio.

They arrived at the hospital soon after. An ambulance left the emergency wing with its siren shrieking, reminding Dana of Sarah's trip to the hospital. She hoped they could persuade the attending physician to allow her friend to accompany them to the ranch. They found Sarah standing on the threshold of her room, talking to the guard. An IV was still attached to her hand and the cart stood beside her. Dana asked if the doctor knew she was out of bed.

"Of course not, but I have a call in to his office. I told his nurse that I'm leaving, whether he approves it or not."

"That's my Sarah."

The guard smiled and winked at her. So Sarah had been flirting with him. It was time for her to leave the hospital before her life became more complicated. A young nurse marched down the hall to Sarah's room, a handful of papers in hand. Instructing Sarah to sign herself out, she removed the IV. While the nurse helped Sarah dress, Dana questioned the guard. He reported that no one had tried to enter Sarah's room, but Dana wondered if the guard had slept on the job. She was relieved to learn that he had been replaced overnight by another off duty officer.

It wasn't long before Sarah was settled in a wheelchair for the trip down the elevator. She seemed to have recovered but Dana worried about a relapse. The ranch was quite a distance from the hospital. But Marc assured her that a Flight for Life helicopter could be called to transport her back. Somehow, that didn't ease Dana's mind.

"I've been thinking," Sarah said when she settled into Marc's truck. "Maybe Todd Warren did have an enemy and the killer isn't after us. Or maybe the killer was just there to rob you and he panicked when the garage door opened."

Dana sighed. "If that were true, why would the killer try to break into the mansion the following night?"

"To rob the place. I'm surprised that no one tried before."

"There have been break-ins. Remember when

the druggies trashed the house looking for the capsules my brother-in-law had hidden there?"

"Yes, but his brother the sheriff was responsible for that."

Dana told Marc about the crooked sheriff who had managed to fool county authorities about his criminal background. He and his brother had formed a vicious drug ring within Stanton County. When was Jeff's friend at the P.D. going to call with his report about them and the other inmates?

They stopped in town to shop for Sarah's new clothes and toiletries, with Marc standing guard. It was nearly dark when they reached the ranch. Dana noticed the silhouetted forms of three cowhands armed with rifles, scanning the roadway. Once the pickup was parked, Marc hurried over to the nearest man to question him while Dana helped Sarah from her seat. She didn't notice another vehicle in the area, but the light was growing dim. Was someone out there, watching them?

Once inside the house, Marc gave Sarah the grand tour. Dana then insisted that Sarah call her husband Harry. He had to be worried. But not nearly as worried as she was about the killer's whereabouts. He must know by now where she and Sarah were staying.

She needed to call her daughter. Punching in the number, she was surprised when Kerrie immediately picked up.

"Why haven't you answered your phone, Mom? I've been frantic since I heard about the tornado. I was just getting ready to come looking for you."

Dana slumped into an easy chair to tell her what had happened. She tried to discourage Kerrie from making the trip because she didn't want her involved, although Kerrie had helped to solve a number of their murder cases. Dana promised to keep her informed, knowing full well that Kerrie might show up at the ranch at any time.

A hand gripped her shoulder and she looked up into worried brown eyes. When she assured Marc that everything was fine, he offered her a glass of chardonnay. Gratefully accepting, she watched as he poured two half-goblets. Jeff stood sullen-faced across the room until Dana offered him her glass, which prompted Marc to fill another. Jeff declined because his job was to guard both women. But Sarah accepted the wine when she descended the stairs a moment later.

"Why so glum, chums? We're safe and sound in Marc's lovely home and I'm ready to party."

Dana was never surprised at anything Sarah had to say, but she was shocked by her behavior. Rising from her chair she said, "You just got out of the hospital. You need to take it easy."

"Easy, peasy, Dana. We survived a tornado. What else can happen?"

Dana told her about the electrical wires found beneath a window, and that a sharp shooter could take aim at their shadows on the drapes.

"Too bad Jenny's not a bomb sniffing dog." Sarah giggled as though she had already been drinking. How was that possible? Taking her arm, Dana towed her into another room.

"Have you been sniffing glue?" Dana whispered.

"No, there was a brandy snifter in my room and I had a little nip."

Dana took the goblet from her hand. "I think it was more than a nip. Not a good idea after your head injury."

Jenny's sharp bark ended the conversation. Dana heard the front door open and the shuffling of feet on the wood floor. Taking Sarah's arm, she escorted her back into the living room and sat her in a chair. Both men and the dog were missing and she wondered what had taken place. Knowing she was a target, Dana refrained from opening the door, but turned off the lights to peer through a draped window. She could make out several dark forms moving about and reasoned that it was the cowhands guarding the house. But when a shot rang out, she stumbled over furniture in the dark to reach Sarah. Together they knelt on the floor.

"Wheresh your gun, Dana?"

"In my room. I didn't think I'd need it in the house."

Sarah hiccupped. "Better call the sheriph."

"My phone's on a table somewhere in this room."

"No worries. One of the men musta called."

They heard another shot and the sound of breaking glass. The sounds were followed by a barrage of gunfire, which prompted both women to flatten themselves on the floor. Dana could hear both dogs barking hysterically and the shouts of men in the yard. After what seemed an eternity, all was quiet. Sarah raised herself to her hands and knees and began to crawl. Dana could barely see her in the dim light that filtered in from the drapes she had parted earlier. She crawled after her, calling her name.

"Where are you going, Sarah?"

"Ta she if anybody's still alive?"

Chapter Eleven

Sarah tried to stand but sank back to the floor. She must have drank an entire snifter of brandy, Dana thought as she pulled a pillow from the nearest couch to place under Sarah's head. She then pushed a recliner against the door and edged toward faint light streaming from the window. Peering into the yard, she could discern no movement or bodies on the ground. Holding her breath, she opened the drapes and backed several steps into the room to make herself invisible to anyone on the grounds. A half-moon had risen above the mountain, allowing her to identify haystacks, but no one hidden behind them.

The doorknob rattled and someone knocked. Should she answer the door? Banging followed and she heard a man's voice call her name. It sounded like Marc. Carefully making her way to the door, she hesitated before pushing the recliner aside. Was the killer imitating Marc?

"What were we drinking tonight," she called.

"Chardonnay" was the answer.

Sighing, she opened the door. Marc and Jeff stood on the threshold, appearing dejected when she switched on the overhead light.

"He got away," Marc said.

"The killer?"

"I don't know anyone else who would open fire on my property."

Marc must regret his invitation for us stay at the ranch. What has he gotten himself into?

Jeff offered to stand guard that night in the house while Marc's cowhands patrolled the ranch's perimeter. He said the sheriff had promised a deputy, who should arrive momentarily. Dana offered to stand watch with her own gun, but was asked to help Sarah upstairs to her room. Jeff said he would wake Dana if he needed help.

Where was her dog? Dana suddenly realized that Jenny wasn't there.

"Out back of the corral in a fenced in area," Marc said. "She'll let us know if anyone approaches from the east. I hope you don't mind. My dog, Bruiser, is patrolling the rest of the property."

She did mind. Jenny hadn't spent a night out of doors since she came to live with her as a pup. Would she think she was being punished? Before Dana could protest, she noticed the grim expressions on both men's faces and nodded her agreement. She helped Sarah up the stairs to her room and into bed. She then tossed and turned in her own bed, worrying not only about Jeff but the killer's possible return. Dana was surprised that Jenny hadn't barked her annoyance at her corral confinement. Maybe she enjoyed the freedom of sleeping outside.

She was in the midst of an unpleasant dream when someone knocked at her bedroom door.

"Time for breakfast," Sarah called from the hallway.

Dana invited her in and was surprised that she looked so well. She seemed cheerful and not the least bit hung over. Sarah said that Marc had freed Jenny from the enclosure and fed her. He didn't think the dog had minded her guard duty because she resisted leaving the corral.

"She hates being cooped up," Sarah said. "And she and Marc's Lab seem to hit it off. Why don't you allow her to roam free on the ranch?"

"Because she's a wolf who might attack livestock on a neighboring ranch. She could get herself shot."

Sarah reminded her that breakfast was waiting. They needed to plan their day and decide whether to place Marc and his employees at risk by remaining at the ranch.

They found Marc and a number of cowhands seated at the long dining table, eating Rosita's breakfast burritos. They stood when the women entered the room. Old-fashioned chivalry, Dana thought, smiling as she took a chair between Marc and Jeff.

Placing a napkin in her lap, she said, "I hope no one needed medical attention last night."

"Fortunately not," the rancher replied. "Some broken window glass and damaged siding are the worst we found. Don't worry about it."

"But I do. We need to find somewhere else to stay."

"He's no doubt watching for you to leave, Dana. It would place you both in even more danger." He glanced at Jeff, who nodded his agreement.

"But he might shoot one of your men. Or you."

Marc smiled at her obvious concern. "We've got a tracker out searching for him and a couple of sheriff's deputies are looking for the black Ford SUV he's driving."

"Any word from your friend at the police department," Dana asked Jeff. "And did you check with the rental agency about the SUV?"

"I'm glad you reminded me." Jeff pulled a folded report from his back pocket. "This just came in on Marc's computer. The name on the rental lease is James Burton but the I.D. was stolen from someone in Colorado."

"So that means he came in from the south."

"Probably. There was also a liquor store robbery in the area about the same time. The bandit smashed the store camera before he robbed the clerk, so there's no image of him. The clerk described him as tall and well-built, wearing large aviator sunglasses and a baseball cap."

Dana thought back over the suspects and was unable to decide on any of them. She asked about Jeff's friend at the police department.

Jeff ducked his head. "I'm afraid he had a family emergency and had to fly to Ohio, where his mother is hospitalized."

"And there's no one else who can—?"

"I'm sure the sheriff has access to the inmate data base."

Sarah finished her burrito before she asked, "Why can't we search for them online?"

"That's possible if you're willing to pay for the finder service."

Sarah glanced at Dana and smiled.

Dana merely nodded. *Of course I will. I'm the*

Bank of America with a destroyed mansion. Her account balance was less than half of the amount she had inherited when they first began their sleuthing hobby. But what good was money if anyone present at the table was shot and killed?

Marc volunteered his computer, which they could use while he and two of his men searched the property for some sign of the shooter. The rancher said if the killer were smart, he would have left through the pasture where the cattle grazed, to hide his footprints.

Jeff stayed behind to guard the three women and lend advice to the inmate search. A late autumn snowstorm had been falling all morning with large wet flakes, accompanied by a strong southwest wind, creating a moderate ground blizzard. An hour later Marc and his men returned, announcing that any tracks had been erased by the storm.

"I don't think the killer's dumb enough to try another attack under the circumstances," Jeff said. "Unless he's desperate." Turning to Dana he asked if she had decided which man would go to such lengths for revenge.

Dana said that she had ruled out the serial killer in California, because he didn't know the area. She was convinced that last night's shooter knew his way around. That left her former brother-in-law Rob Turnsby, his brother, the former sheriff; and Pete Toliver, the young man who killed both wolves and people on Gray Wolf Mountain. Or it could have been one of the homegrown terrorists who kidnapped them in Arizona.

Rob wanted the mansion back and would probably kill to regain possession. But if it were him, he had to know that his former residence had been destroyed. The description nearly fit him but she had never known him to wear a mustache or baseball cap. His brother, on the other hand, had a paunch and couldn't be considered well-built unless he had worked off his flab in prison. He was definitely the meaner of the two brothers, and more inclined to take revenge on her and Sarah.

She thought about the terrorists they had encountered in northern Arizona. They could be anywhere, but the only one she could identify was Mister Clean's clone. Maybe he was wearing a salt and pepper toupee and had grown a mustache. She thought no, he had been too nice to her to take revenge.

Jeff was appraising her from across the room. She couldn't interpret his expression and wondered why he was so uncommunicative. What was on his mind? He must be sorry that he had placed himself in the killer's line of fire by agreeing to protect them.

Dana booted up Marc's computer and scrolled to a people search site. Glancing at her list, she typed in Rob Turnsby's name and filled in the credit card information. When nothing happened for several minutes, she typed in another name. Still nothing. Frustrated, she hit her fist on the desk.

"It's probably the snow clouds blocking satellite reception," Jeff said as the screen went blank. "I'll go out and brush off the transceiver." He slipped into his sheepskin coat and left. A few moments later he returned, brushing remaining snow from his coat. "That's strange. The snow's melting as soon as it hits the dish. I wonder if someone deliberately knocked the dish out of alignment."

Jeff strode over to turn on the television set. Nothing happened. "Either the wind blew the satellite dishes out of sync or someone deliberately cut us off from the outside world." He picked up his cell phone and punched in a number. Shaking his head he said, "Must be heavy snow blocking the signal. There's nothing but static."

Dana shivered, imagining the killer stationed outside the ranch house, ready to burst in with gun blazing. She told herself that she had been watching too many cop shows and John Wayne movies. Rushing to help Jeff close all the drapes, she agreed when he told the others to stay away from the windows. Glancing out as she closed a pair of drapes, she realized that they were trapped in a whiteout, snow so heavy that she couldn't see past the pane. The sky was growing increasingly dark. Maybe the killer would freeze to death out there, if he were unable to get inside.

Marc and two of his men returned, stamping their feet and brushing off snow. "Any tracks have been covered by new snow," he said. "It's nearly zero visibility out there. I don't think we'll have to worry about a shooter in this weather." Nevertheless, he asked each person present to station themselves in sight of a window or door, although not in a direct line of fire. He left for the kitchen and returned with Rosita, who was wringing her hands. "Ay, yay, yay." she said, her lips trembling. "I cannot go home."

Her boss offered her the remaining upstairs bedroom where she would be safe. That seemed to calm her. Sarah didn't seem affected in the least. Smiling, she placed an arm around the housekeeper's shoulders and murmured something Dana was unable to hear.

Jenny barked and they heard a banging sound, which Marc attributed to the wind. But he unlocked his gun cabinet and handed out rifles to everyone present, including Rosita, who claimed to have never held a gun. Marc patiently showed her how to load, cock and fire the rifle; telling her to hold it pointed at the ceiling. He did the same with Sarah and Dana, although Dana had previously fired a Springfield.

They sat and waited, listening to the howling wind. A banshee wind, Dana thought, remembering Irish folklore. Her grandfather called it *bean sidhe* and said the banshee fairy had come to take her grandmother's life one cold and windy night in Cork County, Ireland.

"Must have been a tree limb hitting the outside wall," Marc said. "I don't think anyone can survive for long in a ground blizzard, or even find the ranch house, for that matter."

Jeff agreed. "The wind must have misaligned the satellite dishes."

Marc grunted as he collected the rifles and placed them back in the cabinet, although he failed to lock it. He reminded Dana of her grandfather, a take charge man who didn't seem to suffer fear of anything.

It was then they heard breaking glass.

Chapter Twelve

Jeff stayed to guard the women as Marc and his men raced through the house to find the break-in. Dana's heart pummeled in her chest, knowing that her female companions were equally frightened. It seemed an eternity before Marc descended the stairs to report a rock thrown through an upstairs window in Dana's room.

How had the killer known which room was hers? Or was it a random throw?

"How anyone can see in this blizzard is beyond me," Marc said. "I'm not risking anyone's life to find out. You can die of hypothermia in a short time out there."

Jeff returned his service revolver to its holster. "We must be dealing with the abominable snowman."

Dana reasoned that it had to have been one of the homegrown terrorists. No one else on her suspect's list was crazy enough to place his own life in danger. But a terrorist wouldn't know his way around the ranch in a snowstorm. She didn't want to consider the possibility that one of Marc's cowhands was involved.

Marc said he had blocked off the lower window pane with Dana's dresser, but she would have to share a room with Sarah until repairs could be made. Fortunately, the wind was blowing away from that side of the house, so a minimal amount of snow would filter into the room.

"No problem," Sarah said. "I'd rather not spend the night alone."

"What about me?" Rosita's dark eyes appeared as large as tea cups.

"We can move your bed into the same room, if the ladies don't object."

"Of course not," Dana said. "The room's large enough. But what if a rock comes sailing through Sarah's window?"

"We'll all camp out in the den. We have plenty of sleeping bags in the basement." As Marc spoke the electricity failed. Without hesitation, he said, "Flashlights are in the kitchen drawer next to the fridge, Rosita."

Jeff took the small flashlight from his belt and handed it to her, with a warning to be careful. One of the cowhands followed with his gun drawn.

Marc said he thought sleeping in the den was their only option. "We men will take turns standing guard."

Sarah gripped Dana's arm. "A roaring fire and goblet of Chardennay would certainly calm my nerves."

"Half a goblet," Dana murmured. "We need to keep our wits in case there's a break-in."

"I'm beginning to wish I'd stayed in Texas with

Harry."

"I'm sure he wishes the same."

The darkness was closing in when Rosita returned with flashlights. Sam, Marc's burly foreman, was then dispatched to the basement for sleeping bags, accompanied by Ned, a lanky youth not long out of his teens. They were told to make sure no one had gained access to the basement before they gathered the bags.

Marc warned them to keep their guns handy. "Whoever he is, he seems as invisible as a ghost."

"He'll have some holes in 'im if he's down there," Sam said. "I don't cotton to varmints who try to kill nice ladies."

At least he didn't say old ladies. Dana thanked him and echoed Marc's warning.

Marc struck a match to light a fire. Kindling stacked on the andirons were quickly lighted before he placed logs in the flames. The roar and crackling of the fire helped to relax Dana's tense muscles and she wondered how long the shooter could stand the freezing cold before he succumbed to hyperthermia.

Chairs were pulled in a half circle before the hearth and Marc lighted a number of oil lamps. Rosita then poured them each half a goblet of wine while two men patrolled the house.

"This is cozy," Sarah said, "but I'm hungry."

Marc apologized for them missing lunch and soon the dinner hour. "I don't want Rosita making herself a target by rummaging around in the kitchen. I'll break out some snacks."

"My husband will be afraid I am lost in the storm," Rosita said. "There is no way I can tell him I am safe." She swore softly in her native tongue. "I hope Ramon does not come looking for me."

Dana flipped open her cell phone and punched in the sheriff's number. There wasn't even static. Had the killer destroyed the cell phone tower? She imagined him pushing the tower over with a backhoe. She knew she was giving him too much credit for Mother Nature's work.

"This will soon be over." Jeff's voice belied his conviction.

"What makes you think so," Sarah asked.

"I listened to the weather report this morning."

Sarah laughed. "Do you know how many times our local weatherman has been wrong?"

Jeff shrugged. "Well, at least he hasn't been shot like that weatherman in Texas."

Dana asked about the weather report.

"Heavy snow, high winds and dense fog until eight o'clock tonight."

Dana checked her watch in the firelight. "Four hours to go, Jeff." It was so dark with the drapes drawn that it appeared to be midnight. She prayed the weather report had been accurate. She didn't think they could stand another stormy night.

Marc returned with bagged popcorn and bowls of peanuts and pretzels, which Sarah immediately dipped into. When promised chips and dips, she appeared to relax and enjoy the party, if you could call it that. Better to celebrate remaining alive than to mourn the circumstances, Dana thought. Jeff was right. This all had to end soon.

They were startled when a loud knocking sounded at the living room door. Marc and his men grabbed guns and crept out of the den. Dana could hear Marc asking the identity of the visitor through the door before he opened it. A man's voice answered but she couldn't understand him. Several moments later a uniformed officer appeared with Marc.

"Rosita?" Marc said. "The deputy came to check on us and I asked him to take you home."

Rosita quickly left her chair. Gathering her things, she left without a backward glance. Dana doubted she would return next morning, if ever. No problem. Sarah was an excellent cook and she could handle the household chores. But would Marc want them to stay?

Dana hadn't slept in a sleeping bag in years, not since she and her first husband had camped at Yosemite. Twisting and turning on the hardwood floor, she finally fell asleep before dawn, after listening to men's boots walking about the ranch house during the night. Sarah snored softly beside her, apparently undisturbed. Dana knew that her friend could sleep through an earthquake, and envied her ability to ignore sounds while she slept.

The wind seemed to have calmed during the night and she wondered whether they would find the killer's body in the snow. No further incidents had happened since the second rock was thrown. She still found it difficult to believe that someone had braved the storm to terrorize them the previous night. It didn't fit her conception of any of her suspects, with the possible exception of the terrorist group. One of them had broken into the mansion and made himself at home while she and Sarah were away. It had to be him.

Someone touched her shoulder. Surprised, she looked up into Marc's droopy eyes. "Would you ladies mind preparing breakfast? The lights and cell phones are working again and I received a call from Maria. She's not coming back."

Dana groaned. "I'm sorry, Marc. If you hadn't brought us here—"

"Don't let it bother you. I'm tired of Mexican food and Maria isn't the best housekeeper."

"I'm afraid I'm not either, but I'll do my best."

Waking Sarah was akin to disturbing a hibernating bear, but Dana managed to get her on her feet and up the stairs to her bedroom. While Sarah was in the shower, Dana returned downstairs to search for food. Plenty of tortillas, cheese, hamburger and ingredients for Latino dishes filled the refrigerator and cabinets, but no bacon or pancake flour could be found. Sarah was a genius in the kitchen and could whip up something to satisfy the men.

Glancing out the kitchen window, Dana noticed huge snowdrifts in the yard. There were also tracks in the snow that didn't appear to be large enough for humans. They must have been made by Marc's Labrador. She wondered why he had been left outside during the blizzard, and why they hadn't heard him bark when the killer was throwing rocks. She would ask when Marc returned.

Sarah didn't seem perturbed by the lack of ordinary food when she entered the kitchen, so Dana left to climb the stairs. Opening the door to her own room, she noticed the broken glass and melting snow on the dresser. When she looked out what remained of the window, she could see no footprints of any kind, but something was laying in the snow near a stand of trees in the yard. It appeared to be Marc's dog.

Dana felt sick and left the room for Sarah's.

Sitting on the bed, she cried. It could have been Jenny. Why had he left Bruiser in the storm? Angry, she wiped her tears and stormed downstairs. Marc was standing in the living room, a sad expression on his face. Did he know?

When she reached the landing, she told him that Bruiser was dead.

"I know. He went missing yesterday morning during the storm. I had hoped he was in the barn, but I'm afraid the killer got to him." Marc wiped at his eyes.

"We've got to leave before something else happens. We've caused you enough trouble."

"Don't be silly, Dana. The dog and housekeeper can be replaced as well as the window. But you and your friend are irreplaceable."

Dana briefly hugged him, thinking he was the kindest man she had ever met. But she didn't want to cause him more problems. She knew that roads were probably closed and that it would be days before they could leave. In the meantime she would do her best to make it up to him.

"Breakfast is ready," Sarah called from the kitchen. "Someone needs to set the table."

Dreading an emotional scene, Dana rushed to find plates and silverware. Jenny trailed after her, woofing when they entered the kitchen. She was obviously hungry. Sarah carried a platter filled with breakfast burritos, saying they would have to enjoy Mexican food until someone went shopping.

"No need for that," Marc said. We have a greenhouse near the barn that's growing plenty of vegetables. And there's game meat in the freezer.

"Growing food this time of year?" Dana asked.

"It's heated and well insulated with a fish pond,

so someone could live there for a while."

Dana gasped. "That may be where the killer's hiding."

Marc called the sheriff to report what they suspected. If the killer were hiding on the ranch, they needed more manpower to trap him. Dana knew Marc would prefer to hang the killer from a barn rafter, rather than witness him sentenced to death row. But he needed to stand trial for Todd Warner's death.

"What about Bruiser?" Dana asked.

"We'll build a box to bury him in," Mark said. "The ground's frozen so we'll cover the coffin in straw to store in the barn until spring. I just couldn't do it on an empty stomach."

A shot rang out and Sam, seated next to Marc, fell face forward into his breakfast plate.

Chapter Thirteen

Jeff ordered everyone down on the floor. Then, crawling to the window, he shot once through the broken glass. "I think the bastard's wounded, and it looks like he's headed for the barn."

Marc pulled his foreman into a sitting position as Dana called 911. Sam had a hole in the back of his head, the bullet doubtlessly embedded in his brain for there was no exit wound. She could hear Sarah whimpering in the background.

When Dana finished telling the operator about the shooting, she sat down trembling. What had she and Sarah caused by investigating Todd's murder? Reaching to grip Sarah's hand, she said, "We're leaving the ranch as soon as possible."

Marc bit his lip but said nothing. His generous offer had produced a nightmare, and Dana refused to cause him more pain. Picking up her cell phone again, she called her daughter Kerrie to ask that she rent them an apartment in Cheyenne. There had to be a way to escape the ranch without the killer knowing.

Several hours later, Sam's body was loaded into an ambulance not long after the snowplow had gone by, followed by two deputies. When told of the killer's whereabouts, the two deputies spread out in the snow, followed by Marc and some of his men, with guns drawn. Dana watched through the broken window, praying there would be no more fatalities. She could see the barn and geodesic shape of the four season greenhouse, and hoped the killer wasn't hiding there. Sarah was sobbing, so Dana left the window to comfort her. Hovering nearby, Jenny had placed her paws in Sarah's lap and was licking her.

When Sarah raised her head, she said, "No more murder investigations, Dana. This has to be the last."

"My thoughts exactly. We won't continue to actively participate in the case, but I'm afraid the killer will follow us to Cheyenne. If we're not careful, we could be the next bodies leaving in an ambulance."

Jeff stood silently, slowing shaking his head. He said at last, "I'm assuming you want me to accompany you to Cheyenne."

Dana managed a slight smile. "We won't leave without you, Jeff. I told Kerrie to rent a three-bedroom, furnished apartment."

"How do you propose to leave here if the killer manages to escape?"

"Maybe a delivery van could back to the door so we can sneak inside."

"I advise disguises. You might dress as cowhands in case you're spotted."

"Someone could create a diversion at the other

end of the house."

"Not a bad idea, if the killer isn't captured. They should be able to follow his prints and blood in the snow."

They discussed a number of plans before the door opened and Marc came inside. His expression told them the killer had escaped.

"You were right, Dana. He's been living in the greenhouse. We found an old sleeping bag on the floor and he's been eating greens and melons from the raised beds."

Jeff said he doubted the man would return to the greenhouse, "but you never know."

Dana insisted they leave the ranch as soon as it could be arranged. When told of Dana's plan to use a van, Marc suggested leaving in one of his horse trailers. He could load a couple of mounts into the back, allowing the women to travel in the small living quarters next to the gooseneck. Everyone agreed it was a good plan.

Marc loaned Dana a denim jacket to wear under her parka. His Stetson was a bit large so he stuffed the inner brim with paper. Sarah could wear some of his late wife's western clothing and one of her western hats. Now that the snowplow had gone by they could leave anytime. If the killer were watching, he would wonder who was leaving. Their departure had to be well-planned and carried out in the swiftest manner possible. Marc would drive his pickup with Jeff riding shotgun. But could Marc successfully hitch the trailer and load horses without getting shot?

Loading food into a grocery bag, along with two duffle bags filled with their new clothing, Sarah stacked them inside the door. Marc and his cowhands left when the wind began blowing snow in a minor ground blizzard. Half an hour later, the pickup and trailer parked out front and Jeff jumped out to open the camper door. He then helped to carry the women's belongings to the trailer. As soon as they were inside, he closed the door and returned to the pickup.

Dana and Sarah sat in the small dining booth and held on for dear life when Marc stepped down on the accelerator. They could hear horses' whinnying on the other side of the trailer wall.

"Tell me this isn't happening," Sarah wailed.

To distract her, Dana asked if she had called her husband.

Sarah admitted she hadn't.

"Do it now. He must be frantic, worrying about you."

"I can't tell him what's happening, Dana. He'll board the first plane."

Dana hesitated before she said, "Tell him you'll catch a flight out of Cheyenne. That you'll be home soon."

"I can't leave you alone."

"One less target for Jeff to protect."

"No, I'm staying. I'll call Harry when we reach Cheyenne."

"I'm glad you're staying, but poor Harry will probably have a stroke."

The gravel road was bumpy, forcing them to grip the table between them. Dana knew why Marc wasn't driving cautiously, but wished he would slow down. Her cell phone rang and she heard Jeff's voice asking how they were faring. He apologized for the ride.

"Marc's driving faster than normal because the

black SUV that pulled onto the road behind us is picking up speed. I suggest that you pull bed covers onto the floor and lie on them."

"Will do, Jeff. Please be careful."

The horses' frightened whickers grew louder, their stamping hooves causing the trailer to sway even more on the icy road. Dana wished they had been left behind in the barn. Steadying herself against a trailer wall, she pulled blankets and pillows from the bed, asking Sarah to help her spread them on the floor. She then heard popping and banging sounds. The trailer tilted to the left and Dana fell against the dining booth, striking her upper thigh. Sarah contributed to her pain by falling against her.

Everything seemed to happen in slow motion as the trailer limped to a stop. Dana heard Jeff's voice yell, "Stay down," before the sound of gunshots echoed inside the trailer. The horses were rearing and banging their heads on the ceiling. After what seemed an eternity, the trailer door jerked open and Jeff told them they would be traveling cross-country on horseback.

"Horseback?" Sarah shrieked. "What about our things?"

"We'll lock them in the trailer and come back for them later. Marc is unloading the horses now. Let's go."

Dana said, "Why the horses? Can't we just unhitch the trailer and leave in the pickup?"

"They shot out a trailer tire as well as one on the pickup when we made a sharp turn onto the county road.

"What about the killer?"

"The SUV backed out of range when we started shooting back. We'll be sitting ducks if they catch us changing tires."

All four of us on two horses? Dana cringed, worrying about Sarah riding bareback. Already mounted, Marc reached to pull Dana up behind the saddle. Jeff did the same with Sarah. Then, hitting their heels against the horse's sides, they left the trailer and rode into the trees as the black SUV came roaring toward them.

"Hang on," both men yelled as Dana leaned to encircle Marc's waist. Daring a side glance, she noticed Sarah hugging Jeff in what appeared to be a death grip.

Marc said to duck as they approached a low hanging branch covered with snow. Leaning as low as she could, without falling, she peered back at the road. Surely the SUV wouldn't attempt to follow them. She was wrong. The black Ford was in pursuit, dodging trees and undergrowth as the terrain sloped upward. Dana knew the sports vehicle could follow for quite a distance. There appeared to be two men in the front seat, and she wondered why they didn't shoot at the overburdened horses. Maybe they planned to steal them once they were riderless.

Marc headed for another stand of trees that only a horse and rider could navigate. The SUV would have to find a trail which circumvented the slope. When they reached what appeared to be the end of the grove, the land sloped downward into a canyon containing a stream lined with pines on the opposite bank. Marc's Appaloosa swerved to the right along the edge of trees, with Jeff's mount close behind. If not for the killer following, Dana would have taken time to admire the beautiful animals with their naturally blanketed rumps and streaked hooves. No wonder their pursuers hadn't risked killing them.

They must be worth a fortune.

Where was the SUV? Dana twisted to scan the area. Marc's hand covered hers as she hugged his waist. Patting her hand gently, he turned his head to stare at her with one eye. He mouthed, "Don't be afraid."

She was afraid. Afraid they would be killed like Marc's foreman. Afraid she would never see Kerrie and her infant grandson again. Afraid that Sarah would fall from the horse. She hugged Marc even tighter as the horse slowed and circled back to face Jeff's Appaloosa.

"Think we lost them?" Jeff asked.

"They'll drive back to the edge of the grove and down this side. We need to ride into the canyon along the stream. They won't be able to follow."

Jeff nodded but Dana was afraid of riding double down a sloping, snowy embankment to the canyon floor. She decided to walk and Sarah agreed. But she first tried to call 911. "No cell service here."

"Service is sketchy in this area. This must be a dead spot," Marc said.

It was a play on words that she didn't appreciate.

Digging in their heels, they started down the slope, slipping and sliding on their backsides toward the stream, the men leading the horses. They were halfway down the slope when they heard an engine and car doors slamming. Picking up their pace, they positioned themselves between the horses and the stream. Would their pursuers follow them on foot? Sliding down a snowy embankment, Dana found herself on the ice, her boots and calves submerged in icy water. Friction had burned her backside and she hoped there weren't holes worn in the seat of her jeans. But that was the least of her worries.

Painfully rising from the stream, she looked toward the rise where two men stood watching them; both wearing baseball caps and sunglasses. She screamed when one of them raised a gun. Marc turned with gun drawn, firing before the other man could pull the trigger. Their assailant fell and his companion promptly dragged him out of sight. Frightened by the gunfire, Marc's horse reared and nearly trampled him before the Appaloosa could be brought under control.

A moment later Jeff and Sarah arrived. "Mount up," Marc said as he helped Dana back behind the saddle. "We still have targets on our backs."

Chapter Fourteen

The chilling breeze stung her nostrils as the horses picked up speed along the snow-covered bank. Clinging to Marc, Dana prayed the killer had been shot and that his partner was as inept as Sarah with a gun. The horses headed back in the direction of the ranch, and she wondered whether the injured man had been helped into the SUV. If left to die, his companion could overtake the Appaloosas before they reached the ranch.

Marc must know the area well. Maybe he knew of a cave where they could hide until dark. Another stand of pines came into view where the stream curved sharply to the West. Marc patted her hand again when they reached the trees. Riding into the grove, he stopped and dismounted, but didn't help her down.

"Stay put. I'll check the road from here." Signaling Jeff, he left alone on foot through the trees.

They waited for what seemed hours before Marc returned. "Not safe," he said, out of breath. "I spotted a black vehicle up the road. It's parked and apparently waiting."

That must mean the other man had died, the survivor still out to get them. Seated behind the saddle wasn't Dana's comfort zone. Marc must have read her thoughts because he reached to help her down, as Jeff did with Sarah.

Marc said, "We can walk a ways to get the kinks out, but I'm not so sure the driver didn't leave the Ford to track us."

They shaded their eyes to scan the terrain they had recently traveled. Nothing appeared to be moving, but that didn't mean someone wasn't hiding in the trees, ready to shoot.

Dana frowned. "Isn't there somewhere we can hide until dark?"

Marc thought for a moment. "There's an old, abandoned homesteader's shack about a mile upstream."

"Then let's go." Sarah's impatience was evident when she motioned for Jeff to help her remount the horse.

Dana knew that walking was a cowboy's anathema, so she agreed to ride. She would have preferred to walk, knowing she would require a pillow to sit when they reached the ranch.

A large hawk swooped down at them as they rode along the streambed.

"Somebody must have disturbed her nest," Mark said, kneeing the horse into a gallop. Wincing in pain, Dana ducked her head and gripped his waist tighter. Hearing Sarah screech behind her, she thought of pioneer women riding sidesaddle through the area. How had they traveled through Indian Territory and survived? Groaning, she thought, How soft we've all become.

Marc pulled up short and pointed. "There's someone on foot up ahead." Urging the horse into the icy stream, they crossed into thick pine trees on the opposite bank. Dismounting, he helped Dana down as well as Sarah when Jeff's horse came ashore.

Ground reining the Appaloosas, a grim-faced Marc said, "I recognized the man I shot. I fired him a couple of months ago for stealing tack and saddles. He must have it in for me."

Dana gasped. "Then he was aiming at you, not me?"

"Probably."

"Is it possible he's in cahoots with our killer," Sarah asked.

"Anything's possible," Jeff said. "They could have met at the Ace Saloon and decided to work together."

"What about the man downstream? He could be the killer."

"Or an ice fisherman or hunter."

Jeff thought it best to ride downstream alone to talk to the man, reasoning that he wasn't the intended target. He would keep his gun handy and try to engage him in conversation.

"Probably the only way to tell," Marc said. "Be careful."

They watched as Jeff retraced his ride through the trees to the bend of the stream where he crossed over out of sight. He then rode back toward them on the opposite bank. Riding casually as though out for a Sunday ride, he approached the stranger within a matter of minutes. Dismounting his horse, Jeff extended his hand and the man accepted it.

Dana sighed. He must not be the killer. That meant watching for signs of life in the other direction. She wished for binoculars, but Marc didn't have a pair in his saddlebags. The killer might wait them out, knowing they would come out of hiding after dark. It was difficult to hide in the snow, even without the moon spotlighting them. She looked to Marc, who was intently watching Jeff and the other man. Whispering to Sarah, she led her to a group of trees near the icy shore where they could watch undetected for anyone traveling down the bank.

Some thirty minutes later Jeff returned. He wasn't smiling. "He says he's looking for a lost dog. I heard him whistling before I got there. Seems to be a decent sort of fellow, but I'm not so sure he wasn't lying."

Dana asked Jeff to describe the man.

"Tall, slim, short beard but no mustache."

"Hair and eye color?"

"He was wearing a baseball cap and sunglasses, but I saw some gray hair beneath the cap."

"A Broncos cap?"

"No. Apparently he's a Patriot's fan."

"How old would you judge him to be?"

"Fifty-five to sixty. He's not from around here unless he recently moved into the old Henderson place. I didn't think to ask."

Marc suggested they wait in the grove until dark. The remaining snow would provide enough light for them to find their way back to the pickup and trailer. Dana checked her watch. Two hours until dark. The temperature had dropped and she was shivering, despite her parka. Sarah was as well.

"I know you're cold and hungry," Marc said, but

it won't take long to reach the ranch once it's dark."

Jeff reminded him that they were leaving hoof and boot prints in the snow, which made them easy to follow, even in the dark. Marc shook his head in agreement, deciding to make the trip alone to call the sheriff and gather enough of his men to track down the killer. Advising them to find a place to hide in the trees, he mounted and rode along the bank until he was out of sight. When he passed the location where the stranger had been, he would cross over to make it appear that only one horseman had ridden that way.

"Our hit man will track us across the stream," Jeff said. "We'd better leave for another location."

"But he'll follow our tracks in the snow," Sarah protested.

"Not if we ride downstream in the water."

"Three of us on a horse?"

"I'll take each of you in turn."

"Take Sarah first," Dana said. "I can shoot, if necessary."

Jeff said they needed to hurry. Glancing up and downstream, he helped Sarah mount behind him, then kneed the Appaloosa into the stream. Dana kept watch from behind the thick branches of a pine tree, alternately scanning upstream and watching the Appaloosa grow smaller in the distance. Moments after the horse and rider disappeared, she noticed movement in the trees across the stream. Drawing her revolver from her hidden holster, Dana's hand trembled as she touched the trigger. Whoever was on the opposite bank was in for a surprise, if he crossed the stream.

Minutes later, a doe and her faun crashed through the undergrowth to drink from the stream.

Sighing heavily, she replaced the gun in her holster. Where was the killer? Had he given up and returned to his SUV? Maybe he had a change of heart and decided to take his wounded companion to a doctor. Or the morgue. She doubted either.

It was another hour until dark. An orange ball descended slowly behind the trees, blinding her when she attempted to look to the West. Shading her eyes, she thought she saw a man standing on the bank opposite her. Had he seen her? Shrinking behind the pine tree, she moved in a diagonal direction away from the stream, keeping the pine tree between her and the man. Along the way, she drew her gun and held it by her side. Her tracks in the partially melted snow could be followed by a blind man.

She would have to take a stand. In the meantime, she'd try her cell phone again. Flipping the lid she saw one bar in the right corner. Was it enough? Replacing the gun in her holster, she punched in 911. Seconds passed before she heard a series of rings. Breathlessly, she whispered into the phone when a dispatcher answered.

"This is Dana Logan-Grayson. I need help. The man who killed Todd Warren is stalking me with a gun. I'm in the foothills just off the county road. The sheriff knows all about this case."

"I can't hear everything you're saying, ma'am. Can you speak louder?"

Dana cupped a hand around her mouth and the phone. "No, he might hear me. Please send deputies with their sirens blaring to County Road 951. That should scare him away. Marc Bartlett's horse trailer and pickup are parked nearby on the road."

The dispatcher repeated what she had heard,

telling her to stay hidden. After a pause, with radio traffic noise in the background, the woman said that deputies were on their way. Pocketing her phone, Dana thought she heard snow crunching a few yards away. Holding her breath, she crawled into a thicket which tore at her parka. Shivering from the cold and her still wet clothing, she kept her head down and silently prayed.

The man called her name.

Chapter Fifteen

She didn't recognize the voice, but her ears were hooded by her parka. Was it Marc or Jeff? Or someone else? Afraid to move, she hesitated.

"Dana, it's Marc. Where are you?"

Getting to her feet, she clutched the gun in both hands before she answered. "Over here, Marc." Twilight had descended and the dark form moving toward her didn't look familiar. And where was Marc's horse? Sidestepping behind a tree, she peered out with the gun pointed at him.

"Put the gun down. It's Marc."

I don't think so. Dana glanced in the direction Jeff and Sarah had taken. Getting off to a fast start, she dodged trees, running parallel to the stream. Briefly stopping, she looked back. No one was in her line of sight, but she could hear crusted snow crunching beneath someone's running feet.

Thank heavens I'm still in shape. Whoever's back there obviously isn't. It has to be the killer. She heard him call her name again, this time the voice was out of breath. If it were Marc, he would have said something to reassure her. Taking a few deep breaths, she resumed running until the trees were no longer there. Should she hide or take a chance making her way down the bank? It was nearly dark but she knew he could spot her black parka in the snow. It was then she noticed what appeared to be a horse and rider coming her way. It had to be Jeff.

Zig zagging down the bank to make herself a hard-to-hit target, she called Jeff's name. The horse picked up speed and reached her in less than a minute. Reaching down for her, Jeff lifted her behind the saddle as she told him someone was in pursuit. Reining the Appaloosa in the opposite direction, Jeff signaled the horse to trot down the bank. Moments later a shot rang out and the horse increased speed. Another grove of trees loomed ahead. If only they could reach them in time to avoid being shot.

Dana heard another shot and felt a burning sensation in her left arm. Letting go of Jeff's waist, she touched the sleeve of her parka, feeling a tear in the material and something wet and sticky. She then realized they were safely among the trees.

When the horse halted, she told Jeff she'd been shot. Quickly dismounting, he helped her down. Pulling his gun from its holster, he ran to the edge of the grove and shot twice in the direction they had come. Then, taking her hand, he led both her and the horse deep into the grove. Scraping snow from a flat rock, he seated her and pulled a small flashlight from his belt. Spraying her parka with light, he handed her the flashlight and peeled the parka from her injured arm.

Carefully examining her arm, he said, "Thank

God it's only a flesh wound." He unzipped his own parka, removing it and his shirt. Cutting long strips of material with his pocket knife, he tightly bound the wound. After he dressed, they remounted the horse to find Sarah. Dana knew she must be terrified if she had heard the gunshots.

Before they continued down the bank, Jeff backtracked to the edge of trees. Warning Dana to hold on tight, he fired two shots in quick succession. The Appaloosa's front legs reared off the ground before Jeff could control him, nearly unseating Dana from her perch.

"That ought to keep the shooter in place long enough for us to escape," he said.

"I hope you're right. I don't fancy becoming a dartboard."

Riding down the bank at a gallop, the Appaloosa seemed to be tiring. Dana worried they wouldn't reach Sarah before the killer fired more shots. Her arm burned and ached like a bad tooth.

"We're almost there," Jeff said. "Just around the bend."

She then remembered Marc, who would return to the grove where he left her. Would the killer take him out? She bit her lip until it bled. A few moments later Jeff called Sarah's name. When she didn't answer, he said, "I'm sure this is where I left her."

Traveling further down the bank, they called "Sarah." Still no answer. Had the killer followed Jeff from the ridge and watched as Sarah dismounted. No, there hadn't been enough time. Or had there? Was it possible that he could have watched Jeff as he drove his SUV through the trees? That wasn't possible either, unless he had run along the ridge on foot. Dana's stomach tied itself in knots. Feeling a bit faint, she gripped Jeff's waist tighter. He responded by squeezing her hands.

"Sarah," she called again.

"Over here."

Is that really Sarah? She didn't know what to believe.

Jeff reined in next to a cottonwood tree. A rising crescent moon shone through high, thin clouds, illuminating a crouched figure near the base of the tree. "What are you doing here? I left you up the bank."

Sarah got to her feet. "I saw a strange man walking along the shore and I hid in the trees. When he passed by, I came down here where I could watch for you."

Still astride the horse, Dana pulled her cell phone from her pocket. Punching in Marc's number, she prayed there was enough cell service to get through to him. After four rings he answered.

"Where are you, Marc?"

"With the sheriff's deputies on the road. Somebody shot out all the tires and broke the pickup's windshield."

"I'm so sorry. This is my fault."

"Don't worry. Insurance will take care of it. I'll be on my way there in a few minutes. Where are you?"

She wasn't sure, so she handed Jeff the phone. Before he told Marc their location, he informed him that Dana had been shot and that the killer must still be in the area. "Alert the deputies," Jeff said. "We need all the manpower we can muster."

Handing her the phone, he said, "They'll be here soon. I want you gals to hide in the trees while I keep a lookout for our shooter."

Lightheaded, Dana clung to the tree.

"On second thought, Dana, I'd better check your wound and help you up the slope." He groaned when he removed the makeshift bandage. "Your arm's getting red. I'd better call an ambulance."

"An ambulance, Jeff? How will they get here?"

He pecked her on the cheek. "We'll meet them at the junction."

Wherever that is. The last thing she remembered was falling into Jeff's arms.

<><><>

The siren was so loud that it hurt her ears. Dana opened her eyes to flashing lights and a tightening sensation. Someone was in the process of strapping her onto a gurney near a waiting ambulance. Where were her friends? Someone patted her hand and asked how she was feeling. Squinting, she looked into the eyes of a white-coated man.

She gasped. "Who are you?"

"An EMT, ma'am. You've been shot."

"Just a flesh wound."

"I'm afraid it's worse than that, but we're here to take care of you."

Why didn't Jeff tell me?

Dana asked the whereabouts of her friends. She then heard Sarah say, "I'm here, Dana. You'll be all right." Sarah pleaded with the EMT to allow her to accompany Dana in the ambulance.

"I'm afraid that's not possible, ma'am."

Dana raised her head. "Then I'm not going either."

He said he would ask his supervisor.

Before the EMT returned, Marc stopped by to

ask how she was doing. His expression told her how upset he was. But before he could say another word, the EMT returned.

"We've got to get you to the hospital right away. Your friend can ride up front with me." Before he closed the door, the other medic climbed in with Dana and began to test her veins for an IV. Closing her eyes, the darkness closed in on her again and she awoke in the hospital.

The three of them stood looking down at her, their faces out of focus.

Glancing about the room, she realized where she was, but couldn't remember getting there. "How did I—?"

Sarah bent to gently hug her. "I'm glad you got some rest. You must be exhausted from your ordeal."

"No more than you. Did they catch the killer?"

"Not yet, but they will. Deputies found his SUV abandoned along the county road. He must have taken his companion's pickup. No body was found but there was blood on the ridge where Marc shot him."

Jeff said, "Sheriff's checking with hospitals in the area, so we should hear something soon."

Dana reached to take Sarah's hand. "Call your husband and Kerrie. Tell them we're behind schedule." With that she drifted off again.

Next morning Jeff entered her room, red-eyed and in need of a shave. He had stood watch all night before Marc arrived to take his place. The two men entered the room together.

"They've been pumping you full of antibiotics," Jeff said. "If all goes well you'll be able to leave the hospital in the morning. But I don't think you should go to Cheyenne for a while."

"I can't cause Marc more trouble."

"Don't worry about it," Marc said, smiling. "My life was pretty dull until I met you. I'd like to keep you around for a while."

Dana couldn't miss the fleeting expression on Jeff's face. "I'll see how I feel tomorrow, Marc. I appreciate your hospitality more than you know."

Jeff turned back at the door to give her a brief smile before leaving. Marc followed to take a seat in the hall, his revolver prominently displayed in a hip holster.

Dana slept most of the day, briefly waking to notice Marc staring down at her. Pointing to the hall, she drifted off again. Strange dreams of running and hiding in the woods haunted her until she awoke to find dinner waiting on her bedside table.

"Time to eat, Missus Grayson," a nurse said. "You've been sleeping like a grizzly bear. You didn't even flinch when I changed your bandage."

Dana glanced up to see Jeff smiling at her from the doorway. Clean shaven, he looked much better than the night before. But where was Marc? She felt a tug of disappointment that she hadn't stayed awake long enough to talk with him.

"Sarah's down in the cafeteria with one of the nurses," Jeff said. "And Marc's on his way to the ranch. Some kind of emergency."

"Emergency? Does it have anything to do with the killer?"

"Don't know. I heard him answer a call as he

was leaving."

"I've caused that poor man enough problems."

"He'll survive. You just worry about getting well." With that he closed the door.

Sarah opened the door a moment later, a box of chocolates in hand. "Your favorites," she said. "I wonder if your doctor will allow you to eat them."

"Hand them over. I'm sure the doctor would say, 'Take two and call me in the morning.'"

Sarah frowned. "Maybe chocolate's not good for an infection. I didn't think of that."

"Jeff said that Marc rushed back to the ranch for an emergency. You don't think the killer had anything to do with it, do you?"

"I hope not. But it makes sense that he thinks we returned there last night."

"Maybe he left the area before the ambulance arrived."

"I hope he didn't kill another one of Marc's men."

"Why would he, Sarah? He wants to kill us."

"He killed Marc's foreman, Sam."

"I'm sure he mistook Sam for me. The window was frosty."

"Maybe one of the cowhands caught him breaking into the ranch house."

"I hope he didn't kill Jenny. I don't think anyone's taking care of her." Dana groaned, envisioning her wolf dog attacking the killer, as Marc's Labrador had done. She had to leave the hospital so they could all travel to Cheyenne. Maybe the hospital would transfer her there in an ambulance. It was over two hundred miles and would cost a fortune, but it didn't matter. Saving everyone's lives was more important than her dwindling inheritance.

"Call Marc and ask him to place Jenny in a

kennel until I'm out of here."

Sarah reluctantly pulled a phone from her fanny pack. "I think we've asked too much of him already, don't you?"

When Marc answered, he said one of his prize heifers was in labor and that the veterinarian was there because she was unable to give birth. He would send Jenny to the boarding kennel with the vet when he was finished. Sarah thanked him and clicked off. Smiling she said, "One problem solved."

"And another big one left."

"Two actually. You need to heal before you can leave the hospital."

"I'll talk to the doctor about home care. I can't stand it here another day."

A knock sounded before the doctor walked in. His smile disappeared when Dana insisted on leaving the hospital. After examining the wound and placing her arm back in a sling, he said, "Tomorrow afternoon at the earliest." He said it with such conviction that Dana didn't argue. Before he left, he recommended a follow-up doctor in Cheyenne.

When the door closed behind him, Sarah told her to take a nap while she visited with Jeff.

Dana closed her eyes, mumbling, "You're a married woman, Sarah."

"Not for long. I talked to Harry this morning. He agreed to a divorce."

"Poor, sweet man."

Dana was dozing off when her cell phone rang. When she picked up, she heard her daughter Kerrie's voice. "Mom, Sarah called to tell me you've been shot. How badly are you hurt?"

"I'm fine. I'll leave the hospital tomorrow. We'll arrive in Cheyenne tomorrow night, and I'll tell you how it happened then."

"There's a problem, Mom. The townhouse I found isn't available until Monday. I wish I had a bigger place for the three of you to stay."

"We'll manage, dear. We'll stay in a hotel until the townhouse is ready." Dana reassured Kerrie again about her injured arm, and clicked off as the door opened to admit the sheriff.

"We need to talk," he said.

Chapter Sixteen

"I just received a report about the escapees."

"More than one, Sheriff?"

"Three of them escaped together from the state pen."

"Which ones?"

"Two brothers, Rob and Will Turnsby. And Pete Toliver."

Dana was stunned. She had suspected her former brother-in-law and his sheriff sibling, but she didn't think the wolf killer hated her with such passion. They had all been imprisoned at the state penitentiary, so they must have planned their escape together. But escape just to kill her and Sarah? She hoped they had other reasons.

"There was only one man with Marc's former employee," she said.

"Are you sure?"

"That's all we saw. I suppose the other two could have been hiding in the backseat."

"They might have split up after the escape."

"If that's true, Sarah's in more danger than I am. We need another guard."

The sheriff hesitated. "I can assign a deputy to guard your room, so Jeff Mailer can protect your friend."

Sarah will love that. "Thank you, Sheriff. May I call you Steve?"

"Sure. A peace officer's widow is still part of the law enforcement community." Checking his watch, the sheriff said he had an appointment with the mayor. Promising to stay in touch, he left. She could hear men's voices through the door. The sheriff had probably stopped to talk to Jeff. Before she could close her eyes, Jeff and Sarah entered the room to ask if she approved of the new arrangement. Sarah was beaming.

Dana nodded. "I don't expect the two of you to hang around the hospital all day watching me sleep. But be careful. There are three escapees instead of one."

"Steve told me. We'll probably hang out in the lobby to watch for anyone Sarah might recognize."

"Good idea. Have you heard from Marc?"

Jeff's smile faded. "Not yet. He's probably busy at the ranch."

They waited in her room until the deputy arrived. He was the same young man who had driven her to the sheriff's office. She hoped he would be less inflexible this time. When the others left, Dana asked if the deputy knew the hospital's medical staff. Shaking his head, he said he hadn't been there before. She asked that he check everyone's I.D. before allowing them in her room. "Especially if they're wearing surgical masks." Nodding, he left for a seat in the hall.

It was time for more pain meds. Glancing up at her near-empty I.V., she pressed her bedside buzzer and waited an eternity before a red-faced young nurse entered the room.

"You'd better tell that deputy this isn't a precinct," she said. "He tried to frisk me."

Dana apologized for the young deputy before asking for pain relief. The dull ache had grown to a throb. The nurse checked her wound and applied a new bandage.

"It's healing well but there's still some redness around the wound. Good thing the bullet didn't hit an artery." The pretty blonde picked up her supplies and turned back at the door. "By the way, Missus Grayson, a man asked about you this afternoon."

"Here in the hospital? What did he look like?"

"He was tall and wearing a baseball cap."

"Broncos or Patriots?"

"I didn't notice. I'm not a baseball fan."

You're not a football fan either. "Did he have a mustache?"

"Not that I remember."

Asked if she told the deputy, the nurse said, "I was too busy trying to get away from him."

When the nurse left, Dana attempted to envision her suspects. It had been quite a while since she had seen them. She decided to call the sheriff, who sounded harried when he answered his phone.

"I'll stop by when I'm finished here to question the nurse, myself."

"Thanks, Steve. It must have been the killer. I don't know of another man who would come to the hospital to ask about me. Unless it was my lawyer, and he doesn't wear baseball caps."

Dana clicked off and took a nap. She was awakened some time later by a hand on her arm. The room was dark and she screamed. A shaft of light then startled her as her door opened and a chubby figure stood on the threshold.

"What's wrong, ma'am?" The deputy clicked on the overhead light, blinding her.

"Someone touched my arm."

The deputy scanned the room and opened the restroom door. "Nobody's here. You must have dreamed it."

Dana insisted that he look in the closet and under the bed. Still nothing. The clock on the wall said 10:15. Trembling, she told him to turn off the overhead light and leave the door open. Maybe the deputy was right. She might have been having a nightmare, but she distinctly remembered the warmth on her arm. Unable to sleep, she was afraid of waking again with the killer's hand on her arm. Or her throat. Calling the deputy into her room, she told him to close the door.

"Talk to me, deputy. Tell me where you're from. Are you married? Have kids? Just talk to me."

"I'm from Nebraska. Not married. No kids. What else do you want to know?"

"Why you groped the nurse?" When he frowned, she said, "Never mind. I'll watch TV with the sound off."

He left the room shaking his head.

Dana stared at the IV attached to the back of her hand in the dim light. She considered disconnecting it and shedding her hospital gown for street clothes. She hated hospitals and found this one unbearable. If only she could sleep until it was time to leave. When she closed her eyes, three men's faces cycled through her mind. Amusement seemed to dominate their features as though they were taunting her. Which one hated her and Sarah enough to track them down and kill them? The images finally fused together and she slept.

A stout nurse woke her that morning to take her temperature. "Looks like you'll be going home today."

Groggy from lack of sleep, Dana felt like hugging her. Minutes later her friends appeared at the door. When told she would leave the hospital that day, they discussed how to sneak her into a rented car for the trip to Cheyenne.

"The killer might recognize Jeff's pickup," Sarah said. And he must have seen your new Jeep parked at the ranch."

Dana frowned. "I'm surprised he hasn't vandalized the Jeep."

"Maybe the sheriff can arrange for you to leave the hospital in a patrol car and drive to the county line, where Jeff and I can pick you up."

"I doubt the sheriff thinks I'm important enough to deserve a police escort, Sarah."

"Then how can we get you safely out of the hospital?"

"I'll leave that detail to Jeff."

The day dragged on with Sarah and Jeff popping in occasionally, always smiling. They spent most of the day in the lobby scrutinizing hospital visitors. None of them, they reported, resembled the escapees, whose pictures had appeared the previous evening in the statewide newspaper.

Marc had volunteered to stand guard during the day as long as ranch business didn't call him home. Dana was disappointed that he stayed in the hall most of the time he was there. He must take his guard job seriously. She knew he wasn't happy about her leaving for Cheyenne, and was probably withdrawing ahead of time.

Sighing, Dana picked up the phone to call Kerrie. Her daughter was at work at the newspaper and didn't have time to talk, although she was excited about seeing her mother that evening.

What if the killer follows us to Kerrie's apartment? She thought of her infant grandson and a lump formed in her throat. Maybe the trip to Cheyenne wasn't a good idea. She couldn't risk getting them involved. But returning to the ranch would endanger Marc and his men. What should she do?

Jeff and Sarah arrived to have lunch with her. Jeff appeared uncharacteristically smug when he said, "Problem solved. You're leaving the hospital in a laundry truck. We'll meet you at the laundry and drive to Cheyenne."

Dana cringed. "Laundry truck? Isn't that how prisoners escape?"

Jeff laughed. "Some do and our suspects may have done just that."

"But what if they suspect?" Dana imagined herself crouched in the back of the van with a load of smelly bedclothes.

"I've arranged for a gurney to take you from your room covered in a sheet."

"Like a dead person? But how will I leave the hospital?"

"A woman deputy about your size will leave

146

after dark wearing a sling on her left arm. Marc will pick her up and drive her to the sheriff's office."

"What if the killer shoots at them?"

"They'll be armed and watching for him along with another deputy in an unmarked car."

Dana protested that it was too dangerous.

"That's their job. You'll be the bait to catch him and hopefully his accomplices."

Sarah volunteered to accompany her in the van, but Dana refused. One human bait was enough. It was a good plan if the killer wasn't in the hospital at the time, or bribed an employee to notify him when Dana left her room. Jeff reassured her that the deputies would be standing by in plain clothing to make sure no one followed the gurney.

It had to work. Thank heavens the escapees were unaware that Kerrie had moved to Cheyenne. Her name might also be on their hit list.

Chapter Seventeen

A short, middle aged nurse arrived to disconnect her IV. Dana questioned the nurse about inquires about her, or anyone asking permission for a visit. The woman said she hadn't heard anything and promised to keep her departure from the hospital secret. After Dana dressed, a gurney rolled into her room and she climbed aboard for the trip down the elevator.

"You're a tall one," an attendant said. "Better remove your shoes. Dead people don't leave here wearing Adidas."

Dana placed her shoes on either side of her waist and accepted the sheet. Holding her breath, she hoped the trip to the ambulance bay would be a short one. Someone patted her hand gently, whispering for her not to move. It sounded like Jeff, but he was at the laundry with Sarah. It must be Marc.

Rigid, Dana held her breath until they were

safely in the elevator. "Not long now," the same voice said. The elevator stopped and she heard the door open. The gurney rolled out and she heard another door whoosh open. Taking a deep breath, she held it again, wondering whether one of the convicts was watching.

The sheet was pulled from her face and Marc smiled down at her. There were others present as well. A tall, auburn-haired woman with her arm in a sling was standing by. Younger than Dana but with the same approximate build, she was wearing sweats and running shoes. She wasn't exactly Dana's double, but she could pass for her in the darkened parking lot.

"I'm wearing my sister's wig," the deputy said when she caught Dana staring.

It was then she noticed the laundry truck standing by with its doors wide open. An empty recliner chair sat inside with bags of laundry on three sides. Marc helped Dana into the chair, his face sad when he asked if he could visit her in Cheyenne. Not until after the three convicts were arrested, she said. He might be followed from the ranch.

"I'll take good care of Jenny while you're gone. You might want to send for her. Or both of us," he said with a grin. With a slight wave, he closed the door, leaving her in the dark. She heard a thump on the truck's side, which signaled the driver to begin moving. Then the sound of an overhead door rumbling open told her they were on their way.

The trip to the laundry seemed to take forever. Darkness and the smell of soiled laundry made it seem as though she had arrived in Purgatory. But one thought kept her sane. She would arrive in Cheyenne in time for dinner with her family, leaving the convicts behind.

The truck finally parked and Jeff opened the back door to quickly usher Dana into his pickup. The rear windows were tinted but she slouched low in the seat behind Sarah, who was wearing a large hat to hide her blond curls. Little was said as Jeff drove toward I-25 and the state's capitol. Dana's escape had been well executed and she thanked him.

"Jeff bribed the laundry manager not to tell anyone about our escape," Sarah said when they reached the interstate highway.

Dana asked if anyone else had seen her and Jeff at the laundry.

"Only the cleaning lady, and I gave her a big tip."

"Sarah told her, 'Don't pet burning dogs,'" Jeff said, laughing.

Dana thought of Jenny, and didn't appreciate Jeff's attempt at humor. She hoped Marc would take good care of Jenny until she could send for her.

They decided to remain silent for the remainder of the trip so Jeff and Sarah could concentrate on watching for anyone following. After a few miles, Jeff suddenly changed lanes and stepped down on the accelerator.

"Stay down, both of you," he said. "There's a truck on our tail that seems determined to run into us."

Sarah gasped as she slid lower in her seat. Dana was tempted to look but positioned herself so that she couldn't be seen. In the process, she banged her injured arm. Biting her lip to prevent herself from crying out in pain, she prayed for deliverance. She heard Jeff swear as the pickup swerved back into the other lane.

It had been a good plan, Dana thought, but

something went wrong. It might have been the gurney, or the convicts working together; one following Marc's pickup, the other the laundry truck. Jeff's pickup was traveling dangerously fast. She knew he was a good driver, but could he outdrive the truck pursuing them? Before long she heard a siren and the pickup began to slow. When he pulled off the side of the road, Jeff said, "I'm either going to get a ticket or the patrolman will follow the truck across the median."

Dana heard the siren stop warbling and knew Jeff's ticket was a certainty. She managed to sit up as Jeff rolled down his window. "The truck tailgating us is driven by some escaped convicts, officer."

The patrolman laughed. "Now I've heard it all."

Both Dana and Sarah tried to tell him what had transpired but he was intent on writing a speeding ticket. Jeff pulled his cell phone from his pocket and punched in 911 to report the convict's whereabouts. When he finished, the highway patrolman handed him the ticket and told him to keep it down to the speed limit. He then heard the radio squawk in his patrol car. So they sat and awaited his return.

Trotting up to the pickup, he said, "Sounds like you were telling the truth." He held out his hand for the ticket. "I'll keep an eye out for the convicts. In the meantime, drive carefully and keep your eyes open." Running back to his car, he flipped on the siren and drove across the median to follow the other truck.

Jeff sat at the wheel for a moment before he turned the key in the ignition. "You ladies ready for your escape to Cheyenne?"

Sarah turned her head to smile at him. "Most assuredly so."

Dana flipped open her phone to call Kerrie. When her daughter answered, she could hear the baby crying. Told they were on their way, Kerrie said she had made a reservation at a hotel near her apartment. "It's not exactly a luxury suite, Mom, but there's a convention in town, so rooms are scarce this week."

"No problem, dear. I could sleep on a bed of nails."

Dana dozed for the rest of the three-hour trip. It was past her usual meal time when they arrived, so they stopped at the Hitching Post for dinner before checking in at the hotel. She would wait until morning to visit Kerrie and her grandson. They wouldn't drive directly there in case one of the men had managed to follow them. When she called, Kerrie sounded disappointed but said she understood. Dana didn't tell her about the pickup truck that had followed them. Her daughter had enough to worry about.

Arriving at the small hotel, Jeff parked at the side entrance to watch for anyone who might have followed. When he felt it was safe, they trooped inside the small, neat brick building with a scrupulously clean lobby. Jeff showed the man his I.D. and explained that no one was to know of their presence. The clerk was then slipped a fifty dollar bill.

Shown to their rooms, Jeff went into detective mode, making sure the rooms were safe. When they were ready for bed, Dana fell asleep as soon as her feet were tucked under the blanket. She awoke sometime later to hear Sarah softly snoring in the adjacent bed. Were they ever going to be safe? The three convicts knew that Kerrie was her daughter although she had married Tom after the men were incarcerated. If they asked around, someone might tell them that the couple had moved to Cheyenne, where Kerrie worked for the newspaper. They had to find another safe haven. Maybe Jeff would know of somewhere they could hide.

Sleep eluded her for the rest of the night. Jeff knocked at seven, inviting them to breakfast. He appeared rested and ready for anything that might come their way. What would they have done without him? Dana wished that Sarah would tone down her flirting. It seemed to bother Jeff. She would have a talk with her while they were getting dressed.

"Me flirting with Jeff? I'm just being sociable, Dana. You know he's more than just an employee."

"Exactly. He's a friend as well as our bodyguard. But he doesn't need distractions to take his mind from the job."

Sarah's expression was that of a reprimanded child. "I guess I'll go back to Harry."

"An excellent idea, Sarah. At least you'll be safe."

"You'll come with me, won't you?"

Dana hesitated. "The killer would probably have trouble tracking us to the West Texas outback. But are you sure that's what you really want to do?"

"I miss Harry but it may only be a temporary hideout."

"I guess it's our only option but—"

"Good, let's join Jeff for breakfast. I'm ravenously hungry." Sarah towed her to the door. When it opened, they found Jeff standing guard. Dana wondered if he had overheard their conversation.

Smiling, he offered them both an arm as they walked to the elevator. "I checked the lobby, parking lot and restaurant. There doesn't seem to be anyone lurking about."

Dana sighed with relief. Maybe they wouldn't have to worry about their flight to Texas. During breakfast she wondered how their flight could be accomplished, without leaving a trail. Jeff might drive them to Denver in a rented car in case someone had followed them to Cheyenne. Kerrie and the baby could meet them somewhere before they left. Kerrie was well versed in eluding followers.

Jeff said it was a good plan but seemed disappointed that he wasn't going along. Dana couldn't risk having him around Sarah's husband. Sarah had imagined herself in love with their bodyguard from the moment she met him.

Kerrie called as they left the restaurant, asking when they would arrive. She needed to check in at work within the hour. When Dana told her about the trip to Texas, she sounded relieved. Kerrie suggested a park down the street from her apartment. She would meet them there on her way to the babysitter. Given directions, the trio parked beneath a large tree and waited for Kerrie's Toyota to appear. In the meantime, they watched for any suspicious vehicles lingering in the area.

A black Ford SUV cruised by, raising the hair on Dana's neck. It couldn't be the same one rented by the killer, but Jeff sat bolt upright in his seat as he watched the car turn the corner. It bore a county two license plate, which was assigned to Cheyenne residents. But the killer might have a penchant for black SUVs and rented another. They watched intently as the black Ford turned another corner and headed back toward them.

"Duck," Jeff said. "We can't take any chances."

While Dana crouched between the seats, she

punched in Kerrie's number to warn her away from the park. When her daughter answered, she said she was a block away and would call the police.

"Not yet, dear. We're not sure it's the same driver."

Before Kerrie could answer, a shot rang out and Sarah screamed. She also heard Jeff swear and return fire as the Ford picked up speed. Starting the engine, he pulled into the right lane.

"Call the police, Kerrie."

Managing to sit upright, Dana asked if they were both all right.

"A little glass cut," Jeff said before giving her the license number, which she repeated to her daughter. "We'll follow at a distance to report the killer's whereabouts."

"Be careful, Mom. I can't believe that you and Sarah are involved in another murder investigation."

"I want to see you and the baby, Kerrie, but I can't risk the killer learning where you live."

Kerrie said she understood, but her voice cracked like an adolescent boy's. "Call when you reach your destination."

Dana promised to spend time with her when she returned from Texas. She then clicked off before her own voice betrayed her disappointment.

"Call nine-one-one and report the Ford's location," Jeff said, reciting the street names as they drove past. His voice was strained, which caused Sarah to hyperventilate. Dana choked on her words as she spoke to the dispatcher, who relayed the information to Cheyenne patrol cars. She listened to a patrolman's reply that he had the SUV in sight. She told Jeff to ease off, so they wouldn't be involved in further gunfire. But when they saw the Ford a block away, it was parked halfway on the curb, the driver's door open.

"He made a run for it," Jeff said. The pickup stopped and he opened his own driver's door. "Damn it, I can't go after him because he might circle back."

They heard a siren and watched a patrol car screech to a halt beside the abandoned Ford. Jeff pulled the pickup behind the Ford and got out to talk to the patrolman. Dana saw her bodyguard point in the direction the killer must have taken, and watched as the cop grabbed a microphone from his car to call for backup. A moment later another patrol car arrived, followed by two more. After a brief conference, three policemen scattered, each taking a slightly different route.

Dana patted Sarah's shoulder as she sat blowing her nose. "How we manage to get ourselves into such predicaments is beyond me, Sarah. It's time to retire from our sleuthing hobby."

Hiccupping, Sarah said, "It's not like we wanted in on this murder case. I should have stayed at the ranch with Harry."

"I agree, but will Harry take you back?"

"Of course he will. He doesn't want a divorce."

"Then you've got some sucking up to do, my friend. The poor man is undoubtedly heartbroken."

Jeff returned to the pickup and slammed the door. When asked what was wrong, he said, "Nothing," although they knew he was angry. Jeff had always managed to keep his cool in any number of situations they'd shared before, so something drastic must have happened. Starting the engine, he said he would rent a car to drive them to the Denver Airport, less than two hours drive south. Dana could call for a reservation. If none was immediately available, they could stay at the airport hotel.

Picking up her phone, she called information for the number. Three reservation clerks later, she reserved two tickets to Hobby Airport in Houston. From there they could fly to Midland, where Harry would pick them up. But first, Sarah had to appease her husband.

Handing her the phone, Dana insisted she call before they reached the airport. Sarah reluctantly complied.

"Darlin' Harry," she said when he answered. "I've changed my mind. I never should have left you."

A moment later she said, "You what? Well, you tell that shyster to cancel the divorce. I'm coming home, baby, and I'm bringing Dana with me. You know how much I've missed her. And you too, of course."

Dana glanced at Jeff, who seemed as amused as she was. She held her breath, awaiting Harry's answer. Sarah finally said, "Okay, Love, I'll call you from Houston with the arrival time and flight numbers for Midland."

Dana released her breath with a sigh of relief. She liked Harry, but didn't know what to expect when they reached the ranch. Flying there was simply a temporary solution, like a bandage placed on a festering wound. If the convicts remained at large, she might be marooned at the ranch until the convicts ice fished in hell. She thought of Marc, wondering how he was faring at his own ranch. She also wondered if Jenny missed her.

Chapter Eighteen

They arrived at Denver International Airport at eleven-thirty that morning. Their flight wasn't scheduled to leave until after four, so they stopped for lunch and decided to tour the shops. Jeff stayed with them, constantly watching the crowd for anyone suspicious. Or familiar, for that matter. He had known both Turnsby brothers and the wolf killer, Pete Toliver, so he could spot them all in the airport. Dana regretted not allowing Jeff to accompany them to Texas, but still felt it best. She handed him her gun for safe keeping, intending to buy another when they reached their destination.

Checking in at the ticket counter, Dana noticed a stranger watching her. She pointed him out to Jeff, who said he would keep an eye on him. The attractive older man wore a neat gray beard and well-trimmed mustache, reminding her of CNN's Wolf Blitzer. Everyone has a double, she thought, but why was he staring at both her and Sarah. Had the killer hired him to track them when they left Wyoming? Or was she paranoid?

Dana hated going through security. She heard Sarah yelp behind her when the probe touched her undergarments. She knew the terrorist threat made it necessary, but thought there must be a better way to screen passengers. When they were seated on the plane, she noticed the bearded man walk past and take the seat behind her. Gripping the arm rests, she felt perspiration dot her forehead. Sarah seemed unconcerned and she decided not to cause her worry. She doubted the man would shoot them on the plane, and would think of a way to elude him when they landed.

Once in the air, Sarah fell asleep. It wasn't long before she was snoring. Dana envied her friend's ability to sleep like a hibernating bear, but not having anyone to talk to increased her anxiety. Without a weapon to defend themselves, they were at the man's mercy.

A woman's voice startled her. "Coffee, ma'am?"

"Yes, please." When handed the cup, she asked if there were seats available in the rear of the plane. The flight attendant shook her head. Every seat was taken. Dana opened her tray table with trembling hands, nearly spilling her coffee. She had to think of something. Pulling a brochure from the seatback ahead of her, she read a TSA pre-screening notice for flyers who volunteered information about themselves prior to boarding. Vetted frequent flyers could enter special screening lanes without enduring embarrassing searches. Why hadn't she known that? Had it been that long since she had flown? Dana wondered if Jeff could check out the man's identity from his seat number, if she stayed alive long enough to call him. A woman across the aisle switched on her screen and she decided to do the same. A Bruce Willis thriller was playing and she tried to concentrate on the plot, but the gunplay increased her anxiety. It was going to be the longest flight of her life.

Sighing with relief when the pilot announced their approach to Houston, she decided not to wake Sarah until the man behind them left the plane. Praying that touchdown wouldn't wake her, Dana held her breath during the plane's descent. Fortunately, it was a smooth landing and her friend continued to snore. Seated on the middle aisle, she watched as passengers regained their overhead possessions and filed from the plane. The man behind her wasn't among them. When the plane emptied, she removed her seatbelt and stood to glance toward the rear of the plane. The man was still seated.

Catching her breath, she called for a flight attendant. When she arrived, Dana said, "I can't wake my friend."

The man stood. "I'm a doctor. Perhaps I can help."

"May I see your credentials?" Dana said.

"You doubt my word?"

"I'm afraid I do. You were staring at us the entire time we were at the ticket counter."

He flushed and look away. "You remind me of my late wife." Removing a wallet from his pocket, he handed her his medical I.D. card. He then showed her a picture of his wife. She did resemble Dana.

Sighing, she apologized.

"Well, then, I'll take a look at your friend."

Sarah sat upright in her seat. "I'm awake, Dana, and I don't need looking after."

They shared a laugh as the doctor escorted them from the plane. Because they had a layover, he invited them to dinner at an airport restaurant. Dana gratefully accepted, knowing full well that Sarah would chat him up. Once seated and their orders taken, the doctor asked how long they planned to stay in Texas. Told they were uncertain, he invited them to visit him at his gentlemen's ranch near Houston. He was obviously lonely and admitted he had no children or other close relatives.

"No girlfriend?" Sarah asked.

Dana groaned.

"No, are you interested?"

"Sarah's married," Dana said.

"But I'm returning home to file for divorce."

The doctor pulled a business card from his wallet. Handing it to Sarah, he said, "Call me when it's final. By the way, my name's Brandon Carter. I'll be retiring soon and looking for a traveling companion, if you're interested. Have you visited Australia and Tasmania?"

"No, but I'd love to." Sarah tucked the card in her wallet. "You'll be hearing from me."

Dana groaned again. *Poor Harry. I should turn Sarah over my knee.*

When dinner was over, they each gave the doctor a hug. He waved as he left, reminding them to visit him at his ranch.

"How could you, Sarah? Harry thinks you're going home to reconcile."

"I told you I'm not happy there. And Brandon

Carter is my soulmate."

"How can you tell so soon?"

"His eyes, Dana. So blue and sincere."

"Good grief, I thought you were in love with Jeff."

"He's in love with *you*." Sarah checked her watch. "Time for the flight to Midland. Let's hope they didn't lose our luggage."

"I'm not worried about luggage." Dana scanned the area for anyone suspicious. "I just don't want to arrive at Harry's ranch with a bullet in my back."

"You'll love it there, Dana. Hot and dry, cows as far as the eye can see. No mountains or streams—"

"Then why did you tell Harry you were going back to him?"

"To save our lives."

Dana took her arm and led her to the Texas airline. She hoped that Harry would be waiting for them. She hated deceiving him. Hopefully, Sarah would make a quick, clean break, and they could hide somewhere else.

They arrived in Midland at 10:17 p.m., a few minutes early, to find Harry waiting for them. Beaming, he embraced Sarah and gave her a resounding kiss. Hugging Dana, he then led them to the luggage carousel, his surprise apparent when they only claimed two suitcases. Sarah promised to fill him in on all that had happened during the drive to the ranch.

The two hour drive south placed them at the ranch gate well after midnight. Sarah had talked nonstop about everything that had happened since her arrival in Wyoming. Harry merely nodded, occasionally asking why she hadn't called him for help.

"I didn't want to worry you, dear."

Too busy flirting with Jeff, Dana thought. When Sarah stopped for breath, Dana asked if any strangers had appeared at the ranch asking for Sarah.

"We don't get many visitors, Dana. Some of our rancher friends stop by, dependin' on the time of year. Cattle brandin' and all that, you know."

"I thought you were retired, Harry."

"This is my daughter and son-in-law's ranch. They're traveling in Europe and Sarah and I have been caretakers while they're gone. Otherwise, we'd be vacationing at one of our RV sites."

"I see." Why hadn't Sarah told her that the ranch residence was only temporary?

Harry pulled up to the ranch house and carried their luggage inside. Dana was shown to the guestroom and Sarah followed Harry into the master bedroom. Plopping down on the bed, Dana felt safe at last. She might even sleep the rest of the night.

Following breakfast, Harry took them on a tour of the ranch. The operation was similar to that of Marc's, with the exception of the level terrain. No mountains or streams and not many trees dotted the landscape. No wonder Sarah was homesick for Wyoming, although Dana doubted she missed the snow and cold weather.

Sarah said little all morning although Harry

appeared happy. When they returned to the house, she suggested shopping in the nearest small town. They had few clothes and needed to replenish their supply. Harry offered to drive them there.

"I know you don't enjoy shopping," Sarah said. "Dana and I will drive into town while you feed the livestock."

Harry's smile withered and he handed Sarah the keys. "Take your time, darlin'. I'll be waitin' for you."

Sarah drove as though the devil were after her. "There's not many places to shop for clothes," she said, "but we can make a day of it."

"I never realized how insensitive you can be, Sarah. We just arrived and you're leaving poor Harry in the dust."

"I thought I was in love, but not with him. Why prolong the agony?"

"You're going to break the poor man's heart."

Sarah pulled the pickup off the road and wiped her eyes. "I think you'd better drive. I can't see where I'm going."

Dana climbed behind the wheel and drove until Sarah told her to turn at the junction and proceed into town. Glancing constantly in the rearview mirror, there didn't seem to be anyone following. They were apparently safe but Sarah was miserable. She didn't think she could stay with Harry another day.

They shopped until they were exhausted. After a late lunch, Sarah drove back to the ranch. Harry was waiting and poured them each a glass of red wine. He told Sarah that he had missed her and had counted the minutes until her return. Dana thought her friend was going to burst into tears again. To change the subject, Dana asked again if anyone had come to the ranch asking about them.

"Strange you should ask. I had a visitor this afternoon. I thought it was odd that Sarah's brother showed up unannounced."

"I don't have a brother, Harry. What did he look like?"

"Tall, middle aged, buff."

"Wearing a mustache, sunglasses and a baseball cap?"

"No mustache. I think he had a Broncos baseball cap on, though. I thought he must be a half brother, 'cause he doesn't look anything like you."

"Did he stay long?"

"No, I invited him in, but he said he would come back later."

"Did you tell him where we were?"

"I think I mentioned you went to town."

"You'd better take us back to the airport, Harry. We won't be safe at the ranch."

"Take you back? No way. I won't let some varmint harm you and Dana."

"He might harm you, too, Harry. He's one of the escaped convicts we're running away from."

Harry was silent for several moments. "Now that you're back, I can't let you go, Sarah."

Sarah hung her head. "I came back to file for divorce. I'm sorry I deceived you. I was scared—"

"Get packed," he said, his voice rife with anger. "I'll not play this silly game of yours any longer."

Both women rushed to their rooms and threw clothing into suitcases. Within ten minutes they were on their way back to the airport. Harry drove as though he were an Indy 500 racer until they reached the outskirts of Midland. When they arrived at the airport, he left them standing on the curb as he sped away.

Sarah sighed. "I never realized what a little spitfire he is."

"Now that you burned that bridge, where do we fly to next?"

"We'll fly back to Houston and call Brandon."

"You can't be serious. We just met the man."

When they entered the airport, they found the reservation desk closed. A night watchman called a taxi and gave them directions to the nearest hotel. Dana doubted that anyone could have followed, but she had been wrong before.

The hotel was shabby, but they were both too tired to care. They slept until nine o'clock when Dana awoke to call the airport. Nothing was available until after five that afternoon. Following breakfast in the greasy spoon café downstairs, they returned to watch TV until it was time to call a cab. Sarah had cried periodically throughout the day, and Dana tried to comfort her. She knew divorce was stressful, although she had never experienced one, herself. All three of her late husbands had suffered heart attacks and she considered herself a curse, resolving never to marry again.

When it was time to leave for the airport, they waited downstairs in the lobby for the cab to arrive. A man wearing an orange and white baseball cap walked by the entrance, and Dana feared she would suffer a stroke. When the cab appeared, she scanned the hotel grounds, searching for the cap. No one else was in sight. As soon as they were seated in the taxi, she told the driver to ignore the speed limit as he drove to the airport. During the trip, she turned constantly to peer from the rear window.

"Somebody after you?" the driver asked.

"Escaped convicts," Dana said.

"Who are you? Cagney and Lacey?"

"We've been called worse. Hurry! We don't want to miss our flight."

No one seemed in pursuit but one of the convicts might have followed them to the airport. But how could they have tracked them this far? Dana generously tipped the driver before they rushed inside, reconnoitering the premises. No one present fit the convicts' descriptions, so they were able to breathe easier.

"Brandon is an angel sent to protect us," Sarah said when they were seated in the plane.

"You said the same thing about Harry."

"I'm sure God has more than one rescue angel, Dana. I'll call Brandon as soon as we land. He will probably leave his office by then."

"I hope he meant what he said about staying there. He could be Doctor Jekyll and Mister Hyde, who lures women to his ranch."

"Don't be silly. He has kind eyes."

"So have a number of serial killers who fooled their victims into trusting them."

"Buy a gun before I call him. That should put your mind at ease."

"Good idea."

The engines revved up and the plane started down the runway. Were they flying into greater danger? Dana tented her hands to pray that Sarah's love life wouldn't get them killed.

Chapter Nineteen

Sarah called Brandon Carter the moment they landed in Houston. She said he sounded delighted to hear from her, and invited them to stay at the ranch. He would pick them up in half an hour. Sarah's smile never left her face as they retrieved their luggage and found their way to the passenger loading area. Dana was apprehensive, silently praying they weren't making a mistake. She hoped the doctor wouldn't mind stopping by a gun shop on the way to the ranch. She still had her permit from their stay at the Texas RV resort, where Sarah met Harry.

"Why didn't Brandon choose you instead of me," Sarah said as they stood waiting outside the terminal. "You resemble his late wife."

"He's not much taller than you, for one thing. Some men are intimidated by taller women."

"Tom Cruise married Nicole Kidman and Sammy Davis Junior was shorter than his wife—"

A shiny black Mercedes pulled to the curb and the grinning doctor left the car to help them with their luggage. He then held the door for Sarah to sit in the passenger seat while Dana slid in behind her. When they left the airport, Dana asked to stop at a gun shop.

"Gun shop?" He stared at her in the rearview mirror. "Why in heaven's name would you need a gun? Are you afraid of me?"

Sarah told him they were being followed and apologized for not telling him sooner. "We won't stay long at the ranch because it might place your life in danger."

"Nonsense. I enjoy intrigue. Life has been dreary since Liz died." He asked if they might have been followed to the Houston airport; that perhaps he should take an indirect route home.

"Keep an eye on the mirrors, Doctor Carter," Dana said.

He insisted they call him Brandon, and decided it best to have dinner at a restaurant on the outskirts of the city. They could watch for pursuers from the balcony. Both women agreed. Brandon parked out front where the Mercedes could be seen from the balcony, and they could keep a watchful eye on the door and plate glass window.

Not exactly an appetizing experience Dana thought as she picked up her menu. Sarah was so engrossed in conversation with Brandon that she neglected to serve as lookout, so Dana kept the watch for suspicious diners. As she listened to the couple's conversation, she noticed a man in a baseball cap park his pickup next to the Mercedes. Cautiously opening his door, he peered inside the restaurant through the large front window. Darkness had descended so his image was reflected like that of a ghost. His cap bill blocked his face but she could tell that he was tall, although she found it difficult to tell what his physique was like beneath his denim jacket. When she gasped, Brandon stopped listening to Sarah and asked what was wrong.

"Could be my imagination, but I think I saw the killer."

"Shouldn't we call the police?"

"Good idea. Can you tell the make of the pickup truck parked next to the Mercedes?"

Brandon leaned forward to squint. "The grill appears to be a Ford, but I can't tell the year or color."

Dana picked up her phone and called 911. She knew explaining their dilemma wouldn't be easy. They should have stopped at a gun shop before the restaurant. Exasperated that the dispatcher thought it was a crank call, she handed the phone to Brandon.

"This is Doctor Brandon Carter," he said. "I need to speak to Chief Ashley— I know he's off duty. Put me through to his home."

Sarah's brows raised. If she had not been impressed before, she certainly was now.

Covering the mouthpiece, he said, "We're golfing buddies but I can't remember phone numbers. I have him on speed dial and I left my phone in the car."

Dana glanced back at the restaurant window. The pickup was still there and someone was sitting behind the wheel. Waiting for them to leave? They would be hard to miss at such close range. She listened to Brandon repeat her description of the man and his truck to the chief, telling him to check with the Stanton County sheriff, if he needed verification. He then requested a patrol car to meet them at the rear of the restaurant.

When he clicked off, he said, "Now what would you ladies like for dinner? I'm sure they have take-out."

"No need for doggie bags," Dana replied. "The pickup is gone. I wonder if he's waiting for us along the street."

It wasn't long before they witnessed flashing lights through the window, but a waiter arrived to take their orders, distracting them. Dana worried the lump in her throat wouldn't allow her to eat, but she ordered lobster bisque as the doctor suggested.

Brandon said, "Tell me about this killer who's following you."

"He's someone we helped to place behind bars," Dana said. "But two other men escaped with him from the Wyoming Penitentiary and we're not sure which one followed us here."

"Interesting. Have you notified the police?"

"No, we weren't sure until just now."

"Then I'll drive you to the nearest station where you can fill out a report."

"Let's hope the police have captured him. If not, we'll file a report tomorrow."

"Very well. We'll try to elude him until then."

Why is the doctor so accommodating? Most men would dump us on the curb as Harry did in Midland.

When they had finished dinner, their host called the dispatcher to put him through again to the chief. Ten minutes later, a patrolman entered the kitchen to make them aware of his presence. The aroma of finely prepared food must have made the patrolman hungry for he breathed in the scents with an ecstatic expression. Dana wished for a carry-out bag to give him.

They were ushered out to the patrol car to sit in the backseat. Darkness closed in on them and they huddled together as the car crept from the alley onto the main street. There was no sign of the pickup, and Dana hoped the man had been arrested. If he were still at large, he may have seen them leave the balcony, and was possibly following the patrol car.

Dana asked the patrolman to check on the killer's arrest. When he called in, he was told the suspect had disappeared. They were back to square one. She asked the patrolman if he noticed anyone following.

"Not unless he's driving without lights." It was a dark, rural, two-lane road under an overcast sky, which would make it difficult to spot anyone else on the road.

"Maybe we'd better not go to the ranch," Brandon said. "Would you take us to the Hillcrest Hotel instead?"

The patrolman noticed a wide spot in the road and negotiated a U-turn. He was right. A pickup without lights had been following. Grabbing his microphone, he called for backup. Turning on the siren and overhead lights, he raced back toward Houston. Hopefully, the pickup would follow without taking a shot. She wondered if the good doctor had already experienced enough intrigue. She'd had enough to last the rest of her life.

Moments later Dana noticed flashing lights approaching. Their patrol car slowed and pulled off the side of the road. "Stay put," the cop said as he left the car with his gun drawn. Several minutes later the other patrol cars continued slowly down the road. The car door then opened and the patrolman took his seat behind the wheel.

"Pickup's nowhere in sight. He may have turned around or driven across country when he spotted the other patrol cars."

Brandon insisted that he take them to the hotel, if the patrolman was sure they were no longer followed. Some fifteen minutes later, they pulled into the parking lot of the Hillcrest Hotel. The patrol car drove around back, telling them he would stand guard until they were safely inside. He then opened the back door and they hurried to a side entrance. The doctor arranged for their rooms and escorted them to the elevator. "Don't leave your room alone. I'm in 219 next door. Call if you need anything."

When their own door closed, Sarah gushed, "Isn't he wonderful?"

I hope so. "Yes, a nice, lonely man. I think we'd better look him up in the phone book as well as on the Internet people search. Tomorrow we need to buy a laptop as well as a gun."

"You're so cynical, Dana."

"Maybe, but I'm also careful. Our lives depend on it."

Exhausted, they decided to turn in early. Dana checked the door locks and peered through the peephole in the door. Was that an eye staring back at her? She exhaled slowly as the object moved out of sight. Another hotel visitor must have paused in the hallway. She wished she was as trusting as Sarah. It was going to another sleepless night.

Next morning after breakfast at the hotel, the doctor ordered a taxi to take them back to the restaurant where his car was parked. They were distressed to find all four tires flat and the windshield broken. The doors had also been keyed in long sweeping strokes. Both women apologized and Dana offered to pay for the damages.

Brandon told them not to fret. He had decided to trade in the car for a new one. Dana wondered what his medical specialty was that he could take the vandalism in stride. Retrieving his cell phone, he called for another cab to take them to a car dealership. When they arrived at a Cadillac dealer, he said, "It's a step down but under the circumstances—"

He told them to choose a car they liked. After sitting in several, they choose a crystal red sedan. Brandon wrote a check, signed the papers and they were on their way to a gun shop. Dana suggested calling a wrecker, but he phoned the police chief to check the Mercedes first for prints. Cop shows must have been his favorite TV programming because he seemed to enjoy the excitement. Or he was simply attempting to impress Sarah, who didn't need impressing. She was clearly infatuated.

When they arrived at the gun shop, Brandon recommended a .38 special instead of a Glock. "Easier to handle, he said, and it fits in your purse." He insisted on paying for it. Having a sugar daddy didn't set well with Dana, but Sarah didn't seem to mind. She linked her arm in his when they left the shop. "Dana needs a new laptop to conduct a people search," she said.

Dana gasped, afraid Sarah would say it was to check on him. She insisted on paying for it herself.

"As you wish." He smiled at Sarah and opened the door of the new car. "This is my gift to you, my dear. Would you like to drive?"

Sarah's mouth was agape before she stammered,

"N-no, I-I want you to drive."

This is getting out of hand. She would have another talk with Sarah. Accepting a new car from a strange man was not something Sarah would have previously done. But divorcing her husband of five months wasn't like her either. Was she suffering from early onset dementia? Or had the doctor hypnotized her?

Brandon drove to an electronics store where Dana decided on a tablet with a keyboard. After brief instructions on usage, they were on their way to the ranch. The doctor took what he called the scenic route with frequent stops to check for followers. They didn't arrive at the Bar B Ranch until almost noon. The elaborate ranch house, he explained, was his late wife's design. He thought it belonged in Disneyland, with its turrets and gingerbread trim.

"It's lovely," Dana said, comparing it to the mansion she had inherited from her sister. Biting her lip, she remembered the tornado that had destroyed the mansion. But all that mattered was to stay alive long enough to watch Sarah marry her impetuous physician. She knew her friend well enough to know that was on her mind.

"You'll be safe here," the doctor said, patting Sarah's hand.

Marc had said the same thing to her about his Wyoming ranch, and the results had been disastrous. Brandon had no idea what he was himself getting into.

Chapter Twenty

The house was luxurious, from the massive paintings and plush carpet to the delicate antique furniture. The home had obviously been designed by and for a woman. Dana was surprised that Brandon hadn't replaced the furniture after his wife died.

While they were seated drinking coffee, she asked his medical specialty.

"Psychiatry. I served as a criminal analyst in Dallas for many years until I decided to move here for private practice. It's been very rewarding."

No wonder he's so laid back and into crime detection. "But you were on the flight from Denver."

"I attended a conference there at the Brown Hotel."

"How fortunate we were to meet you," Sarah said.

"Not nearly as fortunate as I am, my dear."

Dana experienced chills. Was Brandon Carter for real? Dana couldn't wait to look him up on the

Internet.

"Tell me more about your murder suspects," he said.

"Two brothers who were involved in drugs and murder, one of them formerly married to my sister Georgie until she died. His brother has a long rap sheet but managed to fool county residents into voting him into the sheriff's office.

"Fascinating."

"The other suspect is a disturbed young man who lived on Gray Wolf Mountain. He began by killing wolves and eventually people."

"And you were involved in their capture?"

"I'm afraid so."

The doctor folded his hands and cocked his head to stare at her. "You both were very brave."

"Or foolish. We didn't think about the men escaping from prison to come after us." She had the feeling he was analyzing her. Why wasn't he questioning Sarah?

An older woman appeared to announce that lunch had been prepared. Dana considered it a reprieve and accepted his right arm. Sarah clung possessively to his left as he led them into the dining room, which was even more elaborate than the living quarters.

"Our clothes were destroyed when a tornado struck Dana's mansion," Sarah said. "We need to go shopping."

Brandon's brows raised. "If you think it's safe."

Dana shook her head. "It's not. We can survive with the clothes we have, if you don't mind jeans and sweatshirts."

"Of course not. I'm a jeans and sweatshirt man, myself, but my wife insisted on—well, never mind.

I'm happy to have such intriguing house guests."

Dana asked if he would mind if their bodyguard flew to the ranch to protect them. She was no longer concerned about Sarah distracting him, but she anticipated that Jeff would concentrate his full attention on her.

"By all means, if that would make you feel more secure." He said there were four bedrooms in the mansion, plenty of room for a former police officer.

Dana thanked him and left the room to call Jeff, who didn't answer his phone. She hoped he hadn't taken another job. Leaving him a message, she returned to the dining room, where Brandon and Sarah had their heads together. She knew they would prefer to remain alone, so she asked if the housekeeper would show her to her room.

Her room at the head of the stairs was perfectly designed for a young female with frilly pink curtains and matching coverlet. Dana placed her new tablet on the corner desk and attached the keyboard, hoping to find the right WiFi connection, without asking Brandon. She wasn't having much luck until Sarah entered the room. Handing her note paper, she said that Brandon had written down Internet instructions.

"You didn't tell him—?"

"Of course not. He thinks you're researching the convicts."

"That, too, Sarah. I'll stay here until dinner to give you and Brandon some privacy."

"We'll have plenty of time for that later. I want him to think of me as a woman of mystery."

"That you are, my friend. After all these years, I've yet to figure you out. Especially when it comes to men."

Dana's sarcasm either sailed over Sarah's head or she chose to ignore it. "Hurry, I want to see what the people search has to say about Brandon."

Sighing, Dana followed Brandon's instructions and managed to boot up and search the Internet to find the doctor's name. When she did, a long list of awards filled the small screen as well as his educational credits.

"He appears legitimate, Sarah. No black marks against him."

"Good. Then it's full steam ahead."

Dana reminded her that she was still married. "You'd better file for divorce before you commit yourself."

They both heard gravel crunching beneath the bedroom window and rushed to determine what had caused the noise. The red Cadillac moved slowly toward the rear of the house, possibly to a garage. Was that Brandon at the wheel?

"He didn't mention other servants," Sarah said. "It must be him. I wonder where he's going in my car."

Dana shivered. "Are you sure he bought it for you, Sarah? Have you seen the paperwork?"

"No, he'll give them to me in due time. I'm sure he wants to find out first whether we're compatible."

"As I recall, he eluded to only wanting a travel companion." Dana's cell phone rang. She didn't recognize the number and was surprised to hear Marc's voice.

"Just calling to make sure you made it safely to Sarah's ranch."

"It's a long story, Marc. We're at the Bar B Ranch near Houston. Sarah decided on a divorce."

There was silence on the other end.

"By the way, have you seen Jeff? I tried calling him to fly down to resume his guard job."

"I hate to tell you this, Dana. Jeff's in the hospital with a bullet wound."

Dana gasped, unable to speak. At last she asked if the wound were serious. When told it was, she wanted to know who pulled the trigger. Marc said he thought it was one of the escaped convicts, but wasn't sure.

"At least one of them's here, Marc. I was hoping Jeff would come to protect us."

"I'll come. I was a sharp shooter during Desert Storm."

"But your ranch—"

"My brother Gary can handle it. There's not that much to do this time of year."

"Are you sure that Jeff's going to survive?"

"He's a tough old bird. He'll be fine."

"I'll call him at the hospital. When can you fly down?"

"First plane out tonight. I'll call with the flight numbers and time of arrival."

"Bless you, Marc. You've done so much already." Dana clicked off and filled Sarah in on what had happened. Sitting on the bed they said a prayer for Jeff's recovery. Dana then called the hospital. She was told that Jeff was in the x-ray lab, so she left a message. She then called her favorite florist to order a huge bouquet sent to the hospital. Carnations, not roses. She didn't want to send the wrong message.

Calling the hospital again, she was put through to the Jeff's room. The phone in his room rang several times before a woman picked up, saying that Jeff was in surgery. Dana asked about the severity of his wound, and was asked if she were a family member.

"No, but he's my bodyguard and I need to know his condition."

"I'm sorry. Only family members may have that information."

Dana hung up, her worry increasing. She would have to ask Marc about Jeff when he arrived.

A knock at the door startled them. Sarah rushed to find Brandon, a smile on his face. Rubbing his short grey beard, he said, "I thought you ladies would like to go shopping at Nordstroms. My treat.

"You've done enough," Dana said. "We can't accept more of your generosity. We'll only go if you allow us to pay for our own clothes and take you to dinner."

He shrugged. "If that's what you want. I'll have Norman bring the limo around."

Limo? Isn't the Cadillac good enough for shopping?

When he noticed Dana's expression, he assured her the limousine was safer than the Cadillac.

Sarah admitted that she had never ridden in a limousine.

They retrieved their purses and told him they were ready. Trooping downstairs, Dana noticed fresh flowers in several vases positioned about the room. Sarah had certainly found her prince charming, but he was a little too charming to suit Dana. She'd never known a man so attentive and generous, although Marc ran a close second.

The sleek, black limousine parked out front and the chauffeur walked around to open doors for them. Dana couldn't recall riding in a limo, but she wouldn't admit that to Brandon. Sarah acted like an adoring teenage fan, and she feared the doctor would take advantage of her.

What would Marc think when she told him Sarah had latched onto a new man so soon after leaving Wyoming? It didn't really matter what he thought. He was flying in to see her, not Sarah. But how could she gracefully convince him that she wasn't interested in a romantic relationship?

The chauffeur reported a pickup following them when they were ten minutes from the ranch. It wasn't an unusual occurrence but it placed them all on alert. Norman was instructed to slow down and allow the pickup to pass, but the other driver adjusted his speed to that of the limousine. Because there was no other traffic on the rural road, Brandon suggested that the driver might be a local rancher looking for a side road. But a moment later, Norman applied the brakes, reporting a road block ahead.

"Road block?" Brandon leaned to look through the windshield. "What kind of roadblock."

"A log, sir. It's stretched across both lanes."

Dana pulled the revolver from her purse and opened the door when the limo came to a stop. Steadying her arms on the roof, she pointed the gun at the approaching pickup truck. The driver ducked his head, the cap hiding his face as he completed a rapid U-turn and drove back in the opposite direction. Dirt and loose rock kicked up from the side of the road, nearly blinding her as the others left the limo.

"I hope he wasn't a neighbor," Dana said. "I nearly pulled the trigger when I saw the Broncos baseball cap."

"I didn't recognize the truck," Norman said. "I don't think he's from around here."

Dana suggested driving around the log. The

land was flat and they should call the highway department to get rid of the road block before it caused an accident. Better yet, they could flag down the large tractor she spotted driving toward them. She told everyone to take their seats and for Norman to drive around the log. If a farmer was in the tractor, he would push the log aside, without being told.

The tractor was moving fast and straight at them. There wasn't time to move the limo from its path. "Get behind the log," Dana yelled seconds before the tractor struck the limousine. The resounding crash sent parts flying, one of them striking Dana's leg. She was momentarily stunned when she fell to the pavement, but managed to pull the gun into both hands to aim at the tractor cab.

"Don't shoot," Brandon yelled. "It's old man Osher. He may have suffered a stroke." Rushing to the cab, he pulled the farmer from his tractor and laid him gently on the pavement.

Dana noticed blood on Brandon's jacket and heard him swear. "He's been shot."

"But how could he drive the tractor?" Dana climbed into the cab to find a large rock mounted on the accelerator. She wondered how one man could have pulled it off. There had to be more men involved.

Sarah called 911 while Dana scanned the landscape for any sign of the culprits. A cloud of dust rose in the distance, which could have been caused by anyone. But why hadn't the killers arrived to finish them off? Were they tormenting them while punishing Brandon for his help?

Dana's nails dug into her palms when she noticed how extensive the damage was to both vehicles. Whoever was responsible must be laughing their heads off and planning even more destruction. They apparently wanted her and Sarah to suffer extreme anxiety before they were killed. But how had they located them? They must have flown on the same planes from Casper and Houston. Probably in disguise. She couldn't remember anyone onboard who fit their descriptions. It was as though they had been embedded with a tracking system.

Their luggage! Had the convicts paid a baggage handler to implant sensors in their suitcases? She wouldn't put it past her former brother-in-law. He must have retrieved his hidden drug money in order to fly to Texas.

Dana asked the chauffeur if he thought the limousine was still drivable. The trunk was smashed and the bumper had been dislodged. There was also a trickle of gasoline on the pavement. Norman checked the rear tires, which he said were still road worthy, so they briefly debated whether to call an ambulance or race to town to the nearest medical facility.

"Let's get him to town," Brandon said, "before something else happens here."

When the farmer had been loaded onto the backseat, the doctor said, "This is no longer intriguing." Kneeling on the floor beside the seat, he held his handkerchief against the wound. "I wish I had specialized in internal medicine."

"Is he going to be all right?" Sarah asked.

"If we can get him to the hospital in time." Turning to shout at Norman, he told him to drive to the nearest hospital.

We need to find somewhere else to stay after we pick up Marc at the airport. Sarah's going to pitch a fit.

185

Chapter Twenty-One

Dana called a taxi while they were seated in the waiting room. The ER doctor said the elderly rancher would probably recover, and had arranged for a hospital room. Deciding that it was time to break Sarah's heart, Dana told her they needed to leave Brandon's ranch. She cringed when Sarah's face fell.

"Brandon's obviously had enough intrigue. We don't want to place his life in further danger."

"I was thinking the same thing, Dana. And I'm so worried about Jeff. We stirred up a yellow jacket's nest, didn't we?"

Surprised at Sarah's reaction, she whispered, "It's not safe to go back for the Cadillac, which I'm sure Brandon needs now that his limo's out of commission."

The ER doors swung open and Brandon walked over to join them. "Osher's conscious," he said with a sigh. "I called his family. They'll be here soon."

When informed of their plans, he attempted to

hide his relief. "Call me when you're settled. Maybe we can get together when this is over." Hugging Sarah, he pecked her on the cheek. He then embraced Dana. "Be careful. I'll worry about you wandering sleuths."

Dana asked the receptionist to direct them to the rear entrance where the taxi would arrive. Sarah turned to wave at Brandon but he had already disappeared. Dana sighed. Leaving his ranch and their new clothing was the best way to elude their pursuers, although she hoped the convicts wouldn't break into Brandon's ranch house looking for them.

The cab driver was waiting. He drove an erratic route through town to discourage anyone who might be following. Convinced they were in the clear, he delivered them to the airport where they could rent a car and wait for Marc's arrival.

"I really liked my Cadillac," Sarah said, as they walked to the nearest car rental desk.

"I doubt that it's in your name and you couldn't accept it, anyway."

Sarah nodded sadly. Dana wondered whether losing the car or Brandon depressed her most.

Dana rented a similar Cadillac, hoping to lift Sarah's spirits. They then looked for a café. Sarah was always hungry and it was approaching dinner time. Deciding on Mexican food, they sat in a rear booth to watch the other customers. Few were present and, from where they sat, they couldn't be seen by passersby. Finally able to relax, they talked in hushed tones about where they would go next. Dana was tired of traveling and suggested they stay in Midland for a while. They could wear disguises, as they had done in Arizona. She was curious about George Bush's hometown and the oilfields where he made his fortune. Marc could chauffeur them around while they sat in the backseat to take in the sights. Checking her watch she realized that it was nearly time for his plane to arrive.

She paid the check and took Sarah's arm. Before they reached the passenger disembarking area, they heard Marc's flight number called, and hurried to greet him. First off the plane, he smiled but was obviously tired. He embraced both women and offered them his arms as they walked to the luggage carousel.

"You both look great," he said. "I was expecting to find two terrified women."

"We're not exactly fear free," Dana said. "And we're awfully glad to see you."

Marc said he had eaten dinner on the plane, but would buy them a drink while they discussed their plans. They found a dimly lighted lounge and sat at a small table in the back. Sarah immediately asked about Jeff and how he had been wounded.

Removing his western hat, he said, "Jeff has a shoulder wound that fortunately missed his lung. A neighbor heard the shot and found him on his apartment driveway."

Both women gasped.

"Did they catch the shooter," Sarah asked.

"I don't think so. When I visited Jeff in the hospital, he asked that I take his place until he recuperates."

Dana wondered whether Jeff had seen the shooter.

"All he remembers is the sound of a car's screeching tires. Whoever it was didn't take time to check to make sure he was dead."

"When did it happen?

"Not long after you left. One or more of the convicts was probably unaware that you were gone and decided to take out your guard to leave you defenseless."

That could have been the reason but Dana felt there was more to the story. She knew that Rob Turnsby's stashed drug sale money would have allowed him to hire a hit man or two to come after them. Her former brother-in-law was probably sitting under a palm tree in Tahiti by then.

"I'm glad you were able to come, Marc. You might have been shot as well."

He smiled. "Would that have bothered you?"

"How can you even ask?"

He reached to squeeze Dana's hand. "I had to come. I've lost sleep worrying about you."

Maybe now she could sleep as well as Sarah. She told him of their plans to stay in Midland for a time. Handing him the keys to the Cadillac, she said it was time to rent hotel rooms for the night. They could explore the outskirts of town for safer lodgings the following day. Marc appeared as tired as they were and agreed.

"But our clothes," Sarah sputtered.

"We'll rough it tonight and go on another shopping spree tomorrow."

Dana awoke next morning feeling rested for the first time in months. She hadn't felt safe with Brandon, but Marc was another story. It was nearly eight o'clock and time for breakfast. The phone rang while she was getting dressed, which woke Sarah. She overheard her say, "We'll meet you in the restaurant in ten minutes."

Twelve minutes later they found Marc seated in an alcove waiting for them. "I just talked to Jeff," he said. "They caught the man who shot him but it wasn't one of the convicts."

"A hired hit man?" Dana asked.

"Apparently so."

"I wonder how many others are looking for us?"

"It might be a good idea to leave this part of the country. Criminals will have a difficult time following."

"I hope you're right, Marc. Where do you suggest we go?"

"Alaska is probably the last place they would think to look, other than Siberia."

Sarah shivered. "This time of year?"

"I have a friend in Fairbanks, with a mountain cabin."

"And he won't mind?"

"Not at all. I've been there several times to hunt caribou, elk, and moose."

Dana placed a call to airline reservations. They could fly to Seattle that evening and catch the midnight flight to Fairbanks. Sarah hesitantly agreed. So it was settled. They would shop for warm clothing and snow boots, if they could find them, and take carry-on luggage to avoid being tracked.

They spent the day shopping while Marc stood guard. Dana felt a pang of sympathy for him. She knew most men hated to shop, but he didn't seem to mind. A smile never seemed to leave his face, even while wedging bags of clothing and shoes into the Cadillac's trunk.

They decided on an early dinner at the nearest restaurant. After their meals had been delivered,

Marc said he had spotted a tall man wearing a hoodie in several of the stores where they shopped. Dana asked why he suspected him and was told the man had walked around, keeping them in view. But he never bought anything.

"I shouldn't have rented the same color Cadillac that Brandon bought," Dana said. "That made it easy for him to follow."

Marc suggested calling the rental agency to have them pick up the car while the three of them took a taxi to the airport. The women could change into new clothes before they left the mall, which meant another quick shopping spree. Hopefully, the Cadillac would arrive at the airport before their plane left for Seattle. He must have known losing more new clothing would make for cranky passengers, so he offered a hundred dollar incentive to the rental agency for a quick pickup.

When the taxi arrived, they discovered it was same driver who had delivered them to the airport the previous day. He asked if they wanted to take the scenic route again, but was told that speed was of the essence. Shaking his head, he mumbled something about cops and robbers. If he only knew, Dana thought as she turned to peer through the rear window. Darkness was closing in, making it impossible to discover anyone following. The driver cut in and out of traffic as though involved in a car chase. She tapped his shoulder, warning him about getting a ticket, but he ignored her.

He must be high on caffeine.

They arrived at the airport in record time and rushed to the rental agency. The Cadillac would arrive before their plane left for Seattle, the clerk said, staring at them curiously. Dana couldn't blame her. How many customers arrived in a taxi instead of the rental car, unless they'd been involved in an accident? She noticed Marc scanning the waiting area, probably looking for the hooded man. She wondered if he were armed and remembered the gun in her purse. She had a permit to carry but didn't think it applied to airline travel. She couldn't dispose of her own gun because someone might find it and use it to commit a crime. Checking her watch, she realized they still had over an hour until their flight. Pulling Marc aside she asked him what to do.

"No problem, Dana. I have a hard gun case in my luggage that I can fit yours into. Guns have to be unloaded and locked in a case, and declared before we board the plane."

"I wonder why Jeff didn't tell me that before we left Wyoming. I gave him my Glock and bought a new gun when we arrived in Houston."

"He probably didn't know. It's a new TSA security law."

"Good thing we haven't checked our luggage." She noticed Marc staring at a man in the waiting room and asked if he looked familiar.

"Could be the same guy but it's hard to tell. He's not wearing a hoodie."

Dana sighed, knowing she would be a nervous wreck by the time they reached Fairbanks. She then realized that Sarah was missing.

"She went to the restroom," he said, pointing. "Maybe you should check on her."

Sarah nearly collided with her when she entered the restroom. "Don't ever do that again," she said, gripping her friend's arm.

"Calm down, Dana. You're losing it."

"You're right. I need to meditate." Spotting an

empty section of seats, she led Sarah toward them. Once seated, she signaled Marc to join them. They didn't have long before they were required to check in.

Myriad thoughts raced through her mind as she silently repeated her mantra. Sounds were magnified as she drifted into a dreamlike state, and she flinched when someone set a suitcase down nearby.

"Twenty minutes are up," Marc said, startling her. "We need to load your gun into my case. And this is not the place."

The followed him to a corner of the building that appeared unoccupied. Dana handed over her revolver and he quickly removed the shells, placing them in a hard, black case and locking it. Snapping his suitcase closed, he led them to the security counter.

The flight to Seattle seemed to take forever and only half an hour remained for them to cross the concourse to board the Alaska Airlines plane. Seated in the boarding area, Dana noticed that nearly everyone was wearing Sheepskin jackets, plaid shirts, cargo pants and mukluks. Remembering the clothes they had recently purchased, she thought they would never fit in. Fortunately, their clothing had arrived in the Cadillac's trunk before they left.

They boarded the plane at a quarter until midnight, taking their seats over the wing. The plane was only half full and passengers were taking advantage of the space. Before the plane taxied down the runway, they reclined in their seats with legs stretched across the aisle. She would have to climb over more than a dozen pairs to get to the rear of the plane. Dana closed her eyes and listened to Sarah snore. Marc was seated across the aisle and hopefully wouldn't fall asleep.

Gazing from her window at glistening snow, which stretched to the horizon, she was reminded of the children's movie, "Frozen." She prayed they wouldn't have to make an emergency landing in the tundra. That thought alone kept her awake for the two and a half hour flight.

Chapter Twenty-Two

Dana nearly drifted off before the pilot announced their landing in Fairbanks. Yawning and attempting to get her bearings, she woke Sarah and helped her unbuckle her seatbelt. Waiting for the other passengers to disembark, she scanned them as they stumbled by, gripping seat backs for balance. When the last one left, Marc stood to help them to their feet.

A flutter of excitement traveled from Dana's stomach to her throat. Neither she nor Sarah had visited Alaska, and it seemed they landed on another planet. They would shop for plaid shirts and mukluks as soon as they were rested, so they wouldn't stand out in the crowd.

Marc said he had made reservations at the airport hotel. It was a day's drive to his friend's cabin and he didn't want to wear them out.

"You'll love it there," he said. "We'll have to shop for a month's worth of food and necessities as well as some firewood."

Sarah frowned. "Sounds awfully primitive."

"It is, but I'll keep the fire going to make sure you stay warm."

"Why an entire month?" Dana asked.

"By then the convicts will be arrested and taken back to prison."

I hope you're right.

When they had claimed their luggage, Marc led them to the hotel shuttle. He had obviously been there before. Once they reached the hotel, they were shown to the second floor in a room next to his. Dana hung a "Do not disturb" sign on the door handle and told Marc they would call him when they awoke. Nodding, he carried their luggage into the room and bid them goodnight.

"Such a nice man," Sarah said, unpacking. "What would we have done without Marc?"

"We've always found a way. I'm worried about Jeff. If it wasn't so early, I'd call the hospital. I wonder why he hasn't returned our call."

Sarah suggested that he might be sedated, and would call when the medicine wore off. Her voice belied her confidence. There was something about the shooting that bothered them both. Why shoot their bodyguard when the convicts knew they were no longer in Wyoming? That didn't make sense.

Dana's insomnia kept her awake until daybreak. Going over everything that had happened since Todd's murder, she felt as though they were cast in a movie with no control over the storyline or the characters involved. She trusted Marc, but the prospect of being marooned on an Alaska mountain, a day's drive from Fairbanks, was more than a little disconcerting. She was just tired from lack of sleep, she told herself. If she could lapse into a coma for the remainder of the day she would view their situation with different eyes.

Sarah woke her at four that afternoon, her stomach growling loud enough for Dana to hear. "Time for a late lunch or early dinner. I wonder what's on the menu."

"Probably sautéed whale, roasted moose and barbequed grizzly bear."

"I'm hungry enough to eat any and all of them, Dana. Get dressed and we'll call Marc."

Dana checked her cell phone for messages. Still no word from Jeff. Scrolling down her list of numbers, she called the hospital. A receptionist said that Jeff Mailer was no longer there. He had been transferred by air ambulance to Denver. When Dana asked his condition, she was told no further information was available to non-family members.

A tear hesitated on her cheek as she clicked off. She couldn't remember Jeff's son's name, but could try to find him online. She told Sarah to accompany Marc to the restaurant. She would join them as soon as she learned Jeff's condition. Dana should have known that Sarah would refuse. She thought she was in love with Jeff, and would forgo food until they talked to his son.

Dana booted up her tablet and accessed the people finder. She found his son Roger and paid the fee to learn his phone number. When she called, his girlfriend answered. Roger had been sent to Iraq on a peace keeping mission. And she didn't know about his father's condition. Dana wasn't sure that a son's girlfriend qualified as family, but asked that she call the hospital and get back to her.

Hanging up, she told Sarah that the situation was hopeless. She didn't know of anyone else related to Jeff Mailer. Maybe Marc knew more than he had told them. She called the main desk and asked to be transferred to his room. The phone rang ten times before she hung up, deciding to go to his room. After they had dressed, they knocked on his door but there was no answer. He had probably grown tired of waiting for them and gone to the restaurant alone.

"Can't blame him, Dana. He must be in the lounge having a beer."

"I think we should call the sheriff to find out if the Turnsby Brothers have been captured. And maybe he knows which hospital Jeff was taken to in Denver."

Back in their room, Dana dialed Sheriff Simmons' number. He was out of the office, the receptionist said, and unless it was an emergency, she wouldn't patch Dana through to him. When asked about Jeff Mailer's condition and new location, she was told to talk to the sheriff.

Dana curbed the urge to throw the phone against the wall. There was no guarantee that the sheriff would get her message, and there wasn't much they could do from Fairbanks. She dialed the hospital's number, hoping to contact someone who was more cooperative. Surprised that a man answered, she asked for information about her bodyguard.

"My friend and I are in danger and need to know how he is," she said.

"I think the best thing you can do is hire another guard. Sheriff Simmons left strict orders that Mister

Mailer's location and condition not be given to the public."

"But he's a good friend."

"I'm sorry. Only family members—"

Dana hung up. Turning to Sarah, she said, "I've lost my appetite but we haven't eaten all day. I'll call Marc's cell phone and ask him to meet us at the restaurant."

Marc didn't answer his phone. They walked into the lounge, which was nearly empty. He wasn't there. They next tried the restaurant and decided to dine without him. Eventually he would show up. He was supposed to be guarding them. Jeff wouldn't have left them unguarded. Maybe they had misjudged Marc.

"You don't think something's happened to him?" Sarah asked.

"I'm worried that the killer followed us here and killed Marc."

"Then we're defenseless, Dana."

"Marc has my gun in his suitcase. I wonder if we can get into his room."

"We can talk to the hotel manager as soon as I finish my lobster."

Dana scanned the early diners. Cold chills caused her hands to shake, her fork clattering to her plate. Why had they come to Fairbanks? Something must have happened to Marc.

"Please ask for a doggie bag, Sarah. We need to check on Marc."

"They don't call them that anymore, but I'll ask." Signaling the waiter, Sarah asked for a carry out box. She then followed Dana to the office. The manager wasn't in but his assistant agreed to check Marc's room.

Inserting the key card in the lock, he slowly pushed the door open. "Mister Bartlett," he called from the threshold. When there was no answer, he called again. Dana insisted that he check the bathroom and followed him into the room. While he pushed back the shower curtain, she picked up the small suitcase containing the guns and handed it to Sarah, instructing her to take it to their room.

"No signs of blood?" she asked when he left the bathroom.

"None. He obviously left under his own power."

"Wait. Both key cards are on the desk. He wouldn't have left without them."

"Visitors often leave without them," he said. "That's not unusual."

"But he's our bodyguard. He wouldn't leave without notifying us."

The balding man gave her a strange look. "I'll call him on the loudspeaker. If he doesn't answer, I suggest you call the police."

Dana was back in her room when she heard Marc's name called. Sarah had already opened the small case but hadn't touch the guns. Marc's .38 was there beside her own, so he had left without protection. Someone must have followed them on the plane, but why kidnap Marc instead of them?

"What are we going to do?" Sarah asked.

"We'll wait a few minutes and then call the police."

Someone knocked at their door as Dana picked up her phone. "Don't answer it," Sarah whispered, gripping her arm. It might be the killers."

Placing a finger to her lips, Dana tiptoed to the door to peer through the peephole. Whoever was standing on the other side of the door wasn't visible.

But a male voice said, "Dana, it's Marc. Open the door."

Afraid to answer, she hesitated. "Prove it," she said at last. "What's my dog's name and breed?"

"Jenny's a wolf dog."

Sighing, she opened the door a crack, leaving the chain attached. Marc stood with hat in hand, a puzzled expression on his face. "What's wrong?"

"You left without telling us. A bodyguard never leaves his post without permission."

Hanging his head, he apologized. "An old friend's staying at the hotel and invited me into his room down the hall. I thought you'd call when you two woke up."

Dana opened the door and invited him into the room. When he saw the opened gun case, his mood changed to anger. "How'd you get in my room?" When they explained, he unclenched his fists but his expression remained hostile.

"We need to leave first thing in the morning for the cabin," he said. "It's an all-day drive."

Dana's words were clipped. "So you've said. I'm not so sure we should go there."

"Why? It's the safest place on the planet."

"What if we're followed?"

"Easy enough to spot another vehicle in the outback."

Dana turned away to retrieve her revolver. Closing the case, she handed it to him. Then, opening the door, she said, "We'll let you know what we decide before morning. In the meantime, I suggest that you stay nearby in case we need you."

Marc said nothing before he left, but Dana could tell by the way he squared his shoulders that he was still angry. What was in his room that he didn't want them to see? She looked to Sarah, who wore a frightened expression.

"I'm not going to the cabin," Sarah said. "I don't trust Marc anymore."

"Nor do I. I'll call for a reservation to get us out of here tonight. We'll have dinner with Marc so he won't get suspicious. I hate to lie but we'll tell him we're planning to go with him."

"What if we can't get a flight out tonight, Dana?"

"We'll think of something."

Dana pulled a phone book from a dresser drawer. Finding Alaska Airlines, she dialed the number. A voice told her that the flight to Seattle was completely booked, but they could get seats for the Anchorage flight at 8:30 that evening. Dana recited her credit card number and the reservation was confirmed. She next called a taxi.

"I thought we were having dinner with Marc."

"I changed my mind. It doesn't feel safe here. What if Marc's friend plans to help him kill us."

"Kill us? Why would he do that, Dana?"

"Nothing about this murder case makes sense. Pack up. Let's get out of here. We'll book another flight to Denver. We need to find Jeff."

Dana peered into the hall. No one was present so they tiptoed to the stairs and hurried out the entrance, where a taxi was waiting. Told to waste no time getting to the airport, they left to the sound of squealing tires. Dana checked her watch. Their flight didn't leave for three hours, but the sooner they left the hotel, the better.

Sarah appeared to be hyperventilating, and her own hands were trembling. They couldn't trust anyone other than Kerrie and Jeff, and they didn't know if Jeff was still alive. She needed to call Kerrie to make sure she and her family were safe. But she would wait until they arrived at the airport.

"I thought I knew Marc," Sarah said.

"So did I. Strange how someone you thought you knew shows his true self. I still can't believe his reaction to us retrieving my gun."

"I didn't see anything out of the ordinary in his room, Dana. No bodies on the floor or blood stains. What do you think he was hiding from us?"

"Whatever it was must have been hidden in a drawer or his suitcase. What do you suppose it could be?"

"Other than a little black address book filled with women's phone numbers, I can't imagine what would make him so mad."

"Unless it's something to do with Todd Warren's murder."

"If that's true, why wouldn't he share the information with us?"

"Whatever it was, it must be something personal that he doesn't want us to know."

The taxi pulled up to the airport and they found the lobby nearly empty. After checking in, they chose an alcove where Dana could call her daughter, then search for Denver hospitals. Kerrie didn't answer her cell phone. Hopefully she was working late at the newspaper office, or on assignment; and that her husband Tom had arrived home from his business trip to Florida. She would try again before their flight left.

Retrieving her tablet from her carry-on case, she typed in Denver hospitals. A list of thirty appeared on the screen, one of them with one star reviews. She prayed that Jeff hadn't been taken there.

"I don't know which hospital he would have gone

to, Sarah. There are Catholic, Adventist, Jewish—"

"Start at the top and work your way down the list. Someone will eventually tell us if Jeff's there. Maybe you should tell them you're his sister."

Dana punched in the first number and was placed on hold, so she called the second. Told he wasn't there, she punched in numbers until someone told her that Jeff was in ICU at St. Vincent's hospital. No other information was available. When she had repeated the information to Sarah, her friend gasped. A man was standing in front of them with hands on his hips.

"Marc? How did you find us?"

"I called the cab company. Why are you running away after all the trouble I've gone to find you a safe haven?"

"I'm sorry," Dana said. "We can no longer trust you."

An ugly scowl ruined his face. "Not trust me? Why?"

Dana ignored the question.

"Where are you running to?"

"Oklahoma to my niece's place," Sarah lied. "It's safer there."

"Then why the flight to Anchorage?"

How do you know that, Marc?

He must have read her thoughts. "The only flight going out tonight that isn't booked solid is to Anchorage."

Dana felt as though she were shrinking in her seat. She stood to face him. "We're leaving alone."

"I don't think so." He pulled his coat aside to reveal his holstered .38."

"If you're going to shoot us, do it now. We're not going with you."

His scowl softened. "I saw the man wearing the hoodie again, Dana. He'll probably follow you to Anchorage."

Sarah laughed. "Tell us another story, Marc. You'll have to drag us from the airport."

"I'm just trying to protect you," he said, raising his hands in surrender.

"Don't waste your time."

He turned and left for the ticket counter. Dana sighed. "He's going to Anchorage, too."

"I guess we can fly around the country until he gets tired of following."

"And our bank accounts are depleted."

"I was joking. It's better than screaming at this point."

Dana punched three numbers into her phone. "This is Dana Logan-Grayson," she said. "A man named Marc Bartlett threatened my friend and me with a gun at the Fairbanks airport. He's planning to follow us on the Anchorage flight, if you don't arrest him."

When asked for a description, she said, "He's tall, well built and wearing a western hat and boots. His age? Early sixties. I have to go. He's coming back toward us."

"Who were you calling?" he asked when he reached them.

"We're trying to find the hospital Jeff was transferred to so we can check on his condition."

"Did you find him?"

"No. Do you know where he is?"

He shrugged and took a seat next to Dana. "You're making a big mistake leaving here, ladies. There's no safer place—"

"So you've said." Dana glanced up to see an

airport security officer rushing toward them, with his gun drawn.

"Hands up, Bartlett. And give me your gun."

Marc glanced at Dana and Sarah with narrowed eyes. "What have you done?"

He stood and raised his hands as the security guard reached for his holstered revolver. Marc grabbed it first as well as Dana's arm. Holding her as a shield, he told the guard to place his own gun on the floor and be seated. He then ordered Sarah to run toward the airport entrance to engage the nearest taxi parked at the curb. Forcing Dana ahead of him, he kicked the guard's revolver under a row of seats as he pointed his own gun at her head. No one tried to stop them as they left the terminal and raced toward the only cab available. When Dana was seated in the middle of the backseat, he pointed the gun at the cab driver and ordered him to drive to the hotel.

"Why are you doing this, Marc?" Dana asked.

"You'll know soon enough."

The cabbie drove erratically, probably hoping to attract a policeman, but none were in the area. Sarah sobbed beside her and Dana tried to comfort her. When they reached the hotel, Marc told the driver to hand over his keys and to sit on the pavement. He then ordered both women to walk ahead of him to the other side of the building. There a late model Chevy pickup truck waited with a bearded man at the wheel. The driver left the truck to bind the women's wrists and they were ushered into the backseat. The pickup then left in a hurry.

"Are you getting even for the trouble we've caused you?" Dana asked.

Marc said nothing, but she noticed his clenched

jaw.

"And who's this bearded man who tied our wrists?"

The driver's laugh sounded vaguely familiar, but Dana couldn't place it. Why was he helping Marc kidnap them? To take them to the cabin to murder them? Maybe there wasn't a cabin and they planned to dump their bodies in the outback. Glancing sidelong at Marc, she noticed his downcast expression as though he didn't want to be there. Was the driver a hit man hired by the Turnsby brothers to take their revenge? If so, how had he convinced Marc to help him?

Dana's gun had been locked in her small jewelry case and placed in her checked luggage. It was probably already on the plane scheduled to leave for Anchorage, so they had no weapon to defend themselves. She asked if Marc had shot Jeff. He shook his head but still said nothing. She had always considered herself a good judge of character but Marc had completely misled her. What reason did he have for his actions? Certainly not to eliminate Jeff from the competition for her affection. She had never given either man reason to believe that she was interested in anything other than platonic relationships.

She stared at the driver, who looked back at her in the rearview mirror. His eyes were hidden behind large, yellow aviator glasses, and he sported a short, neatly-trimmed beard and mustache. Dana noticed red scars behind his ears, and that his hair was coal black beneath his Broncos baseball cap. She gasped and pretended to cough to cover her surprise. Turning to Sarah, she pursed her lips.

The pickup drove onto the nearby highway. After

a few miles the driver took a secondary road which eventually emptied into a narrow, graveled road that was little more than a neglected path. Bumping along over embedded rocks and overgrown weeds, Dana wondered how they could follow a trail to a cabin in the dark, if that's where they were headed. Or were they going to be shot along the trail and their bodies left to the elements.

After all they had been through, why did it have to end this way? She regretted not calling Kerrie, who would never know what had happened to her. Tears ran silently down her cheeks as she pictured her infant grandson, whom she would never see again. She knew Sarah was having similar thoughts about her own family.

Marc's arm touched hers and she scooted closer to Sarah, disgusted to be sitting next to him. He laughed and placed his arm around her shoulder. Leaning toward her, he kissed her cheek. But he said nothing. She felt like spitting in his face but feared what he might do.

"Why, Marc?"

He simply shook his head and smiled.

"I know we were a royal pain, but that's not a killing offense."

"Who said anything about killing you? We're just making sure that you don't get yourselves in further trouble."

"The police will be looking for you. They know your name."

Marc jerked his arm from her shoulder. "You told them my name?"

"Wouldn't you if someone threatened you with his gun?"

"I wasn't threatening, Dana. I just wanted to

make sure the two of you would be safe."

"You have a strange way of showing it."

Marc groaned as he leaned his head against the seat.

"I assume our driver is the friend you were visiting down the hall at the hotel. When are you going to introduce him?"

The driver laughed as he steered around a huge boulder covered with snow.

"You'll both be charged with kidnapping," Dana said.

"You're not being kidnapped."

"Then why did he tie our wrists?"

"To make sure you don't change your minds about going to the cabin."

Dana felt her features harden. "You're a complete ass. I trusted you and thought you were a great guy. I've never been so wrong about anyone."

Marc ducked his head but said nothing.

"Shut up back there," the driver said. "We've heard enough of your whining."

Reasoning with Marc was useless, so Dana decided to remain silent. She was surprised that Sarah hadn't vented her own frustrations. They said nothing until the pickup stopped several hours later, and both men got out to refuel the truck from the back tank. Dana turned to watch as Marc held a flashlight and the bearded man filled the tank. The smell of diesel nauseated her. Motioning to Sarah to try to loosen the rope around her wrists, she attempted to do the same. Maybe they could untie each other's bonds, but before they accomplished the task, Marc resumed his seat next to her.

"Don't try to escape," he warned. "My friend has a bad temper and might hurt you."

"And you wouldn't hurt us, Marc?"

He placed his arm around her and squeezed. "You know how I feel about you, love."

"Then how could you do this to me?"

"It's only temporary."

"Temporary?"

"You'll see. Now be a good girl and cooperate."

You can't be serious. "And you'll be a good boy and take care of us?"

"You know I will."

The driver was back behind the wheel and the pickup started forward.

"How long until we reach the cabin, Marc?"

"A few more hours."

Ice crystals had formed on the windshield and the wipers were having a difficult time controlling them. She thought about their clothing. All they had were the jackets, blouses, jeans and tennis shoes they wore. No mukluks and fur parkas to keep them warm, if they had the opportunity to escape. She hoped the cabin was well stocked with wood for a fireplace as well as food. Her cell phone was useless in this frozen territory, and there was no one to rescue them.

She spent the next hour in prayer, asking that somehow someone would arrive to save them. Grizzlies, caribou and moose would be their only visitors and probably the meat they would be eating, *if* they were allowed to live. Sarah managed to sleep through the night but Dana could only doze. She wondered why the men didn't switch drivers, and reasoned that they didn't want her to know who the friend was until they reached the cabin.

Marc was asleep beside her and she carefully reached to find his gun. She remembered that he was left handed, which would place the revolver next to her. When she felt it, he grabbed her tied hands and squeezed hard enough to hurt.

"Don't try that again, Dana."

"Tie her behind the truck and let her run or be dragged," the driver said.

"No!" Marc shouted. "It's below zero."

"Right you are."

The voice was vaguely familiar but she couldn't place it. And the darkness made his voice sound even more ominous. Why had these two kidnapped her and Sarah? Had the Turnsby brothers paid them handsomely to terrorize and kill them? She wouldn't put it past them. But why had Marc succumbed to money? He obviously had a generous bank account of his own, unless he had flittered away his money and was about to lose his ranch.

It was still dark when they reached the small, weathered log cabin. Marc gripped their arms and led them through ankle deep snow. "You won't be going anywhere in this weather, so we'll untie your wrists."

"Thank you, Marc. That's very kind." Dana forced herself to smile. Turning to Sarah, she nudged her. "We're both grateful for your empathy."

Opening the unlocked cabin door, he said, "Welcome to our humble abode."

Chapter Twenty-Three

Dana agreed that the cabin was humble and surmised that only men had lived there. She and Sarah had their work cut out for themselves to make the cabin livable. Once inside the door, both women held their wrists for Marc to untie. The cabin was colder than a home freezer. She estimated the temperature below zero, and was relieved to see Marc's friend lighting kindling in the rustic fireplace. Hugging Sarah for warmth, she whispered that she should behave herself and refrain from sarcastic remarks. Escaping from the cabin could only be accomplished with subterfuge.

Marc's unnamed friend seemed even more familiar than he did in the truck. Squinting at them, he said nothing as he seemed to size them up. The one room cabin was dark with only one small window on each wall. Marc's flashlight found an oil lamp, which sat on a rickety table. Dana searched for a match to light it, finding a striker box which she used to illuminate a corner of the room. So this was what it was like to live in nineteenth century Alaska. She shivered with revulsion at their living quarters. No privacy to bath and change clothes. That obviously didn't bother the men.

The bearded man left the cabin and returned moments later with a large cooler. Setting the box on the narrow counter, he pulled out bags of food. Handing them cartons of eggs and packages of bacon, he said, "I assume at least one of you women can cook." His voice was vaguely familiar, but strained as though he didn't want to be recognized.

"Sarah's an excellent cook," Marc said. "I'm not sure about Dana."

"What's your friend's name?" Sarah asked. "Or are we supposed to say, 'Hey, you?'"

"Mister Heyou will do."

"I assume this was your idea to bring us here," Dana said.

Heyou merely stroked his beard and chuckled.

Dana's cold chills resumed as Sarah searched the cupboards for a frying pan. She walked over to help. "We'll need soap and water to clean the dishes and utensils," she said.

"There's a well out back and a bucket."

Marc offered to retrieve the water, telling them a bottle of dish detergent was in one of the bags, along with containers of paper cups and plates. Dana noticed the disgusted look he shot his friend as he left the cabin.

When he returned with the water bucket, Sarah had already pulled strips of bacon apart and laid them on several paper plates. While Marc loaded the stove with wood, Sarah scrubbed a cast iron skillet. Meanwhile, Dana studied Mister Heyou, realizing that he always turned away when she stared at him. His shiny black hair looked unnatural, as did his beard and mustache. Was he wearing a toupee and fake mustache, or had he died his hair? If they were there long enough, his roots would begin to show. She hoped they would manage to escape before that happened.

Dim light streaked the dirty windows. She'd had little sleep during the trip and she looked about for beds. She saw none and asked why.

Without answering, Heyou left the cabin, returning with an armload of sleeping bags. At least they appeared to be new. Stacking them against the cabin's only door, he walked over to inspect the frying bacon. When breakfast was ready, they ate standing because the chairs didn't seem sturdy enough to hold them. Marc offered to repair them and the table after they all had some sleep. He seemed his former self but Dana avoided him as much as possible. When the skillet had been washed and put away and the plates disposed of, Heyou tossed sleeping bags on the floor, spreading his own across the threshold. No one was getting past him.

Dana wondered how she could steal the pickup keys without waking him. She hoped he was as sound a sleeper as Sarah. But she needed sleep before they could steal the truck. Sarah spread their sleeping bags near the fireplace and they removed their shoes, pulled the bags around them, and zipped themselves to the chin. Wondering why Marc hadn't asked about her gun, or patted her down, she questioned his role in the abduction. Did he plan to protect them from Mister Heyou? Or was he priming them for whatever evil plan the bearded man had in store? It didn't make sense. A warm, swirling coma eventually overtook her and she slept until the cabin door banged closed that afternoon.

Sarah was still asleep beside her and she decided not to wake her. Pretending sleep herself, she listened for sounds of the men's voices for some idea of what they had planned. It wasn't long before both men entered the cabin and told them to rise and shine. Dana peered at them through narrowed eyes. Neither appeared to have a weapon and she wondered whether she could attack them with chunks of wood from the fireplace.

"Get up, lazy women," Heyou said, laughing. "We're going for a ride."

"Where?" Dana asked.

"To show you the sights. This is beautiful country."

Were they planning to bury her and Sarah in the snow? Dana shook Sarah until she opened her eyes.

"Time for lunch?" Sarah asked.

"It's nearly suppertime," Heyou said. "It'll be dark soon."

Dana crawled from her sleeping bag. "Then why the sightseeing trip?"

"To show you a caribou herd."

"Can't we see them later?"

Heyou stamped his boot on the rough-hewn floor. "Damned spoiled women. Do as I say."

"I guess we have no choice." Dana helped Sarah to her feet and smoothed her hair. "Let's go."

"But, Dana—" Sarah's eyes were frightened.

"It'll be all right," Dana whispered as they followed the men through the door, but she doubted her own words.

A shiny pair of snowmobiles were parked beside the cabin, so someone had made an earlier trip to the mountain. Marc instructed Sarah to sit behind Heyou, and for Dana to occupy the machine with him, which was attached to a sled. The engines started and the snow machines bumped over mounds of snow. When they stopped, the men got off and told them to follow. Hesitantly trudging after them for what seemed half a mile, they stopped to peer into a canyon where a small herd of caribou stood together. The bearded man carried a rifle, which he aimed at a large buck. Pulling the trigger, he laughed as the animal fell to one side as the rest of the herd scattered.

"Think we can repel down to retrieve the buck," Heyou asked.

"No problem," Marc said, "but we'll have to quarter him to pack him out."

Why did they bring us along? Dana watched as Heyou retrieved rope from the sled, along with a hacksaw. Shivering from the cold wind, she asked if they could return to the cabin.

Heyou swept his arm gallantly toward the log building, which could be seen in the distance. Pulling Sarah after her, Dana mounted the snowmobile, happy to see keys still in the ignition. With hands so cold she feared frostbite, she started the engine and drove slowly up the rise. Sarah clung to her waist. They couldn't escape on the snow machines. Their captors probably brought them along on the hunting trip to make them realize that escape was impossible.

Dana had accompanied her first husband on hunting trips in warmer climates, and knew that cutting up game meat took considerable time. It would give them an opportunity to search the cabin for weapons.

By the time they reached shelter, they were numb with cold and found breathing difficult. The fire had died down and Dana placed kindling on the embers. They had no gloves but plunged their hands in the bucket of water. Carefully drying them on paper towels, they stacked wood on the embers.

"We won't have to worry about them murdering us," Sarah said, sneezing. "We'll die of hypothermia. Or pneumonia."

"I noticed some cayenne pepper on the shelf. I'll make some tea to fortify our immune systems."

Placing a kettle of water on the wood stove, Dana conducted a series of jumping jacks and insisted that Sarah join her. They then rubbed one another's arms and backs to stimulate circulation. When the water boiled, Dana measured what she hoped was an eighth of a teaspoon of cayenne into cups of hot water. She then added a teaspoon of honey to the mixture.

Handing Sarah a spoon, she told her to stir the tea before each sip. Demonstrating, she took a small sip and made a face. "It burns going down but it's guaranteed to quell a bad cold."

Sarah took a sip and a murderous expression crossed her face. Coughing, she said, "Are you trying to kill me, Dana? This is terrible."

"Stir and sip until it's gone. It's the only medicine we have to keep us alive."

Sarah groaned but did as Dana suggested.

"If we had orange juice, we could mix it with the cayenne to soften the burn."

"Some vodka would help."

Dana noticed something rolled up in a corner of the cabin. Pulling it near the window, she spread it on the floor. "It's a bearskin, Sarah. We can wrap ourselves in it."

Gagging, Sarah finished her tea and walked over to take a look. "So that's what I smelled when I woke a while ago. I think I'll zip myself into my sleeping bag instead."

Dana searched the cabin. "All I found were a pair of binoculars. Let's have a look out the window."

Rubbing a clean spot on the pane with northern exposure, she noticed something moving on the ridge. A man was seen crawling over the edge, towing a bloody chunk of meat. Dana shivered at the sight of blood. She had seen deer and antelope carcasses before, but this time the blood represented something more sinister. She envisioned their own bodies bleeding to death in the snow. Why had they brought them there?

They watched as the man carried a quarter section of Caribou to the sled, which he wrapped in canvas. He then trudged back toward the ridge, gripped the rope attached to the snowmobile, and disappeared from sight.

"Why haven't they killed us?" Sarah said.

"They probably can't cook." Dana spread her middle fingers apart like a Vulcan from "Star Trek." When I flash you this sign, hit the nearest man on the head with the heavy skillet. I'll take care of the other one. There must be a butcher knife in one of the drawers."

"But what if we kill them, Dana?"

"That's a chance we'll have to take. It's either them or us. We need to find out first why they brought us here, and if they're working with the convicts."

"What possible reason could they have?"

"None that I can think of."

Marc appeared again on the ridge. This time he shouldered an even larger section of bloody Caribou. After he had wrapped it in canvas and placed it on the sled, he hurried back to the ridge, where he stood for a moment looking down into the ravine. He then turned back to wave at the cabin.

If only I could read that man's mind. I wonder if he has a set of pickup keys. I'd rather take my chances with Marc than the bearded one. We need the keys before we can attempt an escape. Heyou won't hand them over unless I can get my hands on Marc's gun. I might have to shoot them both.

She didn't relish shooting either man, especially Marc. "I've been thinking, Sarah."

"I know, I saw smoke coming from your ears."

"At least you haven't lost your sense of humor."

"It's either laugh or cry, Dana."

"Is it possible that Marc killed my gardener?"

"Why would he do that?"

"Maybe a woman was involved."

"Todd's fiancée?"

"That would explain why he was so anxious to help us."

"True, but it's a little late to discover his motive."

"Maybe not. I don't know how Heyou is involved, unless he's simply helping his friend Marc get rid of witnesses."

"Witnesses?" Sarah frowned. "I still can't wrap my mind around this situation. Especially the fact that Marc's foreman Sam was shot in the ranch house. Why would Marc be involved in that?"

"There are a lot of missing puzzle pieces."

"Why were his truck and trailer vandalized by someone in the SUV?"

"Maybe to take suspicion from himself."

"I doubt he's the killer, Dana."

"What mystifies me most is how they managed to follow us."

"You told Marc where we were, remember?"

Dana gasped. "Do you think Marc shot Jeff?"

"It was probably Heyou. He seems a lot meaner than Marc."

Sarah climbed into her sleeping bag and zipped it to her nose. "Maybe Marc's trying to save our lives."

"He has a strange way of showing it."

Dana returned to the window with the binoculars. Moments later, Marc appeared again on the rise, followed by Heyou. Each struggled under the weight of half the Caribou's hindquarters.

"Stay alert and calm," Dana whispered. "And watch for my Vulcan sign. We'll escape first chance we get."

She watched as the snowmobile struggled to pull the heavy sled. Marc left his seat and decided to walk to the cabin. Both men were dressed in heavy fur-lined hooded parkas and knee high boots. Why hadn't they brought similar outer wear for her and Sarah? Probably to prevent them from escaping.

Chapter Twenty-Four

Dana watched the hunting procession approach the cabin. She then slipped into her sleeping bag, telling Sarah to pretend sleep. She could hear the men's voices when the snow machine shut down, but was unable to understand their words. A few minutes later, the snowmobiles started up again and the sound of the engines faded away. Dana left her sleeping bag to look through the window. She watched the men stop at the ridge and load more meat onto the sled. Before they returned, she slipped back into her sleeping bag.

When the cabin door opened, both men stamped their feet on the threshold and Heyou ordered them out of their sleeping bags. When Dana opened her eyes, she noticed that the bearded one held a chunk of meat.

"Wash, slice and cook this," he said.

"Has it been skinned?" Dana asked.

Heyou looked at her curiously. "On second

thought, I'll slice the meat and you can cook it."

I should have kept my mouth closed. Now he won't trust us with a butcher knife.

She glanced at Marc, whose face was impassive. *Why was he involved in the kidnapping? And what would he do if either she or Sarah contracted pneumonia? Allow them to die or rush them to a Fairbanks hospital?*

When Heyou had sliced the meat into thick steaks, Sarah washed and seasoned them before dropping them into two cast iron skillets. *Didn't the men realize that frying pans were lethal weapons? They could attack them in their sleeping bags and steal the keys to the pickup.*

They ate dinner seated on their sleeping bags, with Marc promising to repair the furniture the following day. Tired from their ordeal, the men decided to turn in early, but they first tied Dana and Sarah's hands.

"Potty break," Sarah protested.

Heyou grumbled but untied them and allowed them to leave. There wasn't an outhouse so they were exposed again to the weather. Dana stationed herself at the cabin door to prevent the men from exiting. Sarah in turn did the same. *Thank heavens it was dark.* In passing, Dana said, "Not tonight. We need a plan first."

Sarah's teeth chattered as she nodded her agreement. "I'll follow your lead."

Both men sat by the roaring fire and slowly got to their feet to allow them to slip into their sleeping bags. "It's warmer with two in a bag," Heyou said, laughing.

"We slept just fine alone," Dana said, "but Sarah and I can double up, if necessary."

"Leave them alone," Marc said.

"You're getting soft on me, aren't you?" Heyou's voice was angry.

Dana hoped they would fight so that she and Sarah could disable them. But they must have decided on a truce because they crawled into their own sleeping bags. Dana sighed and slipped deeper into hers. The time would come when both men would let their guards down. They had already forgotten to retie their wrists. They must be exhausted from th Brandon eir hunting foray. Maybe tonight was the opportunity they needed to escape.

Dana lay awake listening to everyone snore as she devised a plan. She knew if they were caught attempting escape, they would be tied up whenever their captors left the cabin. Was it worth the chance? Sarah slept like a bear in hibernation, and she wasn't aware of Dana's plan. If only she had been able to grab Marc's gun. She knew he slept with it and would wake if she tried to unzip his sleeping bag. So tonight was out of the question. Sighing, she turned onto her side and fell asleep.

The men were awake at dawn and woke both women to prepare breakfast. Sarah said that it was too early, but Dana quickly convinced her to get up. Yawning, Dana lighted the wood stove as Sarah stumbled about the cooking area, complaining that the ice was melting in their small makeshift refrigerator.

"You're old enough to know an icebox when you see one," Heyou said. "You need to clean up the mess and cut some new ice."

"I've never seen an icebox," Sarah said, "but my grandmother said she had one."

Dana felt her temper rise. "Why not leave the food in the snow?"

"Because bears and wolves will eat it," Heyou said. "You're not very smart, are you?"

Dana noticed Marc's jaw tighten but he didn't say a word.

"We need parkas and gloves to cut ice. Are you going to loan us yours?"

"No!"

"Then you'll have to cut the ice, yourself."

"Smart mouth bitch, aren't you?"

"If you brought us up here to die of pneumonia, why don't you just march us outside without proper clothing? Then you can cook for yourselves."

"Not a bad idea. We only need one of you."

"We're a couple, Mister Heyou. You'll not split us up."

"A couple?" He laughed. "I know better than that?"

"Really? How?"

"You've both been married."

So you know us, but who are you? She glanced at Marc, who was chewing his lip.

"I'm hungry," Marc said. "Let's stop this stupid bickering."

"I'm not done with you, missy," Heyou hissed. "Guess who's gonna walk alone in the snow?"

Dana turned to Sarah. "Let's start breakfast."

Grumbling, Heyou donned his parka and left the cabin. Dana heard the pickup start and wondered where he was going. Busying themselves at the wood stove, she noticed that Sarah's hands were shaking. Gripping her arm, she whispered that she had a plan, but now wasn't the time to execute it. Turning to Marc, she said, "How can you stand that man? And what's he got on you to make you act this way?"

Marc shook his head. "I'm sorry about this but there's nothing I can do at this point."

"Won't you help us escape?"

"I can't."

"There's a warrant out for your arrest, but the police don't know about Heyou. So you'll take the blame for our kidnapping and go to prison."

"This is your fault. Your's and Sarah's."

The cabin door opened and Heyou walked in holding a small block of ice. Dana noticed him drop his keys in his parka pocket before opening the icebox door. "Still haven't cleaned up the mess," he said.

"After breakfast," Dana said. She then asked how they would like their eggs.

"We told you yesterday, stupid."

"Sorry, Heyou. I was so tired from the long ride that I forgot."

She knew there was a paring knife in the top drawer and slid it open a few inches as she lifted paper plates from the cupboard. Slipping the knife into her jean's pocket, she carried the plates to the stove, where Sarah was turning bacon over in the pan. There was plenty of hot grease sizzling in the cast iron skillet. She told Sarah to pour some of it into the other skillet to fry the eggs. Then, turning back to the stove, she cracked three eggs and dropped them into the pan. Spreading her middle fingers, she moved next to Sarah. "Toss the grease in Marc's face," she whispered. "I'll take Heyou. Smile."

Sarah nodded and bit her lip. "At the count of

three."

Both women silently counted, then turned from the stove smiling. The men were deep in conversation and apparently unaware of what was happening.

Sarah swung first, missing Marc's face but burning his neck with hot grease. Dana was nearly Heyou's size, so she didn't miss his face. She then tried to jerk Marc's gun from his holster as both men screamed in pain. But his hand gripped the gun.

Hurriedly lifting the parkas from hooks near the door, they left the cabin running. Sarah tripped and fell and Dana stooped to help her to her feet. Before they reached the pickup, the cabin door opened and Heyou fired his rifle, although Dana doubted he could see his targets. Scrambling to get inside the truck, Dana reached inside the parka to find the keys. Starting the truck, she backed down the previous tracks.

"Please, Lord, don't let us get stuck." Another shot sounded as she made the turn onto the trail. Thank heavens it hadn't snowed to cover their tracks. Her injured left arm ached and she winced in pain when she turned the wheel.

"Duck, Sarah, he might get off a lucky shot."

"Marc can still see. He might use his gun."

A bullet hole appeared in the windshield between them. Sarah was probably right. Marc was a good marksmen. Dana couldn't drive erratically to dodge bullets because the pickup would bury itself in the snow. She could only pray that the rifle hadn't been reloaded since the caribou was shot. The trail suddenly dipped down out of sight of the cabin.

Crouched low in the passenger seat, Sarah said, "They'll chase on the snowmobiles."

Dana glanced down at the fuel gauge. A quarter

of a tank remained. "It all depends on who runs out of fuel first. I watched Heyou refuel from the back tank. I hope I remember how he did it."

Closing her eyes, Sarah tented her fingers. "Dear Lord, I pray the men at the cabin stop to put snow on their burns before they leave."

They had a few minutes head start, at best, but Dana could only safely drive twenty to thirty miles an hour because the trail was rough and slick in spots. She knew the snow machines would run full out, probably up to sixty miles an hour. The men would catch them soon. She shuddered, envisioning what their punishment might be.

Dark clouds stretched across the horizon. Snow clouds, by the looks of them. A snowstorm could hide them from the men, but they would also lose the trail. The truck fishtailed but she was able to keep it on the trail. Her breathing came in great gulps, her heart pounding as though she had run a marathon.

The fuel gauge had almost dropped to an eighth of a tank when she noticed the first snowmobile. Gasping for air, she increased speed until the pickup began to slide. Letting up on the gas pedal, she straightened their course when the speedometer read twenty miles an hour.

Gradually picking up speed, she watched as the machine drew closer and the one following closed ranks. She saw an arm raised with a pistol pointed at the truck. Crouching over the steering wheel, she slammed on the brakes. The impact jarred the truck and, wasting no time, she stepped down on the accelerator. Peering into the rearview mirror, she saw the first snowmobile crumpled on its side. The second machine appeared to have run into the first, but the driver was staggering away from the wreckage.

If the second was still operable, she knew at least one of the men would continue to follow. She had to put as much distance between them as possible. Glancing over at Sarah, she noticed how pale she was, and feared a heart attack or, at the very least, a stroke.

"Are they dead, Dana?"

"I'm afraid that one of them is still alive. Maybe both. You can sit up now and keep an eye on the side mirror."

Chapter Twenty-Five

Storm clouds raced toward them from the West, and Dana wondered how far the men would chase them without their parkas. She hoped they were smart enough to return to the cabin before they froze to death. But Heyou seemed determined to capture them again. If he caught them now, she knew he would kill them. They had to continue until they ran out of fuel or lost the trail in the storm.

The pickup's dashboard sported an array of buttons which confused her. She knew the truck was in four-wheel drive, but could still get stuck in deep snow. Remembering the shovel in the truck bed, she sighed, reassured they could dig themselves out, if hypothermia didn't overtake them. It was a long drive and they could easily get lost in the Alaskan wilderness.

"Try my cell phone," Dana said, pulling it from her jean's pocket.

"No signal, but I'll keep an eye on it. I'm glad

you charged it before we left the hotel."

The phone had been turned off at the cabin and she hoped the battery was still charged.

The first flakes of snow hit the windshield as the fuel warning light appeared on the dash. Dana mentally went over what she had witnessed during the previous refueling. Stopping the truck before the main part of the storm reached them, she slipped into a parka. Leaving the pickup to place the auxiliary nozzle in the fuel tank, she turned the switch to automatic flow. Her bare hands were numb and she tried several times to raise the mechanical pump to begin filling the tank. Returning to the cab, she rubbed her hands as she watched the fuel indicator swing toward full.

Leaving the truck again to top off the tank, she shut down the system. While she was closing the fuel tank door, she thought she heard the sound of a snowmobile. Perhaps it was only the wind, which had increased to the point of a minor ground blizzard.

Ducking her head, she hurried to start the truck.

"What's wrong, Dana?"

She didn't want to frighten Sarah, so she didn't mention what she had heard. She said they needed to travel as far as they could before the trail disappeared. With a full tank of diesel, they could stay warm for quite a while when they were forced to stop. The original tire tracks were nearly invisible, but she had to continue driving in case one of the men was still in pursuit. She knew they could follow the pickup's tracks until the storm filled them in or there was a complete whiteout.

The whiteout arrived as though she had wished for it, forcing Dana to stop the truck.

"Still no cell signal," Sarah reported.

"And there won't be in this storm. We'll have to hope for the best."

"I wish we had brought along some food. My stomach's growling."

Food was the least of their worries. They could survive for three days without water and they could eat snow. She hoped the parkas would keep them warm, if they ran completely out of fuel. Moisture was seeping through the bullet holes along with the whistling sound of wind. They needed to plug the holes.

"Look in the glove compartment," Dana said. "There must be something we can use."

Sarah rummaged through a stack of papers and a few fast food napkins. Handing over the napkins, she said, "Look at this. The truck is registered to Robin Turnsby. "

"Rob?" Dana shrieked. "Heyou is Rob?" Dana thought her heart had stopped beating. No wonder her former brother-in-law seemed familiar. Closing her eyes, she envisioned shooting him in the groin at the South Dakota cabin. Why hadn't they recognized him? And why hadn't he killed them before now? She then remembered the reddish scars behind his ears. He must have had cosmetic surgery since his escape from prison.

"Why would Marc team up with a man who had killed his teenaged mistress after she had given birth to his baby?" Sarah crumbled the registration in her fist.

A knock on the driver's window frightened them both to silence. They were unable to see past the frosted panes but Dana knew who it was. Ducking below the window frames they heard a man's voice yell, "It's Marc. Please let me in. Heyou's dead."

Dana rolled the window down an inch and was shocked to see Marc's red face beneath a fur hat covered with snow. His lips trembled and he appeared to be holding back tears.

"Please let me inside before I die."

"Step away from the truck and pull your pockets inside out. Then unbutton your jacket." When she noticed his holster, she told him to toss his gun away. Marc did as he was told. In the process he collapsed in the snow.

"They must have opened their duffel bags for warmer clothing after we drove away."

"You're not going out there, are you?" Sarah said. "It might be a trick."

"I'll be careful. Rob was such a wimp, he wouldn't have come this far without a parka. I'm sure Marc's alone."

Opening the truck door against the wind, she looked back at the damaged snowmobile, which was empty. The snow had lessened and her field of vision amounted to about twenty feet. No one was in sight. Cautiously walking around the pickup and looking beneath it, she decided Marc was alone, but he appeared unconscious. She slapped his face and he didn't respond, so she attempted to pull him into a sitting position. It was then she noticed an ugly red gash sliced across his midsection that was dripping blood. When he groaned, she quickly searched for a weapon and found none. He must have been telling the truth. The butt of his gun was visible in the snow so she retrieved it.

Leaving him, she opened the door to enlist Sarah's help. Lifting the backseats upward to provide more floor space, they were able to lift him behind the front seat, where they covered him with the parkas. Dana thought it was probably too late to save him, but he had made it that far and was in good physical condition.

They had to know his involvement with the escaped convicts. Dana turned up the heater and peered through the windshield. The trail had been completely obliterated, so they would have to wait out the storm. The temperature gauge read minus ten degrees.

The storm had dissipated before Marc regained consciousness. The fur hat he had worn was lying in the snow, a reminder of what had happened. Shivering uncontrollably, he attempted to sit but fell back to the floor.

"Dana, I need to tell you what happened." His teeth clattered and he wheezed when he talked, his words difficult to understand.

"Lie still, Marc. We can hear you." Leaning over the seat, she asked, "How did you get mixed up with Rob Turnsby?"

He closed his eyes and groaned. "How'd you know?"

"Truck registration," Dana said. "Did you buy the pickup for him?"

"No, he came to the ranch asking for my help."

"Why would you consider helping him, Marc?"

"We were best friends until he got mixed up with drugs, but he convinced me that he was innocent of strangling that girl. He said his brother killed her." His cough sounded like pneumonia.

"And you believed him?"

He nodded and closed his eyes. Marc was silent for so long that she feared he had died. She knew the hump in the middle of the floor had to be uncomfortable, if he were still alive, but he was too heavy to lift as high as the seat.

Dana reached to gently shake him. "Why did you agree to help Rob kidnap us?"

His voice was weak when he said, "Rob said his brother wanted to kill you and Sarah, but he just wanted to teach you a lesson because you ruined his life. He said that keeping you at the cabin for a month was punishment enough. He promised to then let you go."

"Ruined his life? He was responsible for my sister's death."

"I know now that Rob lied about everything." Marc coughed violently before his eyes closed. "But I wanted to believe him because it would give me a chance to spend that time with you."

Dana groaned. "Who followed us in the black SUV?"

"Rob's brother, Will Turnsby." His voice was weak.

"Is he the one who killed your foreman Sam?"

"Rob said his brother killed Sam."

"Did Will shoot Jeff?"

"He must have, Dana."

"Did he also kill Todd Warren? Or was it Rob?"

When he didn't answer, Dana reached for his wrist. She couldn't find a pulse, so she felt his jugular vein, noticing red burns on his throat.

"Marc's dead, Sarah." Dana's lips trembled and a tear escaped from the corner of her eye.

Sarah's tears triggered her own and they lamented the pain they had caused him. But they couldn't dwell long on his death. They had to concentrate on saving their own lives. There was no one to tell them which direction to take to reach

Fairbanks, and no GPS system to guide them. When the clouds cleared, Dana decided to follow the sun west until they reached a high point in the road. Once there, they could survey the surrounding area to hopefully find civilization on the horizon.

It wasn't long before the truck embedded itself in another snowdrift. Dana pulled a parka from Marc's chest and left the truck to grab the shovel. Glancing at her watch, she realized that they only had two hours left of daylight. Quickly uncovering the tailpipe, she shoveled a path from the back tires to their tracks. She then worked at uncovering the front tires. Sarah took over when Dana was out of breath. Returning to the truck, they warmed up before attempting more shoveling.

"What if we don't make it out of here, Dana?"

"We'll join Marc in the hereafter."

"You think that's where he went?"

"He was a good man who was loyal to a friend who didn't deserve him."

"Amen to that. I hope he was right that Rob passed on too."

"If we manage to make it to safety, there's still Rob's brother Will to contend with."

"Unless he's already been captured."

Dana opened the truck door and picked up the shovel. When the path was cleared, she walked forward to determine where the snow was deepest. They might have to wait until it melted. Scooping up a handful of snow, she chewed as though it were a snow cone. Sarah did the same. They then climbed back into the pickup, hanging their feet out the door to knock the snow from their feet and legs. Shivering, Sarah said she would give anything for a cup of chai tea.

"We'll enjoy a meal fit for a queen as soon as we're rescued," Dana said.

"You're an optimist, my friend."

"Check my cell phone."

Sarah sighed as she turned the phone back on. "Still no signal."

"Then shut it off to save the battery." Dana pulled the gearshift into reverse and slowly backed into their previous tracks. Creeping forward, she stopped when they encountered another drift. Leaving the truck, they scooped more snow and pulled the truck forward until they were again mired in snow. Exhausted, they returned to the pickup. The sun would soon set and the temperature had dropped.

"This can take forever, Dana. What should we do with Marc's body?"

"He's too heavy to lift into the pickup bed, so we'll have to bury him in the snow and mark the grave with something recognizable."

Dana searched the truck bed but could find nothing other than an empty rifle scabbard. Filling it with snow, she leaned the scabbard against the truck. They then pulled Marc's body from the pickup and dragged him to the snow hill they had built. Covering him with snow, they dug a hole with the shovel deep enough to stand the rifle upright. Sarah then said a prayer.

Rushing back to the truck to warm themselves, they discussed everything that had happened since Todd Warren's death. The Turnsby brothers, they decided were Houdinis when it came to escape, and were evil to the core. Their previous drug ring had corrupted young women as well as a middle aged secretary, who had served time in the Wyoming women's prison for previous drug use. Their worst offense was the death of Dana's sister, Georgi. Why had Marc not known? Rob Turnsby had talked Georgi into leaving her lovely home in San Francisco to live in Wyoming, where he had treated her badly and cheated on her repeatedly while stealing her divorce settlement. The silver tongued thief had also used his wiles to trick his friend Marc. Some friend he was.

"What's that?" Sarah said. "A man in a fur coat?"

"I think it's a bear. Looks like a grizzly."

The bear wandered over to the truck and stood upright at Sarah's window. Opening its mouth wide, it licked the glass, causing Sarah to scream.

"Stay calm and don't move," Dana said. "The bear will lose interest and go away."

"They're carnivores, aren't they? We must look like the bear's next meal."

"Close your eyes and meditate. The bear will probably scratch up the truck but I doubt he'll try to break the window. Just don't move."

Dana slowly reached for her hand and held it firmly out of the bear's sight. Frustrated or bored, the bear left Sarah's window and ambled over to the driver's side. Closing her eyes, Dana meditated for all she was worth as the truck cab began to rock.

"He's going to push us over," Sarah whispered.

The bear emitted an angry growling sound and apparently gave up. Strolling off toward the snow hill and Marc's grave, he began sniffing around the rifle scabbard.

"Honk the horn, Dana. He might dig up the body."

Dana leaned on the horn for so long that she was afraid of running down the battery. The noise eventually convinced the bear to move on, and they were thankful for his lack of interest.

"Someone must be looking for us," Dana said. "The airport guard probably called the police. And the taxi driver may have seen the pickup leave the hotel. "We need to write *help* or *S.O.S.* on the truck's roof in case a police helicopter's searching for us."

When they were sure the bear had left the area, they looked in the truck for anything that would stand out against the burgundy pickup. They finally decided to use snow until it melted. Thank heavens Rob hadn't purchased a white pickup, Dana thought as she formed small snowballs and handed them to Sarah, who was perched on the hood. Fearing frostbite, they clapped their hands and rubbed them often. Too bad Marc hadn't been wearing gloves.

Darkness arrived but the large accumulation of snow emitted enough light to make their surroundings seem like twilight. Restarting the engine until they thawed, they leaned their seats back and slept. Dana restarted the engine several times during the night for several minutes when they awoke chilled.

Sarah had coughed regularly during the night and Dana worried she may have contracted pneumonia. She was relieved when the dawn broke across the sky. The few scudding clouds seemed harmless enough. Maybe the sun would melt most of the snow, but it would also melt their distress message. Telling Sarah to stay inside, she made additional balls to place in the shade, which she hilled up under the truck.

Something small and dark appeared on the horizon moving in their direction. Was it someone coming to their rescue? Both women jumped and waved as they yelled, "over here." But as the object drew nearer they recognized a huge rack of antlers.

"A moose," Sarah shrieked as she ran for the pickup. "They're dangerous and that one may not have eaten all day."

"Moose aren't carnivorous. They eat plants."

"What if the rest of the herd shows up?"

"I read that moose are loners and don't travel in a herd."

"But he can do damage to the pickup. Maybe puncture the tires with his antlers."

"Not unless we anger him. Duck so he doesn't see us."

Holding her breath, Dana slid down as far as her long legs would allow behind the wheel. When she glanced up, the moose was looking in the driver's window at her. She could hear Sarah hyperventilating beside her. The bull's breath clouded the glass and he soon lost interest and walked away. But they heard his deep, breathy bellow a moment later. Turning to watch him through the rear window, they gasped when several wolves leaped to his back while others nipped at his hooves. The moose dipped and swayed, knocking most of them to the snow. He then lowered his head to attack, but there were too many of them. Dana leaned on the horn and started the engine. She then backed the truck toward the wolves.

"You're unbalancing nature, Dana. We shouldn't interfere."

"I've seen enough death to last me a lifetime." Peering through the rear window, they noticed the wolves scampering away. The moose looked back at them and dipped his head as though offering his gratitude. He then lumbered off, causing a lump to form in Dana's throat.

"I understand how the wolves felt, Dana. They were probably as hungry as I am."

"Hungry enough to eat a moose?"

"Almost. I keep daydreaming about lobster and a thick, juicy steak."

"In due time, my friend. I'll check the snow level again and make sure our S.O.S. is still intact. You stay in the pickup. I don't like the sound of that cough. Too bad I didn't grab the cayenne pepper during our escape."

"A cayenne snow cone? If we had enough of it, we could melt a path to Fairbanks."

Shortly before noon they heard the sound of a distant engine. Peering through the windshield they spotted a speck in the sky that steadily grew larger. It was the helicopter they had prayed for. Nearly falling from their seats in their haste to leave the truck, they stood frantically waving their arms.

The police chopper descended to a few hundred feet and circled the area. Both women walked down the path they'd earlier shoveled and continued to wave their arms. At last the pilot lowered his craft to a fairly level area. Trudging through knee deep snow, they shouted their greetings.

"Dana and Sarah, I presume," the pilot said, smiling. "I've been searching for you for days."

They thanked him until he waved them into silence. When they told him about Marc, his copilot left with them to retrieve the body. They cried when Marc's face was uncovered. Such a tragedy. Dana asked if there had been any news from Wyoming about the arrest of the escaped convicts. The copilot said a young man had been captured but two older man were still at large.

"Former Sheriff Will Turnsby?"

"Yes, that's the name. A picture of him and his brother were on last night's news."

"How strange here in Alaska."

"We're not as isolated as you might think. We routinely get news from the lower forty-eight. Will Turnsby could have followed his brother to Alaska, so we've been on the lookout for him."

Dana told him that Rob Turnsby's body was back along the trail. He said they would return for it later. Their mission was to locate Rob's pickup and report its location. He seemed pleased that their flight had become a rescue mission.

Liftoff was a thrill for both women as they scanned the snowy terrain on their return trip to Fairbanks. Dana asked how they were able to locate them and was told that someone had called in a tip about the cabin's location.

I wonder if it was Marc.

"A number of people saw what happened at the airport and detectives followed your trail from the taxi driver to the parked pickup truck."

"We need to fly to Denver to find out about our bodyguard," Sarah said. "Our luggage flew to Anchorage without us."

The copilot said they would have to file a police report at the station before flying to Anchorage. There was a body to explain and another to be recovered. That could take some time.

Dana asked if the police would call the Denver hospital to inquire of Jeff Mailer's condition. He said he would personally take care of it.

Great. Now all we have to worry about is Will Turnsby, who led his younger brother into a life of drugs and murder.

Chapter Twenty-Six

The helicopter arrived at the police compound at a quarter past three. Sarah was lifted down first and hurried into the office. The young copilot offered to buy them fast food as they filed their report. Sarah agreed. Anything to quell her hunger.

Several news reporters were standing by with a couple of cameramen from the local TV stations. Dana didn't want to be interviewed because Will Turnsby was possibly in the area. When he learned of his brother's death, he would waste no time going after them. Dana wondered if Rob had been telling the truth about his brother killing Linda Johnsbury, the nineteen-year-old girl who had borne him a child. Had his brother Will actually strangled her? She knew Rob was a coward and that his brother was capable of anything.

A TV camera's light was on and she knew her voice was being recorded. The reporters agreed to hold their stories until after the women boarded a plane, so they sat down for an interview. After fifteen minutes of questions, Dana told them she needed to call her daughter, suggesting they quiz the helicopter crew to round out their news reports. When it was over, the copilot handed them burgers and fries, and offered to drive them to a clothing store before they left for the airport.

Dana called for reservations while drinking bottled water. She and Sarah couldn't seem to hydrate after their long drought. They would need diapers when they boarded the plane, which was scheduled to leave for Anchorage in two hours. Grabbing clothes they thought would fit, Sarah paid for them with the credit card from her fanny pack. Thanks to Marc they hadn't been searched.

They called a taxi the moment they entered the clothing store, which arrived within twenty minutes. Stuffing their purchases in the trunk, they asked the driver to hurry. The older Asian man looked at them suspiciously and asked if they were on the run. They looked familiar and he couldn't remember whether he had seen them on "America's Most Wanted," or the evening news. To avoid being driven back to the police station, they admitted they were the kidnapped women featured on television. That seemed to satisfy him and he asked for their autographs when they reached the airport. They obliged him by scribbling their names on a notepad.

Sarah smiled. "Our fifteen minutes of fame, my friend."

"Let's hope that's as long as it lasts." Pushing open a restroom door, they carried their purchases inside. When they had dressed, they tossed their dirty clothes away and hurried to the reservation counter. From there they scanned the area before explaining to the clerk what had happened. She knew who they were and called her supervisor, who said a sixtyish man had been there earlier looking for them. When he described the man as tall, well-built and wearing a dark mustache and baseball cap, Dana knew it was Will Turnsby. How did he know to look for them at the airport, unless one of the newsmen had already announced their rescue? It must have been the young man from the radio station who seemed impatient to scoop his fellow newsmen.

The supervisor suggested they wait in his office until their flight arrived. Once there, they answered his questions about their kidnapping and rescue. Promising his security officer to escort them on the plane, he said he would tell his clerks not to reserve a seat for anyone answering Will Turnsby's description. Picking up the phone, he called the police to report Turnsby's presence at the airport.

When he left the office, Dana called her daughter's cell number. When Kerrie answered, she sounded on the verge of hysterics.

"Mom, is it really you?" Kerrie burst into tears, telling them that their story had been all over the news.

Dana briefly told her what had happened and that they were on their way to Denver to see Jeff Mailer. Their next stop was Cheyenne. Told the townhouse was ready for them, Dana said they would arrive there in several days. She clicked off when the supervisor announced that their flight was boarding and the security guard was standing by.

Pulling on their new watch caps, they buttoned their denim jackets over plaid shirts and jeans. No one else was dressed like their fellow passengers from the midnight flight from Seattle, but they hoped they were unrecognizable. Their guard marched them to the boarding gate and Dana turned back to scan the lobby. Standing in one corner was a man who resembled Will Turnsby. He promptly ducked from sight.

Was it actually him or was she hallucinating? Dana told the security guard, who lifted his radio to report the sighting to his supervisor. Once they were safely on the plane, he rushed down the ramp to look for Turnsby.

Dana worried that Will would book a flight on another airline and arrive in Anchorage before their Seattle flight left. She prayed he would be apprehended at the airport before that happened. They only had a forty-five minute layover, hardly enough time to buy more clothing at an airport shop and catch their next flight.

Sarah slept the entire trip and seemed refreshed when they landed. Dana, however, felt as though she had completed a twenty mile marathon. Once off the plane they looked for the reservation desk to inquire about their luggage, then rushed off to the shops. They were relieved that someone from Fairbanks had called to arrange for their suitcases to be transferred to the Seattle flight.

"I feel like I'm playing a game of musical chairs," Sarah said as she rummaged through a clothing rack. "I'm tired of shopping for clothes and running for our lives."

"It will be over soon, if we can stay ahead of Will until he's arrested."

"Do you think he would actually kill us, Dana?"

"No doubt in my mind. He's a psychopath and he must know by now that Rob's dead. You know he'll blame us and try to take revenge."

After they had paid for their clothing and dashed into a restroom to change, Dana peered from the door to make sure Turnsby wasn't lurking nearby. Pulling their caps down over their brows, they walked separately to the boarding area. No one in line or the lobby resembled Turnsby, but he must know they would be landing in Seattle. Dana punched in 911 to report seeing the convict in Fairbanks, and warned that he would follow them to Seattle. She gave the dispatcher their flight number and time of arrival, clicking off as they boarded the plane.

Air turbulence resulted in a rough flight, and Sarah was unable to take her usual nap. She did, however, voice a number of fears, including Turnsby sneaking a bomb onboard or shooting them as they left the plane.

"The Seattle police will be looking for him, Sarah. I'm sure they have a picture of him by now."

"What if he had plastic surgery like his brother and shaved off his mustache."

"We'll deal with it like we've always done." Although dealing with Will Turnsby was like eluding a terrorist. His law enforcement training added to the problem and he could be hiding anywhere. "We have a two hour layover for the Denver flight so we might have to spend that time in the women's restroom."

The landing was smooth and they waited until most of the passengers left the plane. Sarah joined a group of passengers walking down the ramp and, because of Dana's height, she walked with two tall business men exiting the plane. A policewoman was waiting and Dana was relieved to notice Sarah talking to her.

Nearly as tall as Dana, the young, slender officer told them to follow her into a room off the luggage area. It was a short walk as they looked about for Turnsby.

"I've been ordered to take the two of you into protective custody."

"We have reservations to Denver," Dana said. "Our friend is in critical condition in ICU."

"Then we can't protect you."

"Can't you stay with us until our plane leaves, and hand us off to Denver police?" Sarah asked.

"I'll check with headquarters." When she clicked off, she looked at her watch. "It's almost lunch time. There's a restaurant nearby where we can sit in a back booth."

Dana told her they needed to buy clothes and change first. The officer laughed, saying she had spotted their Alaskan clothing right away.

The flight to Denver encountered a thunderstorm and more turbulence than their previous flight. Both women were white-knuckled flyers as the plane seemed to buck like a Wyoming bronco. Lunch with the young officer had been uneventful, and they were now more normally dressed for the lower forty-eight, although the clothing had been costly. Sarah's credit card was maxed out, and Dana's purse had not been recovered. Whoever found it at the Midland airport must have had a grand shopping spree with her credit cards and check book. She hoped there was enough left in her account to pay the rent on the townhouse in Cheyenne.

They landed in twilight at Denver International and were met by a burly, middle aged, uniformed policeman holding a sign with their married last names. Turnsby hopefully didn't know their new last names because he was imprisoned at the time of their weddings. They asked the waiting officer to drive them to St. Vincent's hospital, but he also insisted on protective custody until the convict was captured.

Sarah pleaded with him until he relented and they offered to buy him dinner. Dana then remembered they had no way of paying for a meal although Sarah might have enough change in her fanny pack to buy him a donut. Smiling, he said he had already eaten dinner but would drive them to the hospital. Dana could then call her daughter to drive them to Cheyenne and notify her bank and credit card holders.

If Will Turnsby had followed them that far, was he able to hail a cab in time to follow the police car? And was he aware that Jeff was at the hospital? She doubted either possibility but had learned not to trust probabilities.

Collecting their luggage, they followed the cop to his patrol car, frequently turning to watch for anyone following. The airport was crowded, making it impossible to spot anyone hiding from them. When they sat in the patrol car's back seat, people were leaning to stare at them, probably wondering why two sixtyish women were under arrest.

"It's not far," the patrolman said. "I still don't understand why you don't want police protection until the convict's arrested."

"Our friend's in ICU and may be dying," Dana said. "We may already be too late."

"Okay. I'll hang around until I get another call."

When they reached the hospital, he accompanied them inside. Looking about the lobby, he stood near the registration desk as they attempted to get some answers.

"We've come all the way from Alaska to see my brother, Jeff Mailer." Dana crossed her fingers. "We were told he's in ICU, transferred down from Casper."

The clerk searched for the name on her computer. "I'm sorry, he's no longer here."

Both women gasped. "Where is he?"

"It doesn't say, just that he was released this morning from the hospital."

Released so soon? Straight from ICU? "We need to speak with his doctor."

"Doctor Crane's no longer in the hospital. You'll have to call his answering service."

Dana sat in the nearest chair, exhausted. Handing her phone to Sarah, she asked that she call. When Sarah clicked off, she said that Jeff had been transferred back to Casper.

"You're kidding? Why would they send him back?"

"The doctor said he was sent here in critical condition and had recuperated enough to go back."

Dana called Kerrie and asked that she drive to Denver to pick them up, and was told that her daughter would arrive within two hours. She looked up at the cop, who asked if she wanted him to stay until then. She nodded and thanked him. No sense taking chances.

A familiar face stared at them through the glass entry door. No, it couldn't be Will Turnsby. "Officer, it's him," she said, pointing to the door.

When the officer returned he said, "There was nobody there. Are you sure you weren't seeing things?"

"I'm beyond tired but I know what I saw. That was Will Turnsby, officer. How in the world did he track us here?"

"There's an APB out on him." Picking up his radio, he called for backup. "You two had better find a waiting room on another floor."

They found an elevator and rose to the top floor, for all the good it would do. Will Turnsby was the second coming of Houdini. He always found a way to sneak through barriers and police blockades. If he were in the hospital, he would find them, even in a restroom.

"We'd better find some empty beds and crawl under the sheets," Sarah said. "Too bad we can't get into ICU."

"I've had enough of hospitals, but that may be the only way to fool him into leaving."

The elevator door opened and they cautiously peered into the long hall. Seeing no one, they looked into each room, finding all but one room with two beds occupied. Slipping out of their coats and shoes, they placed them in the closet, closed the door, and climbed into the beds. The darkness was comforting and Dana nearly fell asleep until the door opened, emitting enough light for her to realize it wasn't a nurse.

Chapter Twenty-Seven

"I know you're in there, Dana. I saw the two of you sneak in a few minutes ago."

Dana reached for the call button dangling from the bed rail. Pushing it, she heard it buzz in the distance, but how long would it take for someone to arrive?

"How did you manage to follow us here, Will?"

He laughed. "If I told you, I'd have to kill you, but I'm gonna to do that, anyway."

She sat up in bed and swung her legs over the side.

"Stay right where you are. Before I end your lives, I want to know what happened to Rob. How'd you kill him?"

"He killed himself on his snowmobile by running into the back of the truck."

"And why would he do that?" He reached behind him to close the door.

Dana told him about the kidnapping in great

detail, but omitted the part about the hot grease.

"And the wimp let you get away?"

Ignoring the question, Dana said, "Who killed Linda Johnsbury? Was it you or Rob?"

"Since you're not going to live to tell anyone, it was me. Rob was a coward who only wanted the good life. But he didn't want to work for it."

"So you allowed him to be convicted of the murder you committed? He must have hated you for it."

"He was an accessory, so it didn't make a difference."

Keep him talking until someone arrives. "Where was he able to get cosmetic surgery?"

"In Denver. He came down here after he dug up his stash. He got one of those quicky pull-up jobs in a doctor's office. Purty clever, if you ask me."

Why is Sarah so quiet? She must be frightened to death? She then heard her soft snore from the bed nearest the window. "You didn't just escape to get even with Sarah and me, did you?"

"Hell, no, that was Rob's idea. He was mad 'cause you got the mansion when your sister died. He built the place and it should have belonged to him."

"Did he know a tornado destroyed the mansion?"

"He knew and that's when he lost it. He would have killed you, himself, if that friend of his hadn't talked him out of it."

"Marc Bartlett?"

"Yeah, his old friend Marc. He sure had him fooled."

"What do mean?"

"He had him believing that you and your friend railroaded Rob into prison."

Why isn't anyone coming to the room? Dana

dared not try to ring the buzzer again.

"And Marc believed him?"

"He wasn't any smarter than you are. He believed everything Rob told him."

Dana lowered her head. "I can't believe Marc fell for Rob's lies."

"Rob was a master liar. He could have sold snowballs to the Eskimos."

"Yes, he did have a silver tongue, but you were the smartest Turnsby brother. You convinced the county residents to elect you sheriff."

Turnsby appeared to puff up his chest. "That was easy. The suckers didn't even bother to check my background record."

"It's a small county, Will. Mostly ranchers and farmers. They're good, trusting people."

"A bunch of saps," he said. "But that doesn't matter. It's time for your execution."

"Before you kill me, I deserve to know who killed my gardener, Todd Warren."

"Oh, you mean the kid at the mansion?"

"That's the one."

He laughed as though it were a joke. "Rob said he would give me half the drug stash if I killed you. So I hid in your garage and when the door rolled up, the sun blinded me and I thought the kid was you."

"So you stabbed him by mistake?"

"Yeah, we all make mistakes. But not this time." Raising his gun, he pointed it at her.

Dana dropped to the floor and rolled under the bed as the door opened behind him. A familiar voice said, "Put the gun down, Turnsby. You're under arrest."

Dana glanced up to see two long legs of the law. She also saw Will Turnsby lower his arm to place his gun on the floor. Scooting from under the bed, she grabbed the revolver before he had a chance to change his mind. Another officer, who had been standing in the hall, cuffed the convict's hands behind his back and led him from the room.

"How did you know he was here?" Dana asked, still trembling.

"The nurses' station called downstairs when you buzzed them. They knew this room was unoccupied and that a convict was on the loose."

Dana managed a weak laugh. "And Sarah slept through all the excitement."

"Good thing she did. That one likes to talk and could have incited the perp to shut her up permanently."

"He would have done that anyway, officer. You saved our lives."

Dana woke Sarah when the officer left, and told her what had happened. Sarah thought she had dreamed Turnsby's capture, but sleepily got out of bed to slip on her shoes.

"Kerrie will be here momentarily. We need to meet her downstairs."

Her daughter was waiting for them in the lobby with news they were happy to hear. "Jeff Mailer called just before I left. He's back at his apartment and wanted to know where you were. I told him I was on my way to pick you up, and that you'd call when we returned to Cheyenne."

"Did he know who shot him, Kerrie?

"He said he heard Will Turnsby's voice just before the shooting."

"Why was he transferred to Denver? Did he say?"

"Something about a tainted bullet that caused a

life threatening infection in his upper chest. I guess the Turnsby brothers blamed him as much as you and Sarah for their arrests and convictions."

"So it was a case of revenge that cost Todd, Marc and his foreman their lives."

"I'm afraid so, Mom."

"Then I need to call Jeff."

Taking out her cell phone, Dana punched in his number. The phone rang so many times that she nearly hung up before he answered.

"Dana? I was just dreaming about you," he said, yawning.

"Not a nightmare, I hope."

"Anything but. We were having dinner in a restaurant in the Eiffel Tower."

"Just the two of us, Jeff?"

"Sarah was on her honeymoon with a guy who looks like Wolf Blitzer."

Dana laughed. "Really? Sarah will be ecstatic to hear that."

"And you finally realized that I'm the man of your dreams."

Dana gasped. "Are you sure you weren't shot in the head instead of your shoulder?"

"I'm perfectly sane and I resign as your bodyguard. But that doesn't mean that I don't want to spend the rest of my life with you."

"We'll talk about it soon, Jeff. But I want you to know that I've had a similar dream."

"You've made me a happy guy. I'll see you in Cheyenne."

When Dana clicked off, Kerrie asked when she and Sarah were planning to retire from sleuthing.

"We already have, dear."

Sarah yawned. "You know how I love clichés,

and I think I'm safe in saying, 'All's well that ends well, ladies. We're about to start new lives."

"But who do you plan to spend it with, Sarah?" Dana asked. "Harry or Brandon?"

"I might ask you the same, my friend. I didn't miss the fact that Jeff's name wasn't in that lineup."

"There's no one on my radar, Sarah. I want to spend some time with Kerrie and the baby. Then I'll start looking around for a new place to stay, if I'm not completely bankrupt by now."

"I know you well, my friend. And I didn't miss that happy smile on your face when you hung up from talking to Jeff."

"Whatever I decide to do, there will be no more sleuthing."

"I couldn't agree with you more."

Kerrie laughed. "How many times have I heard you both say that? You two are murder magnets and I suspect that you'll be chasing killers in your wheel chairs, or behind walkers in your 90s. That wouldn't surprise me at all."

Jean Henry Mead

Jean Henry Mead is the author of twenty-one books, half of them novels. The former photojournalist has also served as a news, magazine and small press editor; and has been published domestically as well as abroad. She writes the Logan & Cafferty mystery/suspense series as well as the Hamilton Kids mysteries, Wyoming historical novels and nonfiction history and interview books.

Sample chapters follow from:

Diary of Murder

Gray Wolf Mountain

Murder in RV Paradise

Diary of Murder

Chapter One

"There's nothing worse than a Rocky Mountain blizzard," Dana complained. "Not even our San Joaquin Valley fog."

Her friend whimpered like a frightened puppy when the motorhome swerved on the ice. A massive storm had assaulted them without warning, spattering the windshield with flakes the size of sand dollars. They had already decided that March was not the month to travel Colorado.

"We should have listened to the weather report."

"That wouldn't have stopped me, Sarah. I have to know why Georgi died."

"But they said it was suicide." Sarah's grip on the safety handle was turning her fingers blue.

"My sister would never have taken her own life, and I'm going to prove it."

"If we don't get off this highway soon, we're going to kill *ourselves*."

Dana lifted her foot from the accelerator. "If I pull off now, we could wind up in a ditch. Or hit by an eighteen wheeler." Activating emergency lights, she squinted to locate the center line, which had already disappeared under a thickening layer of snow.

Snowfall increased, forcing Dana to adjust the wipers. At their highest speed, they clattered like a band of castanets. The motorhome swayed, causing something to crash to the floor behind them.

"My laptop," Sarah wailed. "I forgot to put it away."

Snow was swamping the wipers. Their only hope was to prevent the coach from leaving the northbound, two-lane highway. Wind had picked up, driving snow in hypnotic swirls. Nauseated, Dana blinked repeatedly, feeling trapped inside a kaleidoscope. Snow was falling so heavily that it seemed they were standing still.

"We'll never get out of this," Sarah shouted over the wiper's clattering noise.

"Sure we will," she shouted back, doubting her own words. "Watch for exit signs and delineator posts."

"I can't see until we're on them, Dana." Her voice bordered on hysteria.

The lonely stretch of interstate between Denver and the Wyoming border had already drifted in, with visibility reduced to less than twenty feet. If they managed to survive, Dana vowed to never leave an RV Park again without a weather report. A brief glance at the temperature gauge told her it was twelve degrees. So why did she feel that she had just stepped out of the shower?

Hours seemed to pass before visibility increased. Then intermittent lights appeared in the midst of a blinding whiteout.

"Snowplow," Sarah said. "Stay a ways behind him."

"Or her."

"Women don't drive snowplows, Dana. At least not

while I lived in Nebraska."

"That was before the snowplow was invented, Sarah."

Their laughter helped to relieve the stress, but Dana's fingers would have to be pried from the wheel when they reached their destination. If they reached it.

"Steer into a skid," her friend advised. "At least I remember that much."

"Maybe you'd like to drive."

"No, no, you're doing fine." Peering through the side window, Sarah said, "An off ramp should be coming up soon. I can't wait to wade through all that white stuff in my tennis shoes."

"And I can't wait to reach Wyoming." Dana swallowed a lump in her throat when she thought of her sister Georgi.

Snow had tapered off by the time they reached Cheyenne, where an early lunch at a truck stop revived them. Sarah replaced her shoes with boots while Dana fueled the motorhome. Impatient to resume their trip, she hurriedly removed ice from the wipers and swiped at the windshield. Road grime coated the front of her parka and their new RV appeared to have developed Progeria, rapid aging disease. Dana sighed, feeling a similar fate.

Snowflakes disappeared a few miles north of Wheatland, and she relaxed enough to loosen her grip on the wheel. Checking the map, Sarah said they had less than two hours remaining. Reaching across the console to pat Dana's arm, she said, "Illnesses often cause people to react in strange ways."

"Georgi would have told me if she were sick."

"Tell me again what her husband said."

"Rob was nearly incoherent when he called. He

found her in bed when he arrived home at noon. Georgi was still in her nightgown and had a hand to her throat as though she were choking."

"What kind of sickness would cause that?"

"I wish I knew, Sarah. That's something we need to find out. We also need to talk to her doctor and insist on an autopsy."

"What if her husband objects?"

"I assume he'll agree, but I really don't know him that well."

They rode the rest of the way in silence. Before they reached the outskirts of town, Dana called her sister's number. Her brother-in-law answered and gave her directions to a rural subdivision. Before they reached the circular drive, they stopped to stare in awe at the elaborately built house with its towers, wings and gables.

"Dana, this place looks like Queen Elizabeth's castle."

"It's actually a Queen Anne colonial. Breathtaking, isn't it?"

A shiny black sports car, with its engine running, was parked in the three-stall garage.

"Nice car," Sarah said. "Looks like somebody's leaving."

Georgi had mentioned the sports car, a birthday gift from her husband. Why was it running now when Rob was expecting them? Dana climbed down from the motorhome and opened the passenger door. "Take a deep breath." she said, "We've got some investigating to do."

A tall, tanned, well-built man opened the entry door. For a moment she didn't recognize him. He seemed older and more haggard than Dana remembered. Rob Turnsby gasped when he noticed her standing on the expansive wood porch.

"I thought you were expecting us, Rob."

"I'm sorry, I forgot how much you look like Georgi."

"I'm a year older but some thought we looked like twins." We were once as close as twins, she thought as she stepped across the threshold.

She wasn't sure why Rob made her uneasy. Maybe it was his standoffishness, as though he didn't want anyone invading his space. He led them into the living room and motioned them into two matching arm chairs. After introducing Sarah, she glanced about the well-appointed room with its mahogany mantle, large landscape paintings, and Oriental rug. The oak floor gleamed as though recently polished. Rob had done well for himself since marrying her sister.

"Can I get you something to drink?"

"Thank you, Rob. I'll have some herbal tea." She glanced at Sarah, who nodded her agreement.

"I was thinking of something a bit more relaxing, after your long trip," he said.

"Tea's fine, if you have it."

"I'm sure there's some in the cupboard." His eyelids appeared to twitch.

Glancing again at Sarah, she noticed her questioning expression.

Rob started from the room but turned back to say, "If you don't mind, I'll have a drink."

"Of course not. You look as though you need one."

His face seemed to have lost its previous tan. "What are you implying, Dana?"

"Nothing, you just seem on edge."

His sigh was drawn-out and heavy. "It's been a

nightmare since Georgi's death."

"Please sit down. The drinks can wait."

"No, I insist." He turned and left the room.

Sarah leaned toward her, whispering, "What's going on?"

"I don't know but we're going to find out." She left her chair and moved to a large, elaborately draped window. From the corner of her eye she noticed a young woman carrying a packing box into the garage. She turned to watch as a shapely redhead slid into the car and backed it from its stall. *Who can that be? Isn't that Georgi's new car?*

Dana resumed her seat. "Keep your eyes and ears open," she whispered.

Patting her short blond curls into place, Sarah nodded and glanced about the room. "What did you say Rob does for a living?"

"He owns a construction company."

"He built this gorgeous house?"

"I believe he did."

"Very expensive house and furnishings. He must be quite successful."

"I've noticed."

"And young."

"Yes, ten years younger than Georgi."

"Sounds like a novel plot."

Dana shifted uneasily in her chair. "Strange that you should say that. Are you aware that Georgi was a writer?"

"Yes, you mentioned it."

"Did I tell you she's been writing mystery novels?"

"No, is that why you had so many in your library?"

"Partly. Her books piqued my interest in the

genre. She was a very gifted writer." Dana quickly wiped the dampness from her eyes. She then nodded in the direction Rob had taken. Raising a finger to her lips, she settled back in her chair, resting her head against the leather back. Within seconds Rob returned with a tray.

"I hope you don't mind that I microwaved your tea," he said. "The kettle takes forever."

Sarah smiled. "As long as you don't microwave dinner."

"My friend's been reading alternative medicine books," she said, reaching to squeeze Sarah's arm. "We need to discuss Georgi's death certificate as well as the funeral arrangements."

"Already taken care of." He set the china tea service on a marble-topped coffee table. "I wasn't sure you would arrive in time, so I took care of the arrangements, myself."

"But Georgi's only been gone two days."

Rob excused himself and made his way to the bar in an alcove adjoining the living room. He returned with a cocktail. "I knew you would be exhausted from your long trip and I didn't want to burden you with it."

"What are the arrangements?"

"Cremation tomorrow morning."

"Cremation? But Georgi wouldn't–"

"She said that's what she wanted, Dana. I'm surprised you didn't know."

"She had a living will?"

"No, but there's an estate will. I thought that would interest you."

"Why?"

"She left you some money as well as her books. You're her only blood relative, other than your daughter, Kerrie, so naturally she would leave you something."

"I see."

"By the way, where is Kerrie?"

"Working as an editorial assistant for a news magazine in California. I haven't called her yet."

Rob seated himself in a burgundy leather recliner. "Georgi didn't leave you much because the majority of our assets are tied up in the construction business."

Dana felt her scalp prickle. "I didn't expect—"

"The housekeeper's packing her books so you can take them with you."

"We'll have to put them in storage for the time being."

"In that case, you're welcome to leave them here until you've finished traveling." He smiled benevolently.

"Thank you, Rob. That's very accommodating. By the way, was that the housekeeper I noticed leaving in Georgi's sports car?" She watched him wipe his shiny upper lip.

"Uh—yes, I'm allowing her use of the car until her pickup is repaired. She's been very helpful about packing Georgi's things."

"What are you planning to do with them?"

"Give them to charities."

"Would you mind if I go through them and keep a few mementos for Kerrie and myself?"

He shrugged. "By all means. I know that sisters have a special bond. I'm sure you'd like some of her things."

"You're most generous." Dana rose and offered Sarah her hand.

"You can do that tomorrow after the memorial service," he said, sitting upright.

"Would you mind if we look through them before the housekeeper finishes packing?"

"Not at all. I'll show you to her room." He glanced at his watch. "I have a business meeting in half an hour. I should be back in time for dinner."

"You're not taking time off to grieve Georgi's death?"

"We all handle grief in our own way," he said. "I have a business to run and I need to stay busy."

Dana shivered as he guided them up the oak stairs to his wife's room, which was filled with packing boxes. He left before she could ask about the official cause of death. Mentally tabling the question for his return, she opened the closet door.

Shocked, she turned to Sarah. "It's empty. My sister has only been gone two days and he's already getting rid of her clothes."

"I wouldn't be surprised if the housekeeper's making off with them, Dana."

"From the looks of her, she's already taken Georgi's place, including Rob and the sports car."

"We need evidence to go to the police."

"I have to stop the cremation so cause of death can be determined."

"How?"

"I'll think of something. Let's go through these packing boxes to see what we can find."

The first carton contained leisure clothing, the second high-heeled shoes. Five additional boxes were filled with formal wear wrapped haphazardly as though dirty laundry. Dana cringed when she noticed the expensive labels. Her sister must have worn them while married to her former husband, a San Francisco lawyer.

While sorting through a box of designer jeans,

Sarah said, "Look at this. A locked, black velvet box. "

"It must be Georgi's jewelry. I'm surprised it's still here."

"It's heavy, Dana. Do you think we should open it?"

"How? Pry it open? I don't feel right about that."

"The key must be here somewhere." Sarah opened dresser drawers to feel beneath them. Disappointed, she turned to the white Victorian desk that matched the four-poster bed. Opening the drawer, she extracted a carved wooden pill bottle, which rattled when she shook it. Removing the lid, she discovered a key.

"This has to be the one."

Dana was surprised when the box opened. Carefully lifting the lid, she discovered a matching book, its black velvet cover etched in gold with the name Georgiana Turnsby. Hands trembling, she opened the cover and discovered a diary. The beginning entry was dated June 21st, which she quietly read aloud:

I had serious misgivings about moving to Wyoming, but it's beautiful here. I miss San Francisco Bay, but the air is so clear that you can see the mountains forever. I'm glad I allowed Rob to talk me into moving to his home state.

"Sounds like she was happy, Dana."

She scanned the next few pages and stopped. "Listen to this:"

I can't tell anyone that I've made a terrible mistake. I should have listened to my friend, Angela. Now, I'm too embarrassed and ashamed to tell anyone. How could I have been so blind that I allowed myself to be fooled and rushed into this. What am I going to do?

"Oh, my." Sarah dropped a black sequined dress back into a packing box. "What do you think she's referring to?"

"If my instincts are right, she's referring to her marriage, but the entry was written nearly two years ago. Why didn't she confide in me?"

"She said she was embarrassed, Dana."

Turning the page, she noticed the next entry was dated four days later.

I've decided to make the best of it. I've secretly transferred half my divorce settlement to an offshore account. The rest has been loaned to my husband for the business. He promised to build me the most beautiful house in the state, and seems so eager to please me. How can I turn him down?

"Sounds as though she changed her mind." Sarah picked up another box and set it on the bed.

"Georgi was a generous person. I'm sure she was willing to help Rob establish himself in business."

"Then why would he kill the proverbial goose?"

"The housekeeper, maybe. Georgi may have discovered they were having an affair and threatened to divorce him."

"Wasn't there a prenuptial agreement?"

"I would hope she was smart enough to have one, but Rob's a former salesman and a very charming guy. He could have talked her into nearly anything." Dana had turned another page when she heard a door slam somewhere in the house. Thrusting the diary into its box, she hid them under a pile of clothing.

Murder on Gray Wolf Mountain

Chapter One

Dana unbuckled her seat belt and landed on the headliner. The side curtain airbag had ruptured, filling the Escalade's interior with gas and debris. Hand-masking her lower face, she felt as though she were choking.

Sarah! Her friend hung from her seat belt, apparently unconscious. Reaching to touch her hair, she called her name repeatedly, afraid the accident had broken her neck. Sarah groaned a moment later, much to her relief. When she was coherent, Dana told her between coughing spells that their SUV had rolled. She then cushioned her friend's head for the drop onto the headliner.

"Are you all right?"

Coughing, Sara pointed toward a side window.

Dana reached with the toe of her shoe, managing to open the driver's window. The passenger frame was bowed inward, preventing the door from opening, so Sarah would have to follow her through the driver's window. Once Dana had crawled onto the ground, she turned and stuck her head back inside. "Hurry, the Escalade might catch fire."

That got her moving. When they were both able to stand, Sarah groaned while rubbing the back of her neck. She then asked whether Dana had swerved to avoid hitting a deer.

Holding the sides of her throbbing head, Dana said, "No animals but I dodged a log before I heard a bang and the steering wheel jerked from my hands."

"I remember now. We were talking about the sale at Macy's and the next thing I knew I was hanging upside down."

"Are you sure you're not hurt?"

"We Caffertys have the skulls of mastodons— How about you?"

Nodding that she was okay, Dana peered at the Escalade, comparing it to a dead chicken with its feet in the air.

Sarah stood back to appraise the damage. "A shredded tire? I thought these new all terrains are guaranteed not to explode."

"Obviously not."

"Looks like it was hit by a cannon ball."

Dana noticed a hole in the fender near the driver's door. "What in the world—?"

"Somebody shot at us." Sarah turned to scan the terrain.

Crouching behind the Escalade, they searched the area for some sign of the shooter. When none was found, Dana crawled back inside to retrieve their cameras and purses. Moments later she handed them through the window to Sarah. Then, circling the vehicle at a distance, they took pictures of the disabled vehicle.

Sarah rummaged through her large leather bag. "Where's my cell phone? We need to call the sheriff."

"Calm down. It's in the side pocket." Shading her

eyes against the afternoon sun, she noticed a dust cloud as a vehicle drove toward them. The older model, single-seated pickup truck was covered in rust and mud. When it stopped opposite them, a man much older than the truck leaned his head out the window to ask if they'd had an accident.

"Pretty obvious," Sarah muttered.

"I got a first aid kit in here somewheres."

When they said they didn't need the kit, he offered them a ride down the mountain. Glancing at her friend, Sarah said, "You have room for both of us?"

The old man opened the creaking driver's door. "Hold on a minute, ladies. I got some stuff to move around."

Stooped and slim as a broom handle, he shuffled around to the opposite side of the truck in his frayed plaid shirt and greasy, ragged overalls. Dana flipped her cell phone open and punched in 911. Wouldn't you know? No cell service. They would have to accept the ride. Offering to help their benefactor, they were waved off as he removed an aging yellow cat the size of a large Chihuahua. He then hauled out a battered plastic box with a cracked lid. Placing the box and cat in the bed of his truck, he retrieved several lengths of rope with hooks attached to both ends. That left something wrapped in a filthy blanket. When it slid to the ground they saw that it was a saber.

Sarah gasped and grabbed Dana's arm. "We don't want to put you to any trouble."

He cupped a hand to his left ear. "What's that you said?"

So he was hard of hearing. Sarah raised her voice.

"No trouble, young lady. I need to clean my truck out, anyhow."

"Young lady?" They looked at one another and

grinned. "We haven't been called young in ages."

His returning grin had several teeth missing. "You two look mighty spry to me. Good lookin' too, if ya ask me."

That settled it. They would have to accept the ride, but neither of them wanted to sit next to him. The old man didn't appear to have taken a bath in months. Turning her back, Dana removed a coin from her wallet and flipped it on her wrist. Covering it with her palm she motioned for Sarah to call it.

"Heads." Sarah whispered, crossing her fingers.

Sighing with relief, Dana showed her the coin.

"No problem. My sinuses are so clogged from all this mountain greenery that I can't smell a thing. But make sure you roll down the window."

The old man introduced himself as Gus Blake. Pulling a dusty rag from his back pocket, he flapped it in the breeze and proceeded to dust the seat. Finished, he bowed low and swept his arm in a welcoming gesture. Both women groaned as they climbed onto the lumpy seat. Something appeared to be growing out of the dashboard—what was left of it—but at that point, they couldn't gamble that something better would come along. There was a chance the shooter might drive down the rutted mountain road to finish them off.

Gus looked harmless enough. He was no taller than Sarah and weighed half as much. And there was no sign of a gun, unless it was hidden in the glove compartment. The cab smelled of grease and Gus, so Dana was quick to roll down the dusty window. Leaning her head far enough to whip her shoulder length auburn hair in the breeze, she inhaled deeply and glanced out of the corner of her eye at Sarah, who didn't seem to mind the scent of ode to a service station. Her short, curly blond hair never looked mussed and her presence made Gus look all the more grimy.

Gus cleared his throat. "You gals lookin' for a good time?"

Sarah laughed and asked what he had in mind.

"Barn dance tomorrah night down to the Grange Hall. I thought you two might like to go as my dates."

"When's the last time you had a date?" Sarah asked.

He shrugged and tapped the steering wheel with a crooked, arthritic finger. "It's been a while. There ain't a lotta single women here on the mountain."

Sarah turned in the seat to face him. "What makes you think we're single?"

"You ain't wearin' no weddin' rings."

"So you noticed that, did you?"

"Well, shore I did."

"You ever been married, Gus?" Sarah asked.

"My third wife died a coupla years ago."

"Three wives?"

"I've lived a long time and my wives just kinda wore out, if you know what I mean."

"No. We don't know what you mean."

"Ranchin' on the mountains takes a lot out of a woman. What with all the snow, high winds and rough country."

Worked them to death, Dana thought, shivering in the afternoon heat. Some men were heartless.

"So what do you do for fun? Cruise the mountain roads looking for damsels in distress?"

"Mostly I drive around lookin' for wounded gray wolves."

"I thought they were protected."

"They used to be but a law was passed that anybody with a gun can shoot 'em on sight."

Dana leaned around Sarah to ask, "But doesn't that upset the balance of nature?"

"Shore does, but the ranchers claim that wolves kill a lotta livestock."

Dana wondered what he did with the wolves when he found them.

"I nurse 'em back to health."

So Gus was a decent sort, after all. Poor old man had to do something with his time, and chances were slim he'd find another wife. Dana tuned them out as they progressed at a leisurely pace down the rutted mountain road toward the tiny town of Concord. Were the bullets that hit the Escalade from someone shooting at wolves? The shooter must have been awfully near-sighted or a terrible marksman to mistake their SUV for a wolf.

Dana knew there wasn't a wrecker service or car rental agency in the town at the foot of the mountain, and she couldn't imagine Gus chauffeuring them all the way to the mansion. The neighbors would think they were slumming. She shrugged. Who cares what the snooty neighbors think? They'd never accepted her or Sarah since Dana's sister died, leaving her the mansion. Let them think whatever they pleased.

There was one small gas station in Concord and she insisted on buying Gus a tankful of gas. He didn't look like he had enough money to buy anything but the barest necessities, and his truck appeared to be held together with duct tape and baling wire. She wondered whether it would make it as far as Casper, where they could rent a car.

After Dana paid for the gas, she plucked her cell phone from her purse to dial 911. When a dispatcher answered, she reported the rollover as well as the gunshots. By the time she had finished, they were halfway to Casper.

"We need to call a wrecker for the Escalade," Dana said.

"Gonna cost ya a purty penny. Better call my cousin Bernie. Tell him Gus sent ya and he'd do it on the cheap."

Dana wondered if Bernie's wrecker resembled his cousin's pickup truck. She thanked Gus, telling him a sheriff's deputy would inspect the Escalade the following morning before it was towed away.

The old man nodded and said little more during the rest of the trip to Casper. It was nearing the dinner hour when they reached the edge of town. Dana had called ahead to reserve an SUV and hoped they would arrive before the agency closed. The aging truck might break down before they reached their rural subdivision.

The rent-a-car agency had already closed and Gus's truck was smoking as though the front tires had caught fire. What were they going to do now?

"Better head for the mansion," Sarah said.

"Good idee, I can hose the truck down in your driveway—if you got one."

Dana cringed, imagining Gus's truck leaking oil on her unblemished driveway. Nodding consent, they chugged off toward the old rural highway. She noticed that Sarah seemed to be holding her breath. An eternity later, the old truck died several feet from their circle drive and Sarah crossed herself, whispering, "Thank you."

Gus squinted at the setting sun when they left his truck. "Would you ladies mind helping me push the truck in the driveway?"

"Tomorrow morning." Dana said. "You can spend the night with us."

The old man turned to squint at the mansion. "Holy jeebers. That big house all yours? Looks like a fancy hotel to me."

"I inherited it from my sister, Georgi."

"She musta been as rich as Mister Romney."

"Not quite." Dana rubbed her throbbing head. "Tell you what, Gus. Leave the truck where it is and I'll buy you a better one tomorrow."

"Can't let you do that, ma'am. Gladys and me's been together nigh onto thirty years."

"Gladys?"

"My truck. I named her after my first wife and that didn't set too well with wives two and three."

Dana sighed. "Come in the house and we'll discuss the problem." *Maybe I can talk you into taking a bath.*

Gus grabbed his huge cat from the truck bed and reluctantly followed them around to the back entrance, which opened into a mud room. The moment Dana closed the door, Bert, their German Shepherd, bounded into the room to greet them. Skidding to a stop, he took one look at Gus and the cat and barked at full volume. Dana grabbed his collar, telling Sarah to retrieve some clothes from a nearby closet. Fortunately, she hadn't taken her former brother-in-law's clothing to the Salvation Army. He didn't need them in prison.

Sarah prepared dinner while Gus was cleaning up. They then ate in the kitchen so the formal dining room wouldn't intimidate their guest. Showered and freshly shaven with a razor he found in the bathroom cabinet, the old man didn't look quite so disreputable, although Rob's expensive clothing hung on him like a youngster playing dress-up. Dana noticed that his eyes were turquoise. No wonder he'd attracted so many wives.

Gus ate as though ending a hunger strike. During dinner, Dana asked about the wolf killings and why he thought she and Sarah had been the objects of someone's target practice. Shrugging, he asked if they'd noticed Gladys's puncture wounds.

Dana dropped her fork. "Someone shot at you?"

"More'n once. I reckon somebody don't like me savin' wolves."

"What happens to the wolves that recover?"

"I load 'em in the back of Gladys and take 'em

further up the mountain to set 'em free."

The practice sounded dangerous and Dana couldn't imagine anyone nursing a wolf back to health.

Gus must have read her thoughts. "I have to muzzle 'em when they get better, but I think they know I'm tryin' to help. I only got bit once." Rolling up a too-long sleeve, he showed them the scars on his arm.

Sarah shook her head. "Why do you do it, Gus?"

"Somebody has to. There's already too many deer and elk around 'cause the wolves are dyin' off. Purty soon we'll be overrun with game animals that'll starve in the winter for lack of feed."

"Then why were wolves removed from the endangered species list?"

"Politics, ma'am. Ranchers are tired of their livestock gettin' killed."

Dana stood to clear the table. "That's a real Catch 22."

"'S'cuse me?"

"We'll talk about it later over a glass of wine."

After the dishes had been done, they gathered in the richly furnished den. Sarah poured them each a goblet of red wine and they settled into soft, burgundy leather arm chairs. Gus reached down to pet their German Shepherd while his cat watched from a nearby chair.

"Better not take the dog to the mountain, ladies. He's the same color as the wolves. There's so many trigger happy hunters around that Bert needs a big orange collar— like the hunters' dogs wear—in case he gets loose."

Dana gasped. "You think someone would shoot him?"

"No doubt in my mind. He's a handsome feller and you can tell where he came from."

Sarah set her wine glass on an end table. "What

do you mean?"

"He's from the Canidae species, like the wolves."

So Gus wasn't an illiterate, despite his obvious lack of education.

"You know a lot about wolves, don't you, Gus?"

"I been studying on 'em."

"What's to be done about the wolves?" Dana asked.

"Don't know, ma'am. Wish I did. All I can do is patch 'em up or bury 'em."

Dana showed Gus to the guest room and they turned in early, exhausted from the day's ordeal. She set her alarm for seven, planning to call a taxi to take them into town for the rental car. She would keep her promise to Gus to buy him a reliable truck after they met with the deputy on the mountain. Glancing out her bedroom window, she noticed that Gladys was missing. Who would have hauled the old truck away at this early hour? Grabbing her robe, she hurried downstairs where she found a note on the entry table. Gus had scrawled a brief message thanking her for her hospitality and telling her that he was able to start his truck and leave for home.

Disappointed, she knocked on Sarah's door before pushing it open. Sarah could sleep through a tornado and it required a bit of shoulder shaking to wake her. When she told her what had happened, Sarah's face fell.

"I like the old guy, don't you? I was hoping he'd stay around a while."

Dana nodded. "We need to get a move on if we're going to meet the deputy. Get dressed and we'll grab a bite. The rental agency opens at eight. No telling how long it will take for the taxi to get here."

Dana noticed a large bruise on Sarah's right leg when she swung them over the side of the bed. She had some bruises of her own and muscles that ached during the night. Yawning, she went back to her own room to dress. It would be a long day.

Later, as she drove the rental Buick up the mountain, Dana noticed a gray wolf racing across the gravel road. Braking, she sat clutching the wheel and inhaling deeply.

"Beautiful, aren't they?" Sarah said.

"Yes, but I don't want to provide Gus with another patient."

"Must be quite a few of them here in the mountains."

"And a lot of sheep and cattle ranches."

"I hope no one takes another shot at us, Dana."

"Amen to that."

The deputy was waiting for them. He had already inspected the Escalade and considered it totaled. He said they were lucky they hadn't been badly hurt in the rollover. When asked if he'd noticed the bullet holes, he said he had and that it had happened before. But they had been unable to track down the shooter.

"Someone must know who's doing it," Dana said. "Doesn't everyone in a rural area know what everyone else's doing?"

The young deputy shifted his weight uneasily. "That's true, ma'am, but there're plenty of places to hide here in the mountains."

"Could it be one the ranchers?" Sarah asked.

"I doubt it. They're a friendly bunch, always looking out for each another."

"Maybe they don't like strangers."

The deputy laughed. "You're the only strangers

I've seen up here in quite a while and I doubt anyone would shoot at a couple of older women."

Sarah frowned. "Older?"

The deputy ducked his head. "Sorry, ma'am. I-I didn't mean—"

"Don't worry about it," Dana said. "At least you didn't say old women."

She asked him about Gus Blake and wondered where he lived. Told his cabin was a mile off the main gravel road, she made a mental note to stop by his place to make sure Gladys had arrived home safely. She also wondered how many patients Gus had in his wolf clinic.

Murder in RV Paradise

Chapter One

The sun cast a deep orange glow across the small Texas lake. Seated near the shore line, finishing their dinner on the resort patio, the two women watched as a duck repeatedly dived beneath the water. When he failed to surface, Sarah rose from the dining table and walked to the water's edge. Shading her eyes against the setting sun, she scanned the lake for some sign of the missing duck. When she failed to locate it, she walked several yards down the bank before turning back to yell, "Where'd it go? I don't see him anywhere."

Sighing, Dana left the remains of her meal to join her friend on the bank. When they were unable to spot the illusive fowl, Sarah decided that he'd made his last dive. Stooping to peer at a large clump of weeds, she said "There he is, in the bulrushes."

"What's that in his beak?"

Sarah removed her sandals to wade into the lake. "Looks like a piece of silk." Halting her forward motion, she shrieked, "Oh, no, there's an arm attached."

As she approached, a large, red-headed duck with light feathers seemed to run on the water before lifting into the sky. A piece of bright blue cloth still dangled from his beak.

Dana removed her own sandals to wade in after her friend, the water chilling her knees. Parting the weeds several yards from shore, she gasped when she discovered a woman face up in the water, her long red hair floating behind her like rosy tentacles. Dressed in skimpy denim shorts and a torn silk blouse, she didn't appear to be breathing when Dana gripped her nearest wrist to find a pulse.

"We've got to get her ashore." Dana grabbed the woman's tanned bare feet, telling Sarah to call 911.

A small crowd gathered when they reached the bank where two men helped to lift the woman ashore. Placing her on the golf course turf, one of them immediately began CPR.

Both women were pelted with questions as soon as Sarah's call ended. But before they could answer, a woman said, "It's Varina Zagori."

Dana heard another woman grumble behind her. "Someone must have killed her."

When she turned to ask why, their fellow RVers had already started back toward the nearest motorhome.

Puzzled, Dana asked, "When will the ambulance arrive?"

"I was told twenty minutes. We're quite a ways from town."

"Why does this always happen? We can't even vacation without a body turning up."

Sarah shook her head. "I saw that woman this morning just after you backed the motorhome onto our lot. She and another golfer were putting on the green behind us and I guess they didn't realize I could hear them."

"What did they say?"

"They paused their game to stare at us before that one"—she indicated the woman on the ground—"said something strange about us."

"What did we do, back over one of her golf balls?"

"No, Dana. She laughed at the way we were dressed and said we must be traveling dikes."

"Why would she say something like that?" Dana realized she would have to lower her voice when people turned to stare. Taking Sarah's arm, she led her some distance from the crowd as a security golf cart raced up with two people aboard. Jumping out, they ran to where the victim lay. Dana doubted the woman would survive, despite everyone's efforts to save her.

As the women watched the assembled emergency team at work, Dana asked in a quiet voice, "What's this about us being—?"

"I shouldn't have told you."

"I'm glad you did. It's a clue to the woman's character if she had a habit of making snap judgments about people she didn't know." Dana ground her teeth. "You know how I feel about nasty gossips, especially those who make racial and homophobic slurs."

"I agree. They need to get a life." Sarah lowered herself to the grass. "But why would someone stop her golf game to say something like that?"

"Maybe it's our height difference."

Sarah smiled. "Our Sew and So club members *did* call us Mutt and Jeff."

"But they said it affectionately. I don't think the Zagori woman was being nice. She probably made nasty remarks about everyone she saw."

"At least the golfer with her said her remark was uncalled for."

"That woman behind us could have been right. The victim might have made someone so mad that he killed her."

"Then again, she might have accidentally drowned."

"Face up in the water? I doubt it."

An ambulance's wail could be heard in the distance, prompting onlookers to move away from those still working on the victim. From the expressions on their faces, it seemed a lost cause.

Before the ambulance arrived, a small white dog sniffed his way to the body, then turned and made his way across the golf course. Was it the victim's dog? If so, he didn't seem to be mourning his owner.

Dana remembered seeing a ring on the victim's left hand. Where was her husband? He should have been home from work by now, if he wasn't retired or there on vacation. Maybe *he* was responsible for her death. Spouses were always prime suspects, but Dana had a feeling there was much more involved than a domestic squabble. From the brief comments she'd heard earlier, Varina Zagori wasn't a popular resident of the RV resort.

A patrol car screeched to a halt nearby, closely followed by an ambulance. She and Sarah waited, knowing the sheriff or his deputy would want to question them. After a brief inspection of the body, the sheriff approached them and they were led to a picnic table for questioning.

A tall, ruggedly handsome man introduced himself as Sheriff Steve Brandson. He vaguely reminded Dana of her amorous friend, Sheriff Walter Grayson, although he was younger and more than a few pounds slimmer.

He wasn't smiling when he asked, "Are you the two women who found the body?"

Sarah said they were. "We seem to be murder magnets. No matter where we go, we manage to find a body."

Dana nudged her friend under the picnic table. When she flinched, Dana said, "We've had the unfortunate experience of becoming involved in a number of murder investigations."

She would have given the sheriff Walter's cell number for reference but didn't want her suitor to know where they were. She knew he would track them down eventually, but hoped for some quiet time before he persuaded her to marry him.

"Please elaborate." The sheriff impatiently tapped his pad with a pen.

With Sarah's help, she managed to fill him in on all the previous murder cases they'd become involved in. When he frowned while taking notes, Dana said, "We seemed to be cursed—always in the wrong place when a body turns up. I'm sure you understand."

His expression said he didn't. "This is no joking matter, ma'am. The two of you need to come to my office as soon as I finish my preliminary investigation."

"But we just arrived from Wyoming, Sheriff." Sarah's face crumpled. "We didn't even know the victim."

"Two older women traveling in an RV discovering bodies is mighty unusual, if you ask me."

At least he didn't say old women. Sarah's piteous expression evolved into a smile. She must feel flattered that they hadn't been referred to as a couple of demented seniors. Then again, maybe she was thinking of the film, "Arsenic and Old Lace."

The coroner's van pulled in behind the ambulance as the sheriff wrote down their names, ages and other vital information.

He told them he would be taking them into town

for further questioning. Dana dreaded the trip in the back of a patrol car. She hoped they weren't considered persons of interest as she watched the sheriff talk to the EMTs, who were loading their equipment into the ambulance. They were taking their time, their siren silent when they left the area.

Another vehicle arrived, which Dana assumed was the forensics team. Deputies were also cordoning off the area with yellow crime tape. How strange that so many law enforcement departments had arrived so soon for a suspected drowning.

Dana remarked how beautiful the resort was as they were herded to the patrol car. "Not the place you'd expect to find a body."

"An RVer's paradise," a deputy replied. "I wish I could afford a nice rig and an RV lot by one of the lakes. You people don't know how lucky you are."

Lucky? In many ways they were. They were able to travel wherever they pleased, thanks to the generous inheritance Dana had received from her deceased sister, Georgi. She bit her lip, willing away the painful memory of her sister's body in the crematorium after she was murdered.

www.ingramcontent.com/pod-product-compliance
Lightning Source LLC
Chambersburg PA
CBHW070832250626
47159CB00003B/749